King of the Teds
Unification

by

Dave Bartram

with Dean Rinaldi

Published by Blue Mendos Publications
In association with Amazon KDP

Published in paperback 2022
Category: Fiction
Copyright Dave Bartram © 2022
Copyright Dean Rinaldi © 2022
ISBN : 9798360638728

Cover design by Jill Rinaldi © 2022

All rights reserved, Copyright under Berne Copyright Convention and Pan American Convention. No part of this book may be reproduced, stored in a retrieval system, or transmitted in any form or by any means, electronic, mechanical, photocopying, recording or otherwise, without prior permission of the author. The author's moral rights have been asserted.

This is a work of fiction. Names, characters, corporations, institutions, organisations, events or locales in this novel are either the product of the author's imagination or, if real, used fictitiously. Any resemblance to actual persons (living or dead) is entirely coincidental.

Dedication

To lovers of Rock 'n' Roll everywhere.

Acknowledgements

Jill Rinaldi for the excellent book cover design. My friend and ghostwriter Dean Rinaldi.

The book launch team, Facebook group admin and the supporting members.

Chapter 1

"Oh my God, Deano's been stabbed! Quick, somebody call the police!"

Stan the bookie reached for the telephone and dialled 999.

"Hello, yeah, we need an ambulance quickly. There's been a stabbing at Stanley Webb Bookmakers on the Milton Road Estate. You better get here quick, he's in a bad way!" Stan yelled down the telephone receiver.

Deano was unconscious and curled on his side with the switch blade still stuck in his chest.

"Somebody better go next door and let Deano's mates know what's happened.

"I'll do it," Terry Downs said as he turned swiftly on his heels and bolted off towards the Milton Arms pub.

Terry was an up-and-coming lad on the estate. He was sixteen and had left school earlier in the year. He had been in the bookies collecting a win for his dad. Terry ran to the Milton Arms pub next door. He stood at the door, took a deep breath and looked around the busy pub. It was Christmas Eve and still early, but the celebrations were well underway with a group of couples slow dancing on the make-shift dance area to *'Lonely This Christmas'* by Mud. Terry spotted Ricky and Kenny at the end of the bar. He bolted over towards them.

"Ricky, its Deano. He's been stabbed in the bookies!" Terry said before stopping briefly to catch his breath.

"What? You're joking," Ricky said as he put his pint down.

"No mate, really. Stan has called the ambulance. He ain't in a good way," Terry said, shaking his head.

"Kenny, get the others, and you better tell Melanie."

Ricky took Terry to one side.

"What's your name?"

"It's Terry, Terry Downs. I live on the next block from you."

"Thanks for letting me know Terry. I really appreciate it. Now, did you see who did it? It's just you and me. No one else needs to know, alright?" Ricky whispered.

"Yeah, I saw him alright. It was that Skinhead bloke," Terry said, frowning.

"Who, Clifford Tate?"

"No, not him. It was his number two, that lairy one, Eddy Boyce," Terry said through clenched teeth.

"Are you sure?"

"Yeah, I'm sure. It was definitely him. I hate those Bedford Boot Boys!" Terry hissed.

"Right, now let's keep this to ourselves, alright? When the gavvers turn up you saw nothing, alright?" Ricky said, patting Terry on the arm.

"No sweat Ricky. I live here mate. I know the rules, and if you need another head to set things straight then I'm here for Deano and the

Milton Road Teds," Terry said as he stood bolt upright and pushed out his chest.

"I'll be in touch," Ricky said. "Good man, well done!"

"ARGHH… NOOOOOO!"

Melanie screamed as Kenny took her to one side and told her that Deano had been stabbed.

The word spread around the pub quickly. The DJ played *'Rock Me Gently'* by Andy Kim but everybody was making their way towards the door. The sound of the ambulance and two police car's sirens drowned out the music. The lights flashed on and off, lighting up the outside of the pub. Two paramedics clambered out of the ambulance and raced around to the back door. They grabbed a collapsible trolley and pushed past the crowd standing at the entrance to the bookies.

"Please, out of the way! Quickly! Quickly!" the driver shouted.

Melanie was on her knees in a dishevelled heap cradling Deano's head. The grief poured out of her in floods of uncontrollable tears. Ricky turned to see Lee collapsed up against the bookies' shelf. He'd knocked betting slips and miniature pens onto the floor. His chin trembled.

Ricky looked down on his friend, Deano the Dog, King of the Teds lying on the floor in a pool of blood.

"This can't be happening," Ricky thought. *"This isn't right. This sort of thing can't happen here. Not to Deano and certainly not on the Milton Road Estate."*

Ricky began to shake his head.

"No! No! Please don't die Deano. You can't die mate!" Ricky thought.

The paramedics carefully prised Melanie away and then manoeuvred Deano's motionless body onto the stretcher.

"Please take care of my friend," Ricky said as the driver passed him by the door.

"Don't worry, we'll do our best for him," the driver said with a sympathetic nod.

Despite having drunk five pints of Watneys bitter, Ricky found he was very quickly sobering up.

"This is bloody unbelievable mate!" Kenny said as he looked around at the gathering crowd.

"You're telling me," Ricky said.

"Do we know who did it?" Kenny said softly.

Ricky nodded and put his finger to his lips. "I'll speak to everyone later."

"Okay, stand back," a plain clothes police officer ordered, "And let the ambulance men do their duty. My name is Detective Sergeant Ray White, and this is my colleague Detective Constable Bernard Jacobs. We're going to need the names of everyone that was in the bookies or has information that will help us with our enquiries."

Much of the crowd began to disperse and head back into the Arms pub.

"You," DS White called out to Ricky.

Detective Sergeant White wore a pair of brown flared trousers, a chequered brown and beige jacket and a white shirt with the top button undone. His brown and cream tie looked as if it had been recently undone and pulled down.

"Yeah," Ricky answered.

DS White approached him and lowered his voice.

"What is your name son?"

"Ricky Turrell."

DS White wrote it down in his notebook.

"Do you live on the Estate?"

"No," Ricky said.

"I need your address."

"Why?" answered Ricky.

"Don't give me that. Where do you live? I might have some questions for you," DS White persisted.

"I didn't see anything. Sorry, but I can't help you," Ricky said, shrugging his shoulders.

"Did you do it? Did you stab him? What was it? An argument over some bird?" the officer said as he held his notebook.

"What? You must be joking! Deano's my friend," Ricky said firmly.

"So you do know the victim. Right then, Deano what?" DS White said with a sly grin.

"What do you mean, Deano what?" Ricky said.

"Don't try giving it the big one son or I'll have you down the factory quicker than you can recount the lyrics from Jailhouse Rock. Do you get me?"

"Like I said Deano Derenzie is a mate, but I didn't see anything, and I don't know anything," Ricky said as he put his hands in his pockets.

"I suppose a good law-abiding citizen like you wouldn't know who the Bedford Boot Boys are either," DS White said, narrowing his eyes, looking for a reaction to his question.

Ricky didn't answer.

"Cat got your tongue Ricky Turrell?"

"I've got nothing else to say," Ricky said bluntly.

"Well, it looks like they certainly know you lot. I mean, they left their calling card in four-foot-high letters on your pub wall," DS White said. "It doesn't take a lot of working out, does it?"

"I wouldn't know," Ricky said.

Detective Sergeant White took two steps closer to Ricky and leaned forward so his face was just a few inches away from Ricky's ear. "Don't you go playing games with me, Mr Ricky Turrell because, my son, I make one hell of a formidable opponent! You can go now but I will be in touch."

"Here Guv," Detective Constable Bernard Jacobs called out.

"Yes, Bernie?"

"Stanley here reckons he didn't see anything. Just four people in the place and no one sees anything," DC Jacobs said. "What do you want me to do?"

"This lot are old-school Bernie. They would rather do prison time than grass," DS White said before turning to Stan the bookmaker. "Get this place buttoned up, Bernie, and take him in. "You," DS White growled, pointing to Stan the bookmaker, "Want to do yourself a favour and give us a description?"

"He's a bit in your face," Ricky thought. *"Not your normal plod those two."*

Ricky turned his back on the officer and walked over to Melanie. He reached down and helped her up off the floor. She looked up at him; her eyes were red from crying and her make-up had run with thick streams of mascara lines below her eyes and on her cheeks.

"Come on Melanie, "Let's get you out of here," Ricky said as he led her out of the bookies' and back into the pub.

"Oh my god Melanie," Donna whimpered as tears streamed down her cheeks. "I can't believe this has happened."

"Where's Kaz?" Ricky asked.

"She's sitting over there by the DJ," Donna said, pointing in her direction. "I got her a coffee. She's had just a little bit too much of that Baileys and Whiskey. You must know she didn't mean all that stuff earlier, you know. That was just the drink talking. Believe me tomorrow she will be devastated when she finds out what she said to you."

"Look its Christmas and Kaz had a couple too many. It's not a problem, we're friends. I'm more concerned with Melanie right now. I don't think she should alone tonight," Ricky said.

"That's okay. Kaz and I will stay over and take care of her," Donna said as she wiped away her tears.

"Good, in the meantime I'll find out what ward Deano is on and then drop by in the morning and take her up to the hospital, okay?"

"Sure," Donna said with a sniffle. "Ricky," Donna leaned forward and whispered, "Do you think he'll make it?"

"Yeah, of course I do. He's Deano the Dog. He ain't going anywhere," Ricky whispered.

"I wish I did believe that," Ricky thought. *"What if he dies? What then?"*

Donna led Melanie over to the table by the DJ where Kaz was sitting with her head in her hands.

"Nasty business," Ronnie the landlord said.

"Yeah, it is," Ricky agreed.

"Do you know who did it?"

Ricky nodded.

"Be careful, because plod will be all over this," Ronnie said cautiously. "Investigations like this can turn up or interfere with all other kinds of business."

Ricky understood that Ronnie was referring to the stolen car parts and car ringing business that he had been doing with his friend Neil.

"Oh shit!" Ricky thought. *"I'm due to start having high end motors nicked for Frank Allen in the New Year. That geezer Frank's been working with in Africa will be waiting. Whatever happens I can't be letting the old bill get a sniff of my business, and letting Frank Allen down just isn't an option."*

Ricky looked around the pub for Neil and Jackie.

"They must have slipped away when all this kicked off," Ricky thought.

"What did the old bill say?" Kenny said, handing Ricky a pint.

"It was just the usual stuff. They were just fishing for information. What did you tell them?" Ricky said before taking a small sip.

"Nothing mate. I told them I didn't see anything. Yeah, I knew Deano and then he started going on about the graffiti on the wall and asking who the Bedford Boot Boys were. I just shrugged my shoulders and made out like I'd never seen the graffiti before," Kenny said.

Ricky waved over Lee, Terry and Steve Parker to the end of the bar.

"Do we know who did it?" Terry Parker whispered.

"It was Eddy Boyce from the Bedford Boot Boys," Ricky said.

"I'll cut his bleedin' throat," Steve Parker hissed.

"I think the first thing we have to do is make sure that Deano gets through this, right?" Ricky said firmly.

The Teds all nodded their heads.

"Then we have to wait for the old bill to move on to the next crime, so we don't all find ourselves banged up alongside Mickey Deacon," Ricky said.

"Mick would be climbing the walls now," Kenny muttered. "He'd be armed to the teeth and going from door to door on the Bedford estate."

"Yeah, well he's not, is he Kenny? Eddy Boyce will pay, there is no doubt about that, but we have to bide our time and box smart," Ricky said.

"What happens if Deano doesn't make it?" Terry said. "What I mean is, who is taking over the Milton Road Teds?"

There were a few moments silence.

"With Deano in the hospital and Mick, his second in command, in the shovel, I'll step up in a caretaker role just until Deano has pulled through," Ricky announced.

"I've been a Milton Road Ted a bloody sight longer than you Ricky, and you too for that matter, Kenny," Lee said, stabbing his finger into his chest. "Why not me? I want to be leader."

"Don't take this the wrong way, Lee, but you ain't ever going to be running a Ted outfit and you know that mate. Deano and Ricky were friends and Ricky has been on the front line in the last three rows. I say it should be Ricky," Kenny said resolutely. "What do you say Terry, Steve?"

"We're just here for a tear up," Terry said as he puckered his lips and nodded his head. "But I'd rather follow Ricky into battle than you Lee. No offence."

"Then Ricky will be running things until Deano is out of hospital and back in the saddle," Kenny said, staring Lee down.

"Sorted," Steve said.

Ricky handed Lee a five-pound note and asked him to get another round in. Terry and Steve said their goodbyes and left the pub.

"How are you going to sort this stuff out with Specs mate?" Ricky said.

"Look, Ricky, I never wanted this to happen. I mean, if Denise had told me that she was up the duff then I most probably would have stayed with her. I don't know, maybe even got married or something," Kenny said, reaching for his beer.

"This has got to be hitting Specs hard, mate. I mean one minute he thinks he's all happily married and taking little Tommy down the park in the push chair, and the next thing she's gone and slung him out on his ear," Ricky said.

"Don't you think I've thought about all that Ricky? Denise probably told me all this stuff about six weeks ago and there's not been a day gone by that I've not thought about what this is going to do to Specs. I can't control it, mate, so I'm not going to worry too much. If I can find a way to work things out with Specs then great, but if not, then that's it. Denise and my son Tommy have to be my priority."

"Relationships eh?" Ricky said.

"Now you can probably see why I used to like just swooping in for some no-strings-attached fun and then move on to the next one," Kenny said with a wry smile.

"Here Ricky," Ronnie the landlord called out while holding up the pub's phone. "This is Tammy, an old friend of mine that nurses up at St Helier Hospital."

Ricky slipped behind the bar and took the phone.

Ricky: Hello Tammy.

Tammy: Hi Ricky. Ronnie told me about your friend Deano Derenzie.

Ricky: Yeah, have you heard anything?

Tammy: No, nothing firm yet. He's still in surgery.

Ricky: So he's alive then?

Tammy: He is one very lucky man. The tip of the knife missed his heart by half an inch.

Ricky: Damn!

Tammy: He lost a lot of blood but fortunately the knife didn't sever any vital organs. He has a whole team in with him.

Ricky: A whole team?

Tammy: His clothing must be removed while other members of the team have to place IV's, take blood samples, take the blood glucose levels, and put the heart monitoring pads on his chest. He'll need to be lifted and turned over so they can check for other wounds. Every person on the team knows exactly what they have to do. I know all these people personally and I hope I can reassure you that your friend is in the best possible hands.

Ricky: Thank you Tammy. Will it be alright to visit tomorrow?

Tammy: The best thing to do is to ask at reception in the morning. I think it's highly unlikely that your friend will be in a fit state to talk with anyone though.

Ricky: Its great just knowing that he's alive, in good hands and even if we just catch a glimpse of him tomorrow then I'm sure his girlfriend, Melanie, will find some comfort in that.

Tammy: Okay Ricky. I have to go now as my shift is just starting.

Ricky: Thanks for your help, Tammy.

The phone went dead. Ricky handed the telephone receiver to Ronnie.

"Thanks for that Ronnie. It's early days but it looks like Deano is going to be alright," Ricky said.

The DJ was playing *'You, You, You'* by Alvin Stardust and there were several people drunkenly dancing, slopping their drinks onto the carpet and singing along.

"You'd never have guessed that Deano was stabbed up next door less than two hours ago, looking at this lot," Ricky thought.

Chapter 2

"What do you think Guvnor?" DC Bernard Jacobs asked.

"I knew it was just a question of time before somebody either got seriously hurt or killed on the Milton Road Estate. Nothing but low life criminals the damn lot of them," DS Ray White said in a dismissive tone.

"I checked with the hospital Guv, and it looks like Deano Derenzie will probably pull through. He's on the critical list but they reckon he'll be alright." DC Jacobs said, reading from his note pad.

"It's about time we brought that wall of silence up the estate crashing down. I reckon half of all the crimes committed in the area are connected to the urchins on that estate one way or another," DS White said, slamming his hand down on the desk.

"What do you want me to do with the bookie, Guv? I've got him in the interview room," DC Jacobs said as he closed his notebook and put it in his jacket pocket.

DS White looked at his watch. It was just after 11.00pm.

"Let him sweat in there for another half hour, Bernie, then sling him out."

"It's Christmas Eve Guv. He won't get a taxi anywhere?"

"Good, the walk will do him good," DS White said, pulling a packet of Players No 6 cigarettes out. He opened the pack and offered one to Bernie before lighting one for himself and slinging the packet on the desk.

"You're enjoying this, ain't you Guv?" DC Jacobs said with a half-smile.

"I've just decided on both our New Year Resolutions Bernie. We're gonna turn that estate and everyone on it upside down. We're gonna give them a bit of aggravation, my son, and shake the tree until the blaggers, drummers and tea leaves start to fall out."

Chapter 3

"**G**et in the motor," Ricky said as he slid in behind the steering wheel.

Melanie, Kenny, Lee, Kaz and Donna all climbed into Ricky's Rover P5B. He started the engine and shifted into drive. The car took off with a squeal of the rear tyres.

"What if he dies?" Melanie said.

Ricky could see that she was still in a state of complete shock.

"That isn't going to happen," Ricky said as he slowed down at a junction.

"But, how do you know?" Melanie asked as her eyes filled with tears.

"Deano the Dog is the main man, top dog and quite possibly the bravest bloke I've ever met. There is no way he's going to just keel over and turn up his toes," Ricky said adamantly.

"Ricky's right, Melanie. Deano will be alright," Kenny agreed.

Ricky turned and nodded to Kenny.

"I don't want him to die," Kaz said, rubbing her hands.

Kenny put his arm around her. "Don't worry, Kaz, he'll be fine. Are you okay, Donna?" Kenny said, turning to face her.

"I just don't believe it. One minute we're all getting ready to celebrate Christmas and now this," Donna said as she turned back from staring out of the side window.

"Whoever did this to Deano needs sorting out and quickly," Lee hissed through gritted teeth.

"Who do you think did it?" Melanie said, wiping tears away from her swollen red eyes.

"My money's on Clifford Tate," Kenny said firmly.

"Clifford Tate?" Melanie said, looking a little shocked.

"That sounds like a possibility," Ricky agreed.

"But why?" Melanie said, shrugging her shoulders.

"Really Melanie?" Donna said in a quizzical tone.

"What do you mean really?" Melanie said sharply.

"If you're talking about that time I was with Clifford, that's ancient history," Melanie said slapping her hand on her thigh.

"Ancient history is what, eighteen months ago?" Donna persisted.

"We don't know who did it," Ricky said to try and calm down the escalating tension in the car. "It could have been Clifford Tate because of that row we had with the Bedford Boot Boys. Deano did him good and proper. I'm not sure that I could let that go either. But he ain't the only one, is he? Let's be honest, Deano and the Milton Road Teds have been knocking people out for years. It could have been any one of them that has got all big and brave with a blade in their hand."

"Deano stabbed, I still can't believe it," Kaz whimpered.

Ricky drove through the town and across to the hospital. He parked up in the car park and the six of them went through to the reception to ask after their friend. Once they got inside they saw

Teddy Boys dressed in their drape suits everywhere. The word had got out and lads from the estate and surrounding areas had gone to the hospital.

"Ricky, mate just give us the word and we're with you to sort out whoever did this to Deano," Everard James, leader of a small group of Teds up on the St David's Estate said.

"How the hell did you hear about this so quickly?" Ricky said as he looked around at all the Teds.

"I got a call from Lee, and I pulled the lads in straight away. We're tooled up and ready to go," Everard said with a fierce expression. "I had trouble from a group of Nazi Skinheads some years back and I'd only just met Deano. When he heard how they were disrespecting me and my lads, he came in with us and made light work of them all. I don't think any of us had ever seen someone have a row like him. He's an animal, but loyal to his own and he had my loyalty, no matter what, from that day. I owe him, we all do, so no matter who or where they are, we're in!"

"It's still early days mate, and the last thing we want to do right now is go out on a witch hunt and start slapping the wrong people about," Ricky said in a reasoning tone.

"I heard it was Clifford Tate," Everard said as he clenched his fist.

"Who told you that?" Ricky asked.

"Well, Lee mentioned him."

"That's what I mean. Lee doesn't know, it's just what he thinks, and we can't go rolling in heavy handed based on a wild guess."

"But do you think it might be him?"

"It's a possibility. What I will do is keep you in the picture and should we need numbers to bring the guilty party down, I will call you mate," Ricky said with a smile.

"I appreciate that," Everard said, shaking Ricky's hand firmly.

Ricky looked over at the reception. The conversation was getting heated.

"Deano Derenzie is my boyfriend and I want to see him!" Melanie cried.

"I'm sorry, Miss, but no one will be seeing Mr Derenzie," the nurse said with a stern expression.

"My boyfriend has been stabbed and I want to see him!" Melanie shouted through floods of tears.

"Okay, can we all calm down please?" A doctor said as he walked into the casualty area. "Miss, we fully understand your concern and, as you say Mr Derenzie has been stabbed, which means that he is in the best possible place, and right now we need to provide him the right care. I will pull no punches. Mr Derenzie is in critical condition, but we have the best team in the hospital right now working hard to save his life. It would help us if you could all calm down and maybe go home and phone in tomorrow for an update. You can be sure that he is being well taken care of."

"Doctor, will he make it?" Kaz whimpered.

"I certainly hope so," the doctor said with a half-smile.

The doors swung open and DS Ray White and DC Bernard Jacobs strode in.

"Well I never," DS White said as he scanned the room. "It looks like the circus is in town Bernie."

"Yes Guv," DC Jacobs agreed with a smirk.

"Alright now, step away please," DS White ordered as he approached the desk.

Ricky, Melanie, Kaz, Donna and several Teds from the Milton Road Estate stepped back and gave the police officers room.

"Are you the doctor?" DS White said.

"Yes."

"Good. I'm Detective Sergeant Ray White and this is Detective Constable Jacobs. We need to talk with Deano Derenzie."

"That's not possible," the doctor said.

"Everything is possible," DS White said in an obstinate tone.

"The patient is in the operating theatre."

"Did he say anything before he was taken in?"

"No, the patient was unconscious, officer."

"Not a name, any name?" DS White persisted.

"Can you please call in tomorrow and we'll know more about Mr Derenzie's condition," the doctor said, looking down at his watch.

"Bernie, make a note of the doctor's name and call him first thing in the morning," DS White said.

"Yes Guv."

"Right!" DS White said loudly, turning with his hand on hips to face the sea of Teddy Boys.

"The heavy mob are now involved so I want a name! You," DS White said, pointing at Lee. "We want the scumbag responsible for this as much as you lot so, who was it? Cough up a name for me."

Ricky shot Lee a fierce look and shook his head slightly.

"I don't know," Lee said, shrugging his shoulders.

"Is that you don't know, or you're not telling us?" DS White said, taking a step closer.

"I don't know," Lee said, lowering his head.

"You do know that by not telling me you could be nicked for hindering a possible murder investigation."

"He said he doesn't know," Ricky said, taking two steps towards the officer.

"Yeah, you heard him," Kenny said, stepping up to join Ricky.

DS White fixed his glare on them before walking slowly over towards Ricky and Kenny.

"So what's this, are you two the big bollocks then?"

"We're friends of Deano," Ricky said.

"Then do your friend a favour and give us a name," DS White said, holding up his note pad and pen.

"We don't know who did it," Kenny grumbled.

"I heard it was a copper," Everard called out.

"You," DS White said as he turned to face Everard James. He looked him up and down and smiled. "You, sunny Jim, are on very thin ice."

"What do you mean by sunny Jim," Everard retorted in a soft, aggressive, tone.

DS White looked him up and down again and then turned slowly away.

"Nothing," DS White answered in a dismissive tone.

"Like we've been saying," Kenny continued. "We don't know who stabbed our friend. If we knew then we'd tell you. Wouldn't we?" Kenny said as he scanned the room for support.

"Yeah, of course," one Ted said.

"Absolutely," said another.

"In a heartbeat," Donna said.

"Who is the guvnor here, the head honcho, you know, the top dog?" DS White asked as he looked around the Teddy Boys.

The Teds all looked at each other and shook their heads as if they didn't understand the question.

"I will get the person responsible for this and if I find out that during the course of this investigation any of you were withholding information, you will be nicked, and I'll make sure the judge throws the book at you! You can contact me, Detective Sergeant Ray White or Detective Constable Bernard Jacobs at the police station," DS Ray White said as he put his notepad and pen back in his jacket pocket.

Ricky watched as the officers left the hospital.

"Typical filth, hiding behind a badge," Ricky thought.

"Melanie, Kaz, Donna, I'll take you home. The doctor's right. Deano is in the best place. We can call back tomorrow," Ricky said.

"No, I'm staying," Melanie said.

"Yeah, we'll stay with Mel and maybe we'll take a taxi back later," Kaz said, putting her arm around Melanie's shoulders.

Donna nodded.

"Kenny, Lee, are you coming?"

"Yes mate," Kenny said.

Lee nodded.

Ricky turned to face the Teds that had made their way up to the hospital.

"The doctor has everything under control. It's probably best if you lads go home now. We don't want the old bill coming up and making a nuisance of themselves," Ricky said. "Everard, it's good to see you mate. We will be in touch."

One by one the Teds left the casualty reception, leaving just Melanie, Kaz and Donna.

Ricky started the car and slowly drove out of the car park.

"Mick would be all over this," Lee said as he looked back towards the hospital.

"All over what Lee? We don't know who is responsible." Ricky said indicating to turn left out onto the main road.

"I'm just saying that Mick would be getting numbers together and getting out there to sort it out," Lee persisted.

"Are you not listening, Lee?" Ricky said, looking over his shoulder. "Mick isn't here, and Deano wouldn't want us creating havoc with anyone other than those responsible."

"It's that jug headed wanker Clifford Tate," Lee growled as a single tear fell from his eye. "I know it. I know in my gut that he did it. He stabbed my mate!"

"You know fuck all, Lee, so stop giving it the big one," Kenny said calmly. "Ricky has it all in hand and when we have something a little more than your gut feeling it'll be taken care of, right Ricky?"

"Damn right," Ricky growled.

Chapter 4

January 1975

"Who is this Double Bubble, Guv?" DC Jacobs said as he read through his notes.

"Leonard Crawford. I nicked him a few years back. He's a right nasty piece of work. From what I gathered he honed his money lending skills whilst in the shovel, and then set himself up on the Milton Road Estate. There's no shortage of customers and when you see the size of him, you'll see why he ain't gonna get knocked," DS White said.

DS Ray White and DC Bernard Jacobs were driving through the Milton Estate in their unmarked Cortina MK3. It was just after 9.00am.

"Why do they call him Double Bubble?"

"If you borrow a fiver this week, you owe a tenner next week," DS White said as he reached down and changed gear.

"That's a bit bloody steep ain't it, Guv?"

"People on benefits and thieves tend to live from hand to mouth, Bernie. Places like the Milton Road Estate have their own little economy and there is always, and I mean always, a money lender somewhere," DS White said as he slowed down and turned on the indicator.

DS White parked the Cortina beside a block of flats. DC Jacobs wore a pair of blue flared jeans, a black polo neck jumper and a black leather bomber jacket. DS white looked from left to right before locking the car door.

"You can't be too careful Bernie. They'd nick the air out of your tyres around here," DS White said, looking up and down the street.

DC Jacobs followed his guvnor through the flats and up the concrete stairs.

"We could have taken the lift, Guv," DC Jacobs said, gasping for breath as they reached the fifth floor.

"Not a chance," DS White said. "I did it once and it stank of piss. I'm in no hurry to do that again."

The two police officers stood outside a blue painted door with four panels and the number 66 in off-white plastic letters.

KNOCK! KNOCK!

DS White waited just a few seconds before pounding his fist on the door again.

"Alright, alright. I'm coming!"

The door opened and there stood Double Bubble in a pair of pale blue jeans and a white vest. He dwarfed the door opening with his 54-inch chest and bulging biceps.

"Detective Sergeant Ray White. Can I help you?" Double Bubble said, crossing his huge arms.

"Yes, thank you, I'd like to come in," DS White said, pushing past the big man.

"You've got some right front," Double Bubble said. "Who's your hoppo?"

DS White strode straight down the hallway and into the lounge. Double Bubble and DC Jacobs followed him.

"This is my colleague Detective Constable Jacobs. So, rather than beat around the bush why did you do it?"

"What are you on about?" Double Bubble said with a quizzical expression, reaching down for his packet of Players No 6 cigarettes.

"Deano Derenzie, why did you stab him? What, did he owe you money? I mean money lending is your game, isn't it?" DS White said with an accusing glare.

"Hold up, I ain't stabbed anyone. You lot ain't gonna fit me up with that one" Double Bubble said, placing the cigarette into his mouth.

"The word around the Estate is that you two don't see eye to eye?" DS White said, reaching down and picking up a hardback notebook.

"Oi, that's mine. You ain't got no right," Double Bubble said, making a clumsy grab for the book.

"I'm the law, sonny Jim, and I've got every right. Now stop giving it the big one, park yourself over there and smoke your fag," DS White said, pointing to the armchair.

"So, what have we here? Looks like a ledger to me, Bernie. What does it look like to you?" DS White said before throwing the notebook across the room to DC Jacobs.

DC Jacobs flicked through the pages slowly and then slowly raised his head and smiled.

"It looks like a money lending ledger to me, Guv."

"Have a look around Bernie and see what else our friend here has that violates his parole conditions."

DC Jacobs left the lounge and briefly glimpsed into every room.

"You're a fucking slag, White," Double Bubble cried out, jumping onto his feet with his fists tightly clenched.

"Now that's not nice, is it? Do you really want to add assaulting a police officer to the list of charges that are piling up here? I reckon with the five years you still owe, and whatever else we find today, you could be looking at… what, eight years? Now add stabbing Deano Derenzie and, well, you ain't going to be coming back any time this century," DS White said with a sly grin.

"I told you. I had nothing to do with that. I was in the Arms having a quiet drink. I've got witnesses.

"Shit witnesses!" DS White yelled.

"Guv, there's a couple of those Chopper bikes in the bedroom. They look new to me."

"Well, well, well. So what's all this then? Is it some kind of new kink that I've not heard of yet? Or maybe, just maybe, they're stolen property just like the television and the stereo."

"What is it you want?" Double Bubble asked as he slowly lowered his fists.

"Good, we're making progress. Who was it that stabbed Deano Derenzie?"

"I don't know," Double Bubble said, sitting down and slouching back into the armchair.

"Nick him Bernie," DS White said firmly.

"Wait a minute. Look, it wasn't me, and I don't know exactly who did it, but Deano and the Teddy Boys have been having a right old barny with the lads up on Bedford Estate. Maybe it was one of them," Double Bubble blurted out.

"That would be the Bedford Boot Boys, right?"

"Yeah, that's them. Look, I heard that Deano pulled a load of Teds together and gave them a right a good seeing to on their own manor. I don't know it for sure, but the word was that Deano smacked this Skinhead leader bloke and knocked all his teeth out," Double Bubble said with a heavy sigh.

"Hmm, a Skinhead leader bloke. Now who would that be?"

"Oh come on, give me a break," Double Bubble pleaded.

"That's exactly what I'm doing right now, giving you a break. What's his name?" DS White said abruptly.

Double Bubble closed his eyes and shook his head. "Clifford Tate."

"Now you see, that wasn't hard, was it?" DS White said in a relaxed, friendly, tone.

"I ain't no grass!" Double Bubble yelled.

"I tend to look at information as a commodity. There are times when it has more value than others. Today we have you bang to rights and could, if we chose, have you carted back to the factory, and you'd be banged up in Brixton before the sun went down. Do we understand each other?" DS White said, shaking his finger back and forth.

Double Bubble nodded.

"Good, because we're going to need some help to clear some of the outstanding crimes on our books. I don't expect you to give up your customers or anything that has a direct impact on your money lending activities. That would be unreasonable and I'm not an unreasonable man. Every man has a right to make a living, no matter how shitty it may appear to others. What I do want is for you to throw me a name every so often. Give me some information that helps to put a few of these animals away. In return, Bernie and I will turn a blind eye to all your enterprises and, should you need it, help to make sure that you're not bothered by others. Am I making myself clear?"

Double Bubble nodded.

"I'm sorry I didn't hear you," DS White persisted.

"You want me to be your informer and in return I'm left alone," Double Bubble muttered.

"That's it. You nailed it in one," DS White said victoriously.

"I could get proper hurt if this ever got out," Double Bubble said.

"No one will ever know. This, Leonard Crawford, is our little secret."

"Call me Double Bubble or DB. I hate my own name."

"Okay, DB, now throw me a bone. What can you tell me?"

"There was a wages snatch in Thornton Heath in November last year. The geezer made out that he was old bill, flashed a moody warrant card and told the bloke that there was a police sting in operation waiting to get the villains planning to rob him," Double Bubble said.

"I've heard of this one Guv. They got away with seven grand in cash," DC Jacobs said. "He convinced the driver to swap cases, so the money wouldn't be at risk when the robbery was supposed to happen. Very clever that one."

"Thank you Bernie," DS White said as he turned back to face Double Bubble. "So, what about this blag?"

"I know who did it."

"Come on then, spill the beans," DS White said.

Double Bubble sighed heavily. "It was Charlie Summers."

"Charlie Summers. I know him. I nicked him a few years back. He's a drummer, turns over people's houses. This is a step up for him," DS White said, looking a little shocked.

"Yeah, he's teamed up with this other geezer on the Estate. I think they met in the shovel or something. Thick as thieves they are, proper best mates. They drink in the Arms," Double Bubble said.

"Well DB that's a good start," DS White said looking over at DC Jacobs. "Bernie hand our friend back his ledger."

"Yes Guv," DC Jacobs said before putting the ledger on the coffee table. "What about the Chopper bikes in the bedroom?"

DS White smiled and stood up. "What Chopper bikes?"

"Okay, right Guv," DC Jacobs said.

"No need to see us to the door DB. We'll let ourselves out," DS White said.

DS White slammed the door shut behind him. DC Jacobs was about to speak when DS White put his finger on his lips indicating that he was not to talk. They didn't exchange any words while walking down to the ground floor. Once inside the car DC Jacobs spoke.

"Can we trust him sir?"

"Bernie, an hour ago we had nothing. Now we can follow up this stabbing with Clifford Tate and get a warrant to turn over Charlie Summers' place. I can see a clean-up coming, Bernie and that Inspector's badge will not be too far behind it," DS White said with a broad smile.

Chapter 5

Ricky and Neil had visited Dingwall motor auction to see four cars they had changed the chassis and number plates of a few days before. The original cars Ricky had bought as accident damaged from the salvage yard for the registration documents had been stripped down and sold off quickly to local garages and motor traders. The two friends watched as the last of their cars passed by the auctioneer. It reached a staggering sixteen hundred pounds.

"That must have been a private buyer, to pay that kind of money," Ricky said with a broad grin.

"So, what have we made today?" Neil said, rubbing his hands together.

"We pulled in just under five grand, so after costs, we'll have about two thousand, two hundred and fifty quid each," Ricky said as he patted Neil's arm.

"Mate, this is easy money," Neil said.

"We just keep our heads down and keep grafting," Ricky said. "Anyway, how are you and Jackie getting on?"

"Good, really good. You know, I always thought she was a bit out of my league," Neil said as he put his hands in his pockets.

"Don't be silly, mate," Ricky said with a warm smile. "You're a good bloke and I'm pleased that you're happy."

"Cheers, you know I always thought it would end up being you and Jackie and then I'd probably end up being your best man or something," Neil said with a chuckle.

"Oh, no," Ricky said, feigning a laugh. "We're just good friends and that's it. Don't get me wrong she's a great looking girl but I only ever saw her as a mate."

"Yeah, you've said that before, but I saw the way she looked at you sometimes," Neil said.

"Well she's your bird now, Neil, so be happy," Ricky said, then rubbed his stomach. "I'm starving, are you hungry?"

"Mate I could eat a scabby horse, scabs and all," Neil said before turning to look over at the café across the road from the auction. "You fancy a full English breakfast?"

"That would do it," Ricky said as the two lads passed by the motor traders, crossed the road and entered Ernie's Café.

"Alright boys," a friendly, buxom blonde woman said as the lads entered the café. "What can I get you?"

"Hello darling, I'll have two mugs of tea and two of your big boy full English," Ricky said as he looked up at the menu board behind the till.

"Do you boys want some bubble and squeak with that?"

"Yeah, go on," Neil said. "We'll have a couple of rounds of toast as well."

"Bloody hell mate, you are hungry," Ricky said as he sat down at the table by the window.

"I never know what time Jackie's going to get home. It all depends on what Doreen has her out there hoisting. Some days she'll be back and home and sorted by half three and other times it's gone eight at night. She's really got the bit between her teeth with all this hoisting lark, and believe me, mate, she's pulling in some serious money," Neil said.

"You have to take it while you can, so good on her," Ricky said before taking a sip from his steaming hot cup of strong tea. "Does she know about us?"

"Yeah, why, is that a problem?"

"No, of course not. It's just important that as few people as possible know what we're up to. Loose lips and all that, you know?" Ricky said.

"Jackie wouldn't say anything," Neil said with a grin.

"No, of course not." Ricky said, sitting back in his chair as the buxom blonde placed two huge full English breakfasts in front of the lads.

"There you go boys, get that down your necks," the blonde said with a friendly wink.

"Cheers, sweetheart," Ricky said as he reached for his knife and fork.

The lads tucked into the breakfast with Neil dipping his toast into the fried eggs while Ricky put a piece of bacon and an egg on top of his toast and poured brown HP sauce over it.

"This place is the business for a tasty bit of grub," Neil said before shovelling a fork full of egg and bacon into is mouth.

"Tell me about it," Ricky said with a chuckle and then ate the last piece of sausage.

"Nasty business about Deano," Neil said after a few moments silence.

"Yeah, I don't think anyone saw that coming, but it looks like he's going to make it," Ricky said, putting his knife and fork together on the empty plate.

"You know, when you first became a Teddy Boy, I thought you were mad. Don't get me wrong I love all the gear and the music but Deano and the Milton Road Teds? Mate they can get proper mental. That night when you lot hit that pub because Specs got a slap from those builders? That was serious shit, mate and I was literally shitting myself as I sat in that van. My hands were shaking, and I was sweating buckets. I only did it because you asked and… well, I suppose I wanted some recognition too," Neil said.

"That was good of you mate, and yeah it can get rough out there," Ricky said as he motioned the buxom blonde to bring over two more mugs of tea.

"You need to get out Ricky," Neil said, his tone becoming more serious.

"Nah," Ricky said, shaking his head.

"Who knows, next time that might be you getting stabbed up."

"I'm part of something Neil. Sure, it can get nasty pretty quickly, but I know I can take care of myself," Ricky said confidently.

"Mate, Deano the Dog is probably one of the hardest blokes in London, and yet he's on the critical list and laid out on his back in hospital. You're my mate Ricky and I just wouldn't want anything like that to happen to you," Neil said as he peered into his empty mug.

"You're a top fella Neil and we go way back. I appreciate what you're saying but I can't step down mate. This is all just starting for me," Ricky said, reaching for his tea.

"Do you remember when we first met?" Neil said, grinning from ear to ear.

"Yes mate," Ricky said with a chuckle.

"You had made friends with Jackie and that, what's his name, you know the bully boy who wanted to fight everyone, came over and wanted to know what you were doing chatting up his girlfriend."

"Yeah, I remember that," Ricky said.

"Jackie was straight in there telling him in no uncertain terms that he was not her boyfriend and then you kicked his bloody head in," Neil said with a huge grin.

"He was bloody big for his age," Ricky said with an exaggerated sigh.

"Yeah, but you beat him, and I saw the way Jackie looked at you and I wished that it had been me that had the balls to do what you did," Neil said as he put both hands on the table.

"Neil, I was just trying to put him down before he hurt me," Ricky said.

"Yeah, but I always kind of hoped that I would have someone look at me that way one day, do you know what I mean?"

"Neil, you're a good-looking bloke with bundles of cash coming in and now you're with the same girl you've just been talking about, what more could you want?"

"No, no, all is good. I suppose it's just funny how life pans out," Neil said as he reached for his fresh mug of tea.

"That can be true, but I've always believed that we have choices. Now I could have carried on just doing my apprenticeship and having just one if not two nights a week out and you, mate, could have just carried on nicking motors to joyride. Now look at us sitting in this café having earned over two grand this week. Neil there are mugs out there only earning that for a full year's graft. We are on top right now and we have to stay that way. You need to keep getting those motors and making a life with your childhood sweetheart," Ricky said as he put his empty tea mug on the table.

"I'm not complaining," Neil said.

"I should bloody well hope not!"

"Have you heard anything from that bird, Michelle, since her old man gave you your marching orders?" Neil asked before turning sharply to watch two office girls pass the cafe.

Ricky shook his head.

"How did he even know that the headlines in the newspaper had anything to do with me?" Ricky said.

Neil began to laugh.

"He was right though, wasn't he? It was our lot smashing seven sorts out of the Bedford Boot Boys."

"Okay, yeah it was, but how would he know?" Ricky said before blowing the steam away from his fresh mug of tea.

"Maybe he was just looking out for his daughter," Neil said.

"Nah, he hated me from the very minute we met. All he could see was Milton Road estate and that was it for me. I do sometimes think, you know, about what might have been with Michelle because she was pretty special," Ricky said with a sigh.

The door to the café opened and two Skinheads wearing skin tight jeans, super high leg Doctor Marten Boots and short sleeved Ben Sherman shirts strolled in.

"Oi fatty, get us two teas pronto," one of the Skinheads shrieked as he approached the counter "And two bacon sandwiches and don't be tight with the bacon."

Ricky watched as the Skinheads sat down. The larger of the two lads produced a pack of Players No 6 cigarettes and a box of matches. The two lads lit their cigarettes, inhaled deeply and then blew the smoke towards the ceiling.

"We should get going," Neil whispered.

Ricky shook his head.

"Yeah, I heard he got right stabbed up. Probably already dead," one of the Skinheads muttered loud enough for Ricky to hear.

"Good riddance, I say. Just another dead Ted!"

Ricky reached into his pocket for his comb and then slowly combed his hair back.

"Don't start nothing," Neil whispered. "I don't want any trouble."

The buxom blonde placed two bacon sandwiches on the Skinheads' table.

"There you go lads," the blonde muttered.

The Skinhead stared hard at the blonde and then took several bites out of the sandwich.

"Not bad!"

"Do you reckon it was Clifford Tate that did it?"

"Nah, he couldn't have," one of the Skinheads said as he turned on his chair to face Ricky and Neil. "What the fuck are you staring at?"

Ricky stood up.

"I'm looking at you. Why, do you want to make one out of it?" Ricky said, opening his arms wide and beckoning them both hands.

"Come on please lads, this is my café," the blonde pleaded.

"You were talking about a good friend of mine, Deano the Dog. Do you want to share with me who was responsible for the stabbing?" Ricky said, standing just a few feet from the Skinheads table with clenched fists and ready to fight.

"We don't know," the second Skinhead said. "It was just talk."

"Who are you then?"

"I'm Ricky Turrell, Milton Road Teds and I'm on a mission to find out who stabbed Deano," Ricky said before taking a small step closer the Skinheads' table. "I will find him and he will pay."

"Shit, I should have brought my knuckleduster," Ricky thought.

"We ain't got nothing to do with the Bedford Boot Boys. We're just repeating what we heard, mate. We're not looking for any trouble with you, Deano or the Milton Road Teds, alright?"

"Fair enough," Ricky said, lowering his arms and unclenching his fists.

Ricky motioned to Neil that they were leaving.

"Thanks for the breakfast sweetheart," Ricky said before handing the blonde a five-pound note.

Ricky and Neil left the café and wandered back over to the auction.

"Shit, Ricky I thought it was going to go off back there," Neil said.

"I couldn't let it slide, Neil, not if there was a chance to find out who stabbed Deano," Ricky said as they strolled up and down the aisle where the next cars were due to go through to the auction.

"Have you seen anything here you fancy?" Ricky asked.

"A clean pair of trousers would be nice. I think I've just shit in these," Neil said making the two friends both burst into fits of laughter.

Chapter 6

"**G**uv shouldn't we have a warrant?" DC Jacobs said.

"Charlie Summers is a known drummer, so we're just going to have a friendly chat. Maybe he can help us with our enquiries. Now, if my memory serves me right, he's likes a flutter so we'll swing by the bookies first," DS White said.

Detective Sergeant White and Detective Constable Jacobs were driving through the Milton Road Estate. DS White had asked for two uniformed officers to follow them in a marked Ford Escort police car.

"This will be the first of many collars to be felt Bernie. I'm going to squeeze Double Bubble dry and clean this place up," DS White said.

"I have to say, Guv, I was surprised that he grassed on his own people. I mean that could get a fella seriously hurt in a place like this if he was found out," DC Jacobs said.

"We'll give him all the protection he needs until we've got all that we want and then we'll either nick him or throw him to the wolves," DS White said with a smirk.

"He'll probably do a moonlight Guv. I mean, that's what I would do rather than face the lot around here," DC Jacobs said.

***

Ricky and Kenny were standing outside the chip shop each with a Saveloy and chips wrapped in yesterday's newspaper.

"Have you heard any more about Deano?" Kenny said.

"No mate. I called the hospital and he's still on the critical list. They're optimistic; it's just time now," Ricky said.

"Have you heard anything about Eddy Boyce?"

"Nothing at all, mate. Even Clifford Tate has gone off the radar after that hit on the Bedford Working Men's Club. Maybe he's retired," Ricky said before taking a large bite out of his Saveloy.

"Maybe, but that Eddy Boyce won't be able to hide forever. Deano, when he's out, will find him. I'd bet my last pound note on that," Kenny said.

"I heard that Jock Addie had a row with a load of Boot Boys in Orpington. I don't know how true it is, but the word is that he bit part of this geezer's ear off," Ricky said.

"I'm telling you mate; Jock has got his eye on Deano's crown. That ugly mug wants to be King of the Teds. Of all the alliances that Deano's built, it was always Jock that played up, you know pushed his luck. With Deano in hospital and Mick banged up, he probably figures that the Milton Road Teds are ripe for a take-over," Kenny said.

"That ain't going to happen Kenny, we'll go toe to toe with the lot of them if we have to. There's no way that we are going to fall under Jock Addie," Ricky said.

"I just hope that Deano pulls through," Kenny said. "Have you seen Melanie?"

"Yeah, I slipped around to Deano's place just to make sure that she was alright. She's keeping herself busy with Doreen," Ricky said.

"Who would have thought it eh? I mean Doreen recruited not just Jackie, but Melanie, Kaz and Donna. She is one very slick operator," Kenny said.

"You have to take your hat off to her. She's been supplying knocked off gear to the Estate since, well before I started school and now she's got what, seven or eight girls out there hoisting for her?" Ricky said.

"She loves Jackie. By all accounts she's raking it in mate. I mean pulling some very serious money from just nicking goods to order. You've got to admit it makes these geezers doing security vans and banks for ten or twenty grand a bit of a joke. If the gavvers nick you on a bank job then you're down for a ten stretch, but Jackie can pull that kind of money in within a few months, get caught, and do what, a couple of months at the most," Kenny said.

"Little do you know mate, but what with Frank Allen's African operation and the motors Neil and I are ringing, I'm making almost two grand a week," Ricky thought.

"Yeah, you can see the attraction. Doreen is a very smart businesswoman," Ricky said.

"Good looking sort too. I mean for an older bird," Kenny said.

"I thought you were done with all that womanising mate, now you're with Denise," Ricky said.

"Yeah I am, but you can't help noticing those cracking little curves on a good-looking sort," Kenny said with his usual cheeky grin.

"Have you seen Specs?"

"Between you and me, mate, I think that he's following us about. I mean I've taken Denise and Tommy over to the park and I've caught sight of him a couple of times. Once could be a coincidence but not when it's three or four times. Yesterday as we pushed the pram down to the shops, I saw him duck into a bus shelter. I called out to him. I mean I know that it's messy, but we still live on the Estate and we're going to see each other no matter what, so I thought it could be an opportunity to talk things through, maybe find some way to keep everyone happy," Kenny said.

"What did he say?"

"He just stared at us and stomped off."

"You can't blame him," Ricky said.

"Mate I know, and believe me I do feel bad about the whole thing, but what can I do? Tommy is my son, and I can't turn my back on him or Denise like my old man did me," Kenny said shrugging his shoulders.

"I suppose not, mate. Hold up, that's that big mouth copper DS White and his side kick," Ricky said.

DS Ray White and DC Bernard Jacobs came to a stop in their unmarked Ford Cortina.

"Have a look. They've brought uniform with them for back up," Kenny muttered.

Ricky and Kenny watched as the two officers got out of their car and marched towards the bookies. As they entered the busy, cigarette smoke filled shop, it went quiet.

"Well what do we have here Bernie?" DS White said, waving the smoke away from his face.

"Villains!" DC Jacobs said as he crossed his arms.

"Charlie Summers you're looking very affluent and just the villain I was looking for," DS White said.

"Oh come on Mr White, give me a break. I ain't drummed a gaff in years. I went straight," Charlie pleaded.

Charlie wore a pair of flared blue trousers and an open neck shirt with a heavy gold chain under his brown leather jacket.

"Oh really, so that wages snatch had nothing to do with you?" DS White said.

There were a couple of gasps and whispers among the bookies' customers as the uniformed officers strutted around the shop.

"You must be joking, Mr White. That's far too heavy for me," Charlie said, holding his hands up.

"There is only one heavy mob, Charlie Summers, and that's us. A little birdie tells me that you've moved up in the world and we need to have a chat," DS White said, motioning the two officers to take him.

"Come on leave it out Mr White. I've got twenty quid on a dead cert at Chepstow," Charlie implored.

As the first officer attempted to take Charlie by the arm, he shrugged it off. The second officer tried to grab his other arm, but Charlie turned quickly and shoved the officer so hard that he lost his balance, tripped, and fell clumsily to the floor. The men in the betting shop let out a raucous cheer. One of the customers quickly trod on the officer's hand. Charlie saw an opening and made a dash for it. As the first officer tried to give chase Ricky spotted young Terry in the crowd. He stuck out his leg, tripped the officer and then quickly pulled his leg back as the officer toppled over in a heap. Outside there was a growing crowd as word quickly spread to the Arms pub, the chip shop and the newsagents that the police were attempting to make an arrest. Charlie barged past DC Jacobs and bolted out of the door.

"Get him!" DS White yelled out as he swivelled abruptly on his heels and gave chase.

The crowd outside cheered as Charlie scarpered along the pavement and past the community centre. DS White and DC Jacobs pushed past and followed in hot pursuit. Charlie Summers began to flag after his short, enthusiastic, burst. DS White sprinted along the pavement, reached out and grabbed Charlie by the shoulder and swung him around. Charlie fell backwards against the graffiti painted wall and held his hands up in submission. DS White punched him hard in the stomach taking what little breath he had left, away. Charlie choked and fell forward gasping for air.

"Right, so we've got assaulting a police officer to add to the growing list of charges. You'll do ten years for this," DS White hissed as he pushed Charlie back against the wall. The two uniformed police officers caught up to them and handcuffed Charlie.

"That's well out of order," one of the onlookers yelled.

"Typical old bill," another shouted.

"Guv, I think we need to get him out of here quickly," DC Jacobs said as the crowd continued to grow and become increasingly vocal.

"Filth!" an elderly woman cried out.

"The only good copper is a dead one!" another bystander shouted.

"You can't show any kind of weakness to this lot, or they'll be all over you," DS White said while puffing out his chest and standing firm.

DS White turned to swiftly to the uniformed officers.

"You two, get this slag back to the factory and bang him up until I get back."

The two officer's frog-marched Charlie back to their Ford Escort and forced his head down as he was shoved into the back of the car. With his shoulders pulled back, DS White strutted military style back to the betting shop. The crowd became increasingly vocal.

"You'll get yours, copper!"

"Harry Roberts had the right idea!"

As the police car began to drive away with Charlie Summers inside, Ricky spotted what looked like young Terry, run out in front of the car causing it to brake hard. When it came to a stop, he threw a house brick at the windscreen. It cracked from top to bottom. The officer slammed on his brakes and came to a screeching halt, leaving two thick tyre lines on the road. The growing mob let out a huge cheer as the figure ran off towards the flats.

Kenny began to sing:

"Harry Roberts is our friend, is our friend, is our friend"

Almost as one, everyone joined in as DS White strolled over to join DC Jacobs in their Cortina.

"Harry Roberts is our friend, he kills coppers!"

"I fucking hate old bill like him," Kenny hissed. "They don't care whether you did it or not, they just want the clean-up."

"I'm going to have to find young Terry. He's got some balls on him and could make a useful addition to the Milton Road Teds," Ricky thought.

Chapter 7

Ricky put on his new vinyl single *'Sweet Music'* by Showaddywaddy while he got ready to go out. His flat was really taking shape with all the new furniture and goods supplied by Doreen. He reached into the top of his wardrobe and took out an eight-inch round gold tin. Ricky smiled as he opened it and looked down at the twenty-, ten- and five-pound notes that were tightly packed right into the middle of the tin. He counted out five thousand pounds and wrapped an elastic band around the notes before putting the wad inside his leather bomber jacket.

Ricky had overheard, while making a cup of tea when he was at work at Harrington's, that a run-down tyre bay was up for sale on the industrial estate.

Ricky checked his image in the mirror. He opted not to wear the full drape suit and instead selected a pair of black trousers, shoes and a light blue shirt with an open collar. Ricky turned his stereo system off and put the vinyl record back in its sleeve.

The Rover P5B had just been given a full valet by a new company that had opened just a few doors down from Harrington's. Ricky figured that if the place was good enough for Harrington's, then maybe he would use it too, but at the same preferential rates.

"Now that is one good looking motor," Ricky thought as he fired up the throaty V8.

Ricky checked his rear-view mirror, slipped the shifter into gear and then allowed the car to edge slowly out into the road. The motor burbled sweetly as he increased the pressure on the throttle pedal.

Ricky drove the car across town and onto the industrial estate where Specs had been hauled off to and beaten up the year before. He slowed down, indicated and pulled into the tyre bay.

The tyre bay had four outside bays with a roof that covered the length of a car. Next to it was a red brick office, a storage area, and a shop. Above the upstairs window was a weathered sign reading: London Tyre Co.

"Yes mate, how can I help you?" a young lad dressed in blue overalls said with a welcoming smile.

Ricky guessed that the fitter was in his late teens and liked his attitude immediately.

"Can you check the tyres, do the wheel balancing all round and check the tracking alignment?" Ricky said as he handed over his car keys.

"No problem," the fitter said.

"Where's your boss, Keith?" Ricky said.

"Is there a problem?" the fitter asked.

Ricky shook his head and smiled.

"No, I just want a word."

"He's in the office," the fitter answered, before pointing towards a half-painted timber door.

"Cheers."

Ricky knocked on the door twice and then opened it. Inside, the office was packed out with boxes of tyre inner-tubes and tyres, several stacks deep.

"Yes mate, can I help you?" an older man, who Ricky guessed to be his early sixties, asked. He was skinny, wore brown stained overalls and had combed several strands of hair over his balding head.

"It's Keith, isn't it?" Ricky said before closing the door firmly behind him.

"Like I said, can I help you?" Keith said cautiously.

Ricky pulled up a threadbare chair and sat down on the opposite side of Keith's shabby desk. He reached out his hand.

"Hello Keith, I'm Ricky, Ricky Turrell."

Keith shook his hand.

"I've been led to believe that your business is up for sale," Ricky said as peered around at the stock.

Keith looked shocked.

"Who told you that?"

"A friend told me in confidence. Don't worry I've not mentioned it to anyone else because, Keith, I'm interested in buying it."

Keith picked up his half-drunk mug of tea and sat back in his black swivel chair.

"Are you serious or just another daydreamer?" Keith asked bluntly.

"I'm very serious and I'm a cash buyer," Ricky said confidently. "Why are you selling?"

Keith placed his mug back on a pile of paperwork and sat forward.

"I'm looking to retire. I've had enough of all this chasing a pound note. This is a young man's game. I'm not going to try and bullshit you Ricky, because it will make no difference to the price that I want. This place is in need of a complete refurbishment from top to bottom and some kind of campaign to get customers back through the doors. I'm not losing money but it's not exactly pouring in either," Keith said, fixing his gaze on Ricky.

"Okay, I'm still interested," Ricky said with a slight grin. "What's the magic number to make you walk away?"

"Twenty grand," Keith said as he pushed himself further into the back of his chair. "It needs to be pound notes because I'll be saying that it was sold as a going concern for a pound to avoid any tax."

Ricky sat bolt upright and looked Keith up and down, before slowly revealing a smile. He reached into his pocket and pulled out the five thousand pounds from his inside pocket and placed it on the desk.

"Here's five grand and I'll bring you another five grand before you close tonight. I've had a quick look around and you've probably only got a couple of grands worth of stock and I don't know how saleable that is. So, ten grand for assets that have all seen better days and a questionable good will is bloody good money."

Keith gazed down at the pile of money and then back up at Ricky.

"That ain't going to be enough."

Ricky shrugged his shoulders before reaching over to pick up the cash.

"Okay," Ricky said dismissively.

"Alright, alright hold your horses," Keith said, holding up his right hand. "So you can get me another five grand today?"

"Yes," Ricky confirmed.

"When do you want me out?" Keith asked.

"Today works for me," Ricky said as he slowly withdrew his hand from the pile of cash. "We can get a solicitor to do all the legal stuff next week, but you can pack up your stuff and leave at closing time."

Keith gathered up the bundle of notes and began to count it out loud.

"It's all there," Ricky said. "Have we got a deal?"

Keith smiled, exposing a row of tobacco stained, crooked and broken teeth.

"Yeah, we have a deal."

The two men shook hands.

"Right, I'll be back with the rest of your money in the next couple of hours. Just leave the books and whatever else you have on the desk for when I get back," Ricky said as he rose from the chair.

Keith, still counting the money, looked up and nodded.

Ricky left the office and walked back to his car.

"It's all done mate. I've balanced all the wheels and checked the tracking alignment. It didn't need doing," the fitter said with a broad smile. "If you follow me, we can sort the bill out with Keith."

"What's your name?" Ricky said.

"Doughnut."

"Doughnut?" Ricky questioned.

"Yeah, ever since I was at school people have called me Doughnut because of my puffy cheeks," Doughnut said, making a playful grab for his cheeks.

Ricky held out his hand.

"Good to meet you, Doughnut. I'm Ricky Turrell, the new owner of London Tyre Co."

"What! Oh no, does this mean I'm out of a job?"

"No, far from it, Doughnut. This is the start of something new and exciting, and I will need good guys with your kind of attitude. We're going to be doing some great things here," Ricky said before taking back his car keys and handing Doughnut three one-pound notes. "That's a drink for you."

Ricky got back into his car and smiled at Doughnut as he edged back out onto the industrial estate.

"Yes!" Ricky thought. *"This is going to be perfect to wash my money through, plus the inside space will be perfect for ringing a few motors once the doors are closed. I'm bagging over two grand a week now from Frank Allen and with what Neil and I are doing, this will be the bloody business."*

It was then that a tyre distribution lorry pulled up. Ricky watched as the driver bounded out of the cab with his paperwork.

"Hold up, I know him," thought Ricky.

He watched as the driver went around to the back of the truck, opened the shutter doors and handed Doughnut several tyres. Ricky turned the ignition key off and got out of his car. He walked towards the driver as he approached the front of his truck.

"Hello mate, it's Justin, ain't it?" Ricky said.

The driver stopped and looked Ricky up and down.

"That's right, can I help you mate?"

"It's Ricky from Harrington's," Ricky said.

"Course it is. Sorry mate the mincers aren't what they used to be. I really do need to get me some bins," Justin said with a chuckle. "How are you, Ricky?"

"Yeah, good. Can have a private word?" Ricky asked as he began to walk towards the back of the truck. Justin followed him.

"What's up?"

"Right, this is straight off the press, so you've got to keep quiet, alright?" Ricky said firmly.

"Yeah course," Justin replied.

"To cut a long story short, I've just bought this place," Ricky said.

Justin looked up at the weathered and beaten sign.

"Oh okay."

"Yeah, I know, it's going to need a bit of work and that's where we may be able to help each other," Ricky said softly.

"What have you got in mind?"

"Do you ever get any tyres left over?"

Justin paused for a few seconds.

"Sometimes," Justin said cautiously.

"Good because I want them all. I'll pay you a fixed amount, whether it's a mini tyre or a Jag one," Ricky said.

"A unit price then?" Justin said as he rubbed his chin.

"That's it. I'll take everything you have week in and week out."

"Okay, you have my attention," Justin said. "We're talking cash, right?"

"Absolutely," Ricky said as he patted his trouser pocket. "What kind of numbers can you get?"

"I could probably get maybe twenty tyres a week," Justin said, scanning Ricky's face for a reaction.

Ricky shook his head. "That ain't enough."

"Well, I could do some kind of deal with some of the other drivers and make it maybe thirty or forty. The distribution depot is a right shambles and they won't even miss them," Justin said with a wry grin.

"That's a good start," Ricky said, slowly nodding his head.

"Tell you what; why not just take the whole truck? I mean there's over three hundred tyres on board on a good day," Justin said as he took a step closer to Ricky

"What do you mean?"

"The distribution centre is in Milton Keynes and all my drops are around London. So, I could just stop off at my usual place for breakfast and then, with a spare set of keys that I'll give you, the truck could… well, just disappear," Justin said revealing a broad smile.

"I like that," Ricky said. "Leave that with me, alright, and I'll make some plans and get back to you. In the meantime, get whatever you can, that's you or any of your trustworthy mates. There will be pound notes waiting."

"I had a feeling today was going to be a good day," Justin said.

"Yeah, funny that, me too," Ricky said.

Justin drove away and Ricky followed him for a while before returning home and taking most of what was left in his gold tin. He returned to his new business to pay Keith off. Ricky decided that he would call into the Milton Arms for quiet celebratory drink.

"You're looking pleased with yourself," Ronnie the landlord said as reached down for a pint glass.

"It's been a good day Ronnie," Ricky said.

Ronnie began to pour him a pint of Watneys bitter. Ricky looked around the pub. It was still early but he spotted Melanie, Kaz and Donna over by the jukebox and Kenny sitting alone at Deano's table.

"Have you heard any more about Deano?" Ronnie said, tipping the pint glass to one side.

"Yeah, I checked in this morning and he's over the worst now, so I'll get myself up there again tomorrow to see if there's anything he needs."

"I'm pleased to hear it. Tell him I said hello and there's a couple of pints waiting for him," Ronnie said as he put Ricky's beer on the bar.

"I will mate," Ricky said.

Melanie had chosen one of the new records Ronnie had added that morning and put her money in the slot. *'Goodbye My Love'* by the Glitter Band played, with all three girls dancing in front of the jukebox.

"Are you alright Kenny? You look a bit hacked off mate," Ricky said as he put his beer on the table.

"Ah, it's nothing," Kenny said.

"Must be a pretty big nothing to look like that mate," Ricky said.

"It's Specs, he's really pushed his luck."

"Alright, what's up?" Ricky asked, pulling out a chair.

"Denise has taken Tommy down to the park while I was at work and he's kind of pounced on her and started giving her all the come back to me stuff. He's slagged me off like a two-bob coin and told her that he still loves her and all that kind of rubbish," Kenny muttered.

Ricky shook his head and took a sip of his pint.

"When Denise tried to leave, he grabbed her and started telling her that she had to come back. The harder she tried to pull away, the harder he held on, and then he finally pushed her over and gave her a right old mouthful telling her what an unscrupulous two-timing slag she was," Kenny said.

"It would be kind of hard to argue with that," Ricky thought.

"I mean it's out of order ain't it, Ricky?" Kenny said.

"I can't say that I blame him for wanting to talk to her, mate, but he really shouldn't have touched her though."

"That's what I thought," Kenny said. "But when Denise told me why she had been crying I decided that it was about time that Specs and I had a word. There were things that needed to be said and ground rules firmly put in place."

"This isn't sounding too good," Ricky thought.

"Anyway, I found him. Took a while but I did find him. I tried at first to reason with him, but he was trying to walk away and when I stopped him the silly bastard threw a punch. I didn't have a choice, my instincts just kicked in and I let him have it."

"Oh no," Ricky said.

"Yeah, I kicked seven sorts of shit out of him. All I could think of was him grabbing Denise and little Tommy being in the pushchair, so I just unloaded and gave him a right good hiding," Kenny muttered.

"Bloody hell Kenny, is he alright?"

"I don't know, but he was on the ground when I left him. Deano, when he gets out of hospital, will be right pissed off with me," Kenny said. "I had no choice, Ricky. I'm just hoping that Deano sees it that way."

"Well either he will, or he won't. Those are the only two options mate," Ricky said before taking a sip of his pint.

"Oh great, thanks Ricky. I needed to hear that like I need a hole in the head," Kenny said.

Melanie's choice of record finished and then *'The Bump'* by Kenny pounded out of the speakers. Kaz looked over at the table, smiled at Ricky and walked over with her empty glass.

"Hi Kaz, are you alright? Can I get you a drink?" Ricky said, motioning the barman to bring over three drinks for the girls and another pint for Kenny.

"Yeah, I'm fine. Can I have a word please Ricky?" Kaz said awkwardly.

"Yeah sure, what's up?"

"In private," Kaz said, turning swiftly and walking away from the table.

Ricky got up.

"I won't be a minute mate," Ricky said and followed Kaz to the bar.

"What's up Kaz?"

"Look I know we've not really said anything since Christmas, Ricky, but Melanie and Donna both told me what an absolute arse I was on Christmas Eve. I think you know that I kind of fancy you, but all that I said and did is so not me. It's no excuse, but I had far too much to drink and got all caught up in the Christmas spirit," Kaz mumbled.

She took a deep breath and continued.

"What I'm trying to say is that I was out of order and I'm sorry."

"Hey, Kaz don't give it another thought. We're mates alright, and we've all been guilty of having one too many," Ricky said with a warm smile.

Young Terry slammed the pub doors open and ran into the middle of the pub.

"Quick, it's Specs! He's on the roof!"

Ricky, Kenny, the three girls and most of the pub raced out of the pub and onto the pavement outside where a large crowd from the chip shop and bookies was already forming. Ricky looked up and saw that Specs was standing on the edge of the twelve storey flats opposite.

"Oh no Specs!" Donna screamed out.

"Specs, come down, come down," Melanie called.

Specs leaned forward and looked down at the increasing number of people calling for him from the street below.

"Specs!"

"Specs come down!"

Specs turned around so his back faced the crowd below. He edged slowly towards the end of the building. He closed his eyes and let out a short breath before opening his arms like a great eagle and falling backwards.

Melanie let out a terrible scream and fainted.

Ricky watched in disbelief as his friend plummeted from the building. He turned away just as Specs hit the cold concrete.

Chapter 8

"*I can't believe it, what have you done?*" Ricky thought.

Melanie's legs had collapsed under her, and she fell to her knees with her head in her hands, crying uncontrollably. With tears streaming down their faces Kaz and Donna were trying to console her. Ricky could feel the shock and disbelief from all those standing outside the Arms pub. Within just a few minutes an ambulance arrived alongside a police car and the Cortina used by DS Ray White and DC Bernard Jacobs.

Ricky turned to Kenny. He looked somehow older, grey and traumatised.

The police officers set up a crime scene with a photographer taking multiple pictures of Specs and the immediate area. Ricky watched as DS White leaned down and reached into Specs' pocket and pulled out a driving licence and what looked like an envelope. The officer stood up, opened it and read the message. He peered over at Ricky, Kenny, Lee, Terry and Steve Parker all dressed in their Teddy Boy drape suits. As he crossed the road towards them, he put the letter and Specs' driving licence into his inside pocket.

"You lot, yeah, you Teddy Boys, over here," DS White called out.

The five Milton Road Teds followed the officer away from the crowd and stopped outside the community centre.

"I take it you all know the deceased, Samuel Townsend?" DS White said.

"Specs," Kenny mumbled. "Everyone knew him as Specs."

"Does anybody know his next of kin?" DS White said.

"He has a sister, Emma," Kenny replied. "She lives on the Estate."

DS White opened his note pad and wrote down the address.

"Specs, okay, but what I don't understand is why a young man like Specs, with his whole life ahead of him would end it all and jump off a block of flats," DS White said, peering at each of the Teddy Boys in turn.

Ricky felt a pang of shock ricochet through his entire body. His legs felt weak, and he felt mentally exhausted. He wanted desperately to close his eyes and wake up to find that this was all just one terrible dream.

"Would somebody have pushed him?" DS White said. "Maybe it's the same bunch of lads that stabbed your friend Deano Derenzie. I mean that was touch and go. By rights he should be pushing up daisies now having been stabbed in the chest with a switchblade. So, could they have come back to do a number on him?"

Kenny began to shake his head.

"No, no it isn't anything like that," Kenny replied in a barely audible voice.

"Well what then?"

The five lads remained silent.

"Let's get this right, your mate Specs, a fellow Teddy Boy, has just jumped off a block of flats and had his brains spread all over the concrete and none of you lot have a clue why," DS White said. "I'm thinking I should cart the lot of you back to the station and bang you up in a cell for a few hours. Maybe that will help you focus and give me some answers."

"That won't be necessary," Kenny said. "This could be my fault."

"Kenny!" Ricky said with a glare.

"You, button it!" DS White said, pointing his finger at Ricky.

"It's okay Ricky," Kenny said, shrugging his shoulders.

"You don't have to say anything," Ricky said.

"Yes, yes I do," said Kenny.

"Come on son, let's get you down the nick so we can a have a chat and try to get to the bottom of this," DS White said.

"Ricky, mate. Can you go and see Denise for me? Tell her what's happened and that I might be home a little late," Kenny said.

"Sure Kenny, consider it done," Ricky said.

DC Jacobs was taking the names of witnesses when DS White motioned him over. The two officers and Kenny got into the Cortina and drove away.

The crowd began to disperse when young Terry pushed through and called out.

"Ricky, can I have a minute?"

"Yeah sure, Terry," Ricky said as he turned back to face him.

"Look I really don't want to be insensitive what with what's just happened to Specs, but I might need your help with something," Terry said, lowering his voice and looking around him.

"What's up?"

"I was out the other night, just walking around thinking, when I've seen this toffee-nosed bloke in a suit pull up outside the off licence in the High Street and he's left this nearly new Range Rover's engine running. I couldn't help but take a closer look. I've opened the door and before I knew it, I slammed the gear lever into drive and floored it. Ricky, she drove like a beauty, and I mean really smooth. I drove it about for a good hour as the petrol tank was virtually full. Anyway, it started to rain, and the roads got a bit slippery, but I just couldn't help but give it a boot-full, so the rear wheels were spinning. Well, I hit the throttle just a bit too hard on the corner and I clipped the kerb. The next thing I know me and the Range Rover have gone straight through the front of a jewellers. I've jumped out and my first instinct was to run, but then I've seen all this gold laying on the ground. There were bracelets, chains, rings, watches and all sorts. I emptied this carrier bag full of paperwork in the car and ran like a mad man filling it up with everything I could get my hands on. As soon as I heard the sirens I had it on my toes. Over the wall and into the night," Terry said.

"How can I help you, Terry?" Ricky asked.

"I need to sell it, you know turn it into cash," Terry said, opening his sports holdall bag.

Ricky looked down at the stolen jewellery. The bottom of the bag was littered with gold.

"Have a word, Terry. You can't walk about with all that gear. Not with that slag DS White on the estate," Ricky said.

"I know, I just want to get it sold and I didn't know who else I could trust."

"What do you want for it?" Ricky said while still gazing down at the gold.

"Ricky I haven't got a clue what it's worth," Terry answered, closing the bag.

"I could make a few calls," Ricky said.

"What do you have in your pocket?" Terry asked.

Ricky reached into his pocket and pulled out a wad of notes. He counted out two hundred and eighty pounds.

"That'll do," Terry said.

"Terry the gold is worth a lot more than that mate."

"So take it off my hands for what you've got, and if you get a lot more then you sort me out later. I trust you Ricky," Terry said, handing Ricky the bag.

"Are you sure?"

"Yeah, course," Terry said before taking the money and quickly stuffing the notes into his pocket.

"I can get myself a drape suit now," Terry said with a broad grin.

"You'll look good in it," Ricky said with a slight nod of his head. "Don't be a stranger alright? If you see me in the Arms, come on over and we'll have a pint. Look, Terry I need to get myself over to Kenny's bird's place."

"Sure, catch you later Ricky," Terry said.

Ricky walked, at pace, through the flats until he found the flat that Denise had recently begun to share with Kenny.

"What do I say?" Ricky thought. *"I'm sorry Denise, but since you turned Specs' life upside down, he's gone and jumped off the flats. I hope you can be happy now."*

Ricky pounded on the door. It opened a few seconds later. Denise stood there in her floral ankle length dressing gown.

"Ricky, Kenny's not here," Denise said pulling the dressing gown cord tightly across her waist.

"Can I come in?"

"Err, it's late and I've just got Tommy off to sleep," Denise said.

"It's important," Ricky said, taking a single step into the flat.

"Sure, come on in, why don't you?" Denise said sarcastically as Ricky closed the door behind him and walked down the hallway into the living room.

Denise followed him and stood in the doorway with her arms folded.

"What's so important that you need to come barging into my home Ricky?"

"Denise, I have some bad news."

"Kenny… is Kenny alright?" Denise said, as she quickly unfolded her arms and stepped forward.

"It's Specs, Denise. He's jumped off the flats," Ricky said, lowering his voice and shaking his head slowly. "I'm sorry Denise, but I think he's dead."

"Kenny, where's my Kenny," Denise yelled.

"Kenny is okay. The old bill has taken him in for questioning and he asked me to put you in the picture," Ricky said.

"What, do you they think Kenny has something to do with it?"

"No, it's a suicide, but they need to know what Specs' state of mind was and Kenny offered himself up," Ricky said.

"You can't trust the old bill Ricky, you know that. What if they try and pin it on Kenny?"

"Fuck me Denise, I've just told you that your husband, the man you stood at the altar and took an oath with, is splattered all over the concrete outside the community centre and all you're banging on about is the gavvers fitting Kenny up," Ricky thought. *"You really are a nasty piece of work."*

"I'm going to call a friend and see if I can get a solicitor down to the police station just to make sure the old bill don't take liberties," Ricky said.

"Good, thank you Ricky. Tommy and I can't lose Kenny, not now," Denise said with a heavy sigh.

"Denise, I'm at a bit of a loss here. I've just told you that Specs is dead. Do you not have any remorse?"

"I've made peace and forgiven myself. I told Specs the truth and that he needed to move on, but oh no, he followed me around like a lost dog. There's nothing there Ricky. I never loved Specs. I needed a father figure for Tommy, and I didn't believe, back then, that Kenny would step up. But he has now and for that I'm grateful and as harsh as this might sound, with Specs finally out of the way Kenny and I can live out our lives together as we should," Denise said.

"What you wanted, Denise, was somebody to pay the bills and keep your lazy arse from working, and Specs, who clearly loved you, was just a convenience. You're one hard, selfish, bitch and on that note I'm out of here," Ricky said as he stepped around her, walked up the hallway and left without turning back.

***

At the police station Kenny was led through to the interview room. The room was a bland magnolia colour, with just two wooden chairs and a table in the middle.

"Take a seat," DS White said.

Kenny sat down and put his palms flat on the table.

"Bernie, can you organise us some tea. I like mine strong with three sugars. How do you take yours Kenny?" DS White asked as he took a packet of Players No6 Cigarettes from his inside jacket pocket and put them on the table.

"I'm okay," Kenny said.

"Get him one anyway," DS White said.

"Yes Guv," Bernie said, closing the door firmly behind him.

"You want a smoke?" DS White said as he put a cigarette between his lips and lit it.

"No, thanks. I'm okay," Kenny said.

"Right then Kenny, it's time for you to tell me how your friend wound up brown bread," DS White said before leaning back in his chair and blowing the cigarette smoke towards the ceiling.

***

Kenny took his time and explained how he had got Denise pregnant but didn't know anything about it and how she then married Specs. He stopped mid-way through his story and took a sip from the tea that DS Jacobs had brought in. Kenny continued with his story and ended with there being an altercation between him and Specs after he tried to force himself on Denise.

"Women, eh Kenny," DS White said. "The things they do to us blokes. In my job I've seen this a hundred times where birds just wander through life leaving carnage and decimation in their wake. Well, it's a sad story Kenny, but the law is the law, and it looks like you're going to have to go down for this."

"What? But I didn't do it," Kenny shrieked and then spilt his tea.

"Well, you might not have thrown him off the roof Kenny, but the circumstances leading up to his demise does lead directly to your door. With a good brief you may get away with doing just a short stretch, maybe five or six years. It'll depend on the judge and of course how helpful we say that you've been throughout the investigation."

"But I didn't do it!" Kenny cried out.

"Bernie, go and see what you can dig up on our friend here," DS White said.

"I've already done it Guv," DC Jacobs said, opening the brown cardboard file he held in his hand. "

DS White took it from him and opened it out on the table in front of Kenny.

"Interesting Kenny. It looks like you've been before us a few times. No stranger to the authorities," DS White said.

"That was years ago," Kenny pleaded, "I was just a kid."

"It says you were cautioned once and arrested twice for fighting. Do you like to fight Kenny?" DS White asked as he closed the file.

"I was just a kid," Kenny said as he looked down at the table.

"Don't bullshit me!" DS White shouted before slamming his fist down onto the desk. "I know that you and the Milton Road Teds have been up to all sorts, what with fighting the Bedford Boot Boys and the lads from the Cambridge flats. This is common knowledge Kenny, and we know that you were right there in the middle of it all and still up to your old antics. You're a Teddy Boy thug Kenny, who turned on one of his own over some little council house slag, and now he's plastered all over the estate. We nicked and incarcerated your friend Michael Deacon so you, my friend, are not innocent. You've just been lucky not to have been caught but it was only a question of time before you ended up in front of someone like me."

"I never meant for any of this to happen," Kenny pleaded.

"How many times have we heard this, Bernie?" DS White said.

"Every day Guv," DC Jacobs said.

"Yeah, every day we have people tell us how they never meant to rob a place, steal a car or beat the shit out of someone. Believe me Kenny, we have heard it all," DS White said, lighting a second cigarette. "Look, it doesn't need to be this way."

"What do you mean?" Kenny asked, wiping a single stray tear from his face.

"I don't think you're a bad guy and I do understand that stuff like this happens. Believe me, in my job I've seen it all. So, I think we can find a way through this," DS White said before drawing hard on his cigarette.

"How?" Kenny said, perking up.

"I just need you to tell me a few things. Help me to understand what's going on," DS White said.

"I ain't no grass," Kenny said adamantly.

"I don't expect you tell me directly Kenny. I understand your working-class code and so all I'm going to do is ask you to either nod or shake your head. There will be nothing written down and if you do this small service for me then you can leave here with your code intact and just your conscience to deal with. There will be no arrests, no court appearance and definitely no prison time. Will that work for you?" DS White said with a smirk.

Kenny hesitated for a few seconds and then nodded his head.

"Good, you know it makes sense," DS White said enthusiastically. "Now, was there a big, organised fight between the Milton Road Teds and the Bedford Boot Boys?"

Kenny nodded his head.

"Thank you. That was just a tester because we already know that there was. I like to know that we are working together," DS White said. "Was it Deano Derenzie that bashed up Fat Pat the doorman?"

Kenny shook his head.

"Are you sure? Because he was in a bad way and a man like him has a reputation to maintain," DS White said as he stubbed out his cigarette.

Kenny nodded.

"Okay, was it Deano Derenzie that beat up Clifford Tate?"

Kenny hesitated before reluctantly nodding his head.

"Not a tooth left in Clifford Tate's head. It would make sense that Clifford Tate would want to stab Deano Derenzie. Was it him?"

Kenny shook his head.

"No, really? Okay so maybe it was Clifford Tate's number two, Eddy Boyce?"

Kenny nodded his head slowly.

"Excellent so now we know that it was Eddy Boyce that stabbed Deano Derenzie. Now Kenny, I am a man of my word, so no one will know of our agreement."

There was a loud knock on the interview room door. It swung open and a smartly dressed middle aged man in a black pinstripe suit, holding a briefcase, stepped in.

"Good evening officers. My name is Gerald Hart, solicitor, and this is my client. There will be no more questions until I have had an opportunity to talk with him."

"We have finished here. Your client was just filling us in on the deceased's state of mind prior to him committing suicide," DS White said, leaning back in his chair and looking the solicitor up and down.

"Well, if you've finished," Gerald Hart said before beckoning Kenny to stand up and join him at the door.

Kenny stood up and brushed his clothes down. He wiped his face with the back of his hand and walked over to the solicitor.

"Kenny," DS White said, "I'm sorry for your loss."

After Kenny and the solicitor left the room, DS White closed the door.

"That was a right result Guv, nice one," DC Jacobs said.

"Yeah, we'll track down this Eddy Boyce and pull him in. That will make a nice collar," DS White said. "Something isn't sitting right though."

"What's that Guv?" DC Jacobs said.

"Why does a low life nothing, like Kenny, from the Milton Road Estate, have a high-priced brief rushing down here to his rescue at this time of night," DS White said, glancing down at his watch. "There's more to this and I'd bet a month's wages on it. Bernie, I'm sure we'll be seeing more of Kenny."

Chapter 9

Ricky drove up to the hospital and collected Deano. The doctors had ordered him home to rest, but Deano wanted to see his mates and Ricky had laid on a 'welcome home' do with Ronnie at the Milton Arms.

Ricky parked his car outside the pub and strolled in alongside his friend Deano the Dog. As the pub door swung open, their ears were met with the sound of *'Trocadero'* by Showaddywaddy. Both Ricky and Deano beamed as everyone in the pub stood, raised their glasses and cheered as one.

"It's good to have you back in the Arms," Ronnie the landlord said, handing him a pint of bitter.

"Cheers Ronnie," Deano said. "I've missed this place."

"This place has missed you too," Ronnie said.

"Hey, don't you go drinking too much Deano, because I have plans for you," Melanie said, standing up on her toes and planting a huge, exaggerated, kiss on his cheek.

"You might have to do all the work," Deano whispered with a cheeky wink.

"I wouldn't have it any other way, Deano the Dog." Melanie whispered back.

One by one people from around the pub came over and shook Deano by the hand. Melanie and the twins were by the Jukebox when Deano took his usual seat at the end of the bar. *'Young*

Hearts Run Free' by Candi Staton played as Deano drank the last of his pint.

"Well, other than Specs, which we'll talk about at another time, what's been going on? What don't I know…Lee?" Deano said as he turned sharply to face him.

"There's been no trouble from the Bedford Boot Boys, Deano, or the Cambridge Flats lot come to that, but Jock Addie and the Croydon Teds have been busy," Lee said.

"Busy, eh? Busy doing what?" Deano said, slowly leaning forward.

"All I heard was that he had an all-out row with this lot over in Orpington. By all accounts he's pulled a shed load of Teds together and given them a right good hiding. I don't know how true it is Deano, but I heard that he bit part of this bloke's ear off and he's stood up with claret running down his face and gobbed out the bloke's ear."

"Really. Who was this lot in Orpington?"

"It was a mix of Skinheads and Boot Boys. They're only about ten or twelve in number but proper handy lads by all accounts," Lee said.

"Okay, anything else?"

"I'm not sure if I should say," Lee said.

"Then just say it Lee," Deano said.

"It's only what I've heard, so I don't want to cause any trouble," Lee said.

"Ricky, do you know what Lee's on about?" Deano asked.

Ricky shook his head.

"You, Kenny?"

"No mate. Whatever it is Lee, spit it out," Kenny said.

Lee took a deep breath.

"Okay the word going about is that Jock Addie has been saying that you, Deano, are all done now and that he's going to take the top slot and become number one. The new King of the Teds," Lee said.

There was a few seconds' silence as the words sank in amongst the lads. Deano began to chuckle and then laughed out loud.

"What a liberty," Deano said. "The scariest thing about Jock Addie is his breath."

"Yeah, his breath is so bad I wasn't sure if I should hand him a pack of mints or a toilet roll," Lee said.

"I heard his breath was so bad that even his own lads will only talk to him over the phone," Kenny said.

Terry and Steve Parker just nodded their heads and nursed their pints of bitter.

"I'll tell you what though," Kenny said. "His sister is a right good-looking sort."

"Well, you would say something like that, wouldn't you Kenny," Deano said abruptly.

From behind the bar Ronnie, Melanie and the twins carried out several oval plates of sandwiches, sausage rolls and cheese and pineapple on sticks. They put them on the table.

Ricky looked up and saw that Neil and Jackie had entered the bar.

"Bloody hell, Jackie you look incredible!" Ricky thought.

Jackie wore a short pleated black skirt, a red open neck blouse and a black matching jacket with gold buttons and heels.

Ronnie served them both a drink and then they approached the table.

"Deano, it's good to have you back," Neil said.

"Still wearing the Ted gear, I see," Deano said. "Good man, one of these days we might have to put you to work."

"You alright?" Ricky asked. "You've got a bit of a limp."

"I got bit," Neil said.

"It wasn't Jock Addie, was it?" Deano said.

The lads burst out laughing so hard, beer slopped from their glasses out onto the table and carpet.

Neil looked confused and shrugged his shoulders.

"I don't get it," Neil said.

"Private joke," Ricky said. "What happened?"

"It was a bloody great Doberman Pinscher. It came bounding down this driveway and sunk his teeth into my arse. The poxy mutt blooded me," Neil said.

"I'd give up the day job as a postman, if I were you," Kenny said.

"Yeah, I might just do that," Neil said looking over at Ricky.

Ricky couldn't take his eyes off Jackie. She looked directly at him just for a second and smiled. Ricky beamed. People from around the pub were taking handfuls of sandwiches and looking over at Deano. Ronnie brought him a pint and told him that there were eleven more being held for him from friends around the pub.

"Deano," Ricky said softly, "I took the liberty of having your PA Cresta checked through mate. I had one of my mates, Monkey, rebuild the carb, give the engine a full service, put in a new battery, install new brakes and give it a fresh MOT."

"Cheers Ricky, but you didn't have to do that. Hold up a minute, you didn't have the keys," Deano said.

"Well, we couldn't have you stranded on the side of the road and Melanie was good enough to let me have your keys. I told her what I planned to do after she mentioned that you broke down again just before, well you know when," Ricky said.

"That has well and truly earned you more than just a few brownie points," Deano said.

Ricky found his eyes straying towards Jackie. She glanced over and held his gaze for just a few seconds, and Ricky felt an incredible jolt ricochet through his body that felt intensely intimate. His eyes wandered from her eyes to her ruby red lips and back again.

"It's what mates do," Ricky said. "Besides it's just great to have you back!"

Ricky wandered over to the table where Neil was eating a ham and tomato sandwich.

"Are you alright mate?" Ricky asked.

"Yeah, other than the bite on the arse all is good. I didn't let it stop me though. I still took the Jaguar. I'm right up to date with everything on order. Is there anything else coming through?" Neil said.

"I'll have another order shortly. As soon as I know I'll let you know mate," Ricky said as he reached for a sausage roll.

"It's going well, Ricky. I've managed to save quite a few quid. I've been thinking about a holiday. You know something overseas. I mean there's no point in making the cash and doing nothing with it. Besides, I think Jackie could do with a break too. She's been hoisting for Doreen six days a week without a day off for over a year now" Neil said.

"Where do you fancy going?"

"I thought the Caribbean," Neil said.

"The Caribbean! Oh my, look at you," Ricky chuckled. You've not even been to Spain before,"

"Nor have you," Neil said.

"Now that my friend is true, and we both deserve a break," Ricky said.

"No offence mate, but I don't want you coming with us," Neil said.

"As if," Ricky said with a forced chuckle. "I meant that since we're in the same business we should co-ordinate the dates so we can get ahead of the game, and both get away at the same time."

"Yeah, right, that makes sense. I couldn't imagine you wanting to play gooseberry to me and Jackie," Neil said.

"Neil, mate, I love you to death, but I just cannot get Jackie out of my head," Ricky thought.

"What are you talking about?" Jackie said.

Both Ricky and Neil turned to face her.

"Wouldn't you like to know," Ricky said, playfully punching her arm.

Jackie smiled.

"Come on then," Jackie said. "What were you saying?"

"I was just saying to Ricky that we have both been grafting for some time and a holiday might be nice," said Neil.

"What the three of us?" Jackie said.

Ricky's heart began to pump so fast he held his hand over his chest.

"No, just you and me, palm trees and the ocean," Neil said.

"Now that sounds one up from a dirty weekend in Brighton," Jackie said. "Give me plenty of notice, okay, don't you just go booking it as I can't let Doreen down."

"No, of course not," Neil said holding out his hand.

Jackie took it and pulled him in close and whispered in his ear. Ricky could see Neil's face light up.

"Anyway, I'll catch up with you in a while," Ricky said.

"Damn Neil, what is Jackie playing at? In fact, what the hell am I playing at? Jackie is Neil's bird and I have no right to be flirting. He's my mate and I've had my chance with Jackie and blew it over Michelle," Ricky thought.

Deano met him halfway across the bar.

"I need a word Ricky," Deano said.

"Sure mate," Ricky said, following him over to the bar.

"It sounds like you stepped up, and Specs aside, you've kept things in check here while I was in hospital. I appreciate it mate," Deano said.

"I couldn't do anything about Specs," Ricky said.

"Mate, I know. It's a nasty business. He was a good mate, a solid Ted and an integral part of the Milton Road Teds. He will be missed," Deano said.

"For sure," Ricky said.

"You're my number two, right?" Deano said.

"Yes mate," Ricky said, nodding his head slowly.

"Good, because I have some business to take care of. It might get violent and brutal, and I need to be one hundred percent sure that you are with me. Can I count on you Ricky?" Deano asked.

"In a heartbeat Deano," Ricky said as an overwhelming rush of excitement washed over him.

"This must be mad, and I must be off my rocker, but I have missed that rush of having Deano around, the rows, the conflict and the respect of being a hard-core Teddy Boy," Ricky thought. *"We're back on!"*

"Good man, I knew you were one of us the first time I met you. You, Ricky Turrell, are destined for great things. I will need to put a few things in place and then I'll call on you, okay?" Deano said.

"Ready when you are," Ricky said, rubbing his hands together.

"Right, so get the King of the Teds a drink in then," Deano said, patting him on the shoulder.

Chapter 10

Detective Sergeant Ray White and Detective Constable Bernard Jacobs were on their way to the Milton Road Estate having just visited the home of Eddy Boyce.

"Do you reckon he's had it on his toes, Guv?" DC Jacobs said.

"No, he's on the manor somewhere. His mates are hiding him, you can believe that," DS White said.

"Should we give some of his mates a tug, take them back to the factory?"

"No Bernie, what we need here is a bit of patience. Sooner or later, someone will tell someone something and then someone will tell us," DS White said.

"Can I take Saturday night off Guv?"

"Why?"

"I've met this bird Guv, lovely little sort and I wanted to take her out on Saturday if there's nothing urgent.

"Bernie what has your dubious social life got to do with me? Is the bird a WPC?"

"Yes Guv."

"Good, she's one of our own. At this moment in time there is nothing pressing, but if Eddy Boyce turns up then you're with me, alright?" DS White said as he slowed down the car and parked outside the block of flats.

"Cheers Guv," DC Jacobs said.

The two officers got out of the car and walked through the concrete entrance and up the stairs to Double Bubble's flat.

KNOCK! KNOCK!

The front door opened. Double Bubble stood there in his underpants and vest.

"Not you lot," Double Bubble said.

"Yeah, the heavy mob and we need a word," DS White said.

"Not now, I've got company."

"Really," DS White said, pushing past him and walking into the living room.

"Hello darling, I'm Detective Sergeant Ray White and this is DS Jacobs. We just need a word with Leonard, I mean Double Bubble."

The girl pulled the dressing gown across her exposed thighs.

"I know who you are," the girl said.

"Well then you have me at a disadvantage," DS White said. "What is your name?"

"Trudy."

"Well it's nice to make your acquaintance. Are you two an item?" DS White said, looking over at Double Bubble.

"Not exactly," Double Bubble said.

"Oh, so she's a brass then," DS White said. "This must have cost a few bob; an overnighter or maybe you're just working off what you owe?"

"Fuck you!" Trudy yelled as she stood up and stormed off to the bedroom.

"Leonard, do us all a favour and see the brass out. We need to talk."

Double Bubble left the room. Through the closed doors the officers could hear a harsh exchange of words in the hallway and then the front door slammed shut. Double Bubble sauntered back into the living room. He had put on a pair of jeans and socks. The tight white vest was stretched to its limits across his fifty-four-inch chest.

"If you weren't old bill, I'd crush the pair of you like the maggots you are," Double Bubble said making fists with his huge hands.

"Yeah but we are," DS Ray White said. "So stop giving it the big one son, and take a seat. Bernie, you go and stick the kettle on and make us all a nice, friendly, cup of tea."

Double Bubble sat in the armchair and faced the DS.

"We didn't stop you in the middle of anything, did we?"

"No, we were done," Double Bubble said.

"Good, so we can get right down to business then."

"What business?"

"You know what kind of business. Don't be a smart arse. It doesn't suit you. I'm talking about the kind of business that is keeping you on the outside and having brasses like that Trudy to take care of you."

Double Bubble sighed and rubbed his chin.

"Now first and foremost I wanted to thank you for serving up Charlie Summers. He was recognised and he'll do an eight stretch for that blag. Now I'm hungry for more, DB, so my little cock sparrow, what else have you got for me?"

"I don't know anything," Double Bubble said curtly.

"Do I really have to remind you about the terms of our agreement? There must be faces on the estate that don't impact your business. Maybe someone has done you a wrong turn. I'm happy to take that," DS White said.

"Tea's up Guv," DC Jacobs said as he carried three mugs of steaming hot tea into the room.

"Nice one," DS White said. "Now DB, you were just about to say?"

"Martin Benn," Double Bubble said.

"Yeah, I know him. He's a fence, right?"

"Yeah, well, he's about to take a truck load of televisions in. He's been lining up buyers and said that they'll be with him this Friday. He's been selling them like hot cakes," Double Bubble said.

"I'm grateful for the info, but surely people on the estate will be borrowing money from you to buy them?"

"Yeah normally, but he's letting people have them on tick with interest," Double Bubble said.

. "So, your friend is taking business that would normally go your way?" DS White said.

Double Bubble nodded.

"You're a vicious bastard, DB, but it makes sense to take out one of your competitors. Right, we'll keep an eye on Martin Benn and then turn him over on Friday when he takes delivery of the televisions. If you hear of any change of plans, be sure to let us know. I want him bang to rights. A nice clean collar and caught with his hands in the cookie jar." DS White said.

"Yeah of course," Double Bubble said.

"Now that wasn't too painful, as it?" DS White said. "Now if my info serves me correctly Deano Derenzie will be out of hospital."

"Yeah, the flash bastard was in the Arms bold as brass giving it large the other day," Double Bubble said.

"It doesn't sound like you like him too much DB."

"He's just a flash git. It's a shame that bloke didn't finish him in the bookies."

"Well, it's that bloke that did him in the bookies that I'm interested in," DS Ray White said

"You know who it is?"

"Do you?"

"No, all I heard was it was some Skinhead from the Bedford Estate, but I don't have a name. If I knew who it was, I'd buy the bloke a drink," Double Bubble said.

"Is this Deano Derenzie the type of guy that would go looking for him?"

"Too right he will."

"Good, so when you hear where and when I want you to contact me straight away okay? I want the clean-up," DS White said.

"If I hear anything, I'll let you know."

"What is it between you two?" DC Jacobs asked. "I mean it sounds like you really hate him."

"I just don't like him or what he stands for," Double Bubble said with a sneer. "Nothing more, nothing less. I just don't like him!"

"Fair enough," DC Jacobs said.

The officers drank the last of their tea and put the mugs on the coffee table.

DS White stood up and put his hands in his pockets.

"One last thing DB."

"What's that?"

"What do you know about the Bank of America job in Mayfair?" DS White said.

"That wasn't anybody from this estate," Double Bubble said, shaking his head.

"Are you sure?"

"If it was, there would have been a whisper somewhere. Besides, a job like that was almost certainly done by someone on the inside. Stands to reason, doesn't it? I mean eight million quid and a safe the size of a small bungalow. That takes inside knowledge and there are only a few firms in London these days with the clout to pull off a job like that," Double Bubble said.

"That's what I was thinking," DS White said. "But it doesn't hurt to ask the question."

Double Bubble followed the officers down the hallway and just as they approached the front door DS White stopped and turned back to face Double Bubble.

"What do you know about a Teddy Boy called Kenny?"

"He's a nothing. Just one of Deano's little mob," Double Bubble said as he shrugged his shoulders. "Why?"

"So he's not connected then?"

"Connected?"

"You know what I mean DB. Is he a player or does he work with anyone serious?"

Double Bubble began to laugh.

"The only things that Kenny is interested in is dressing up with his boyfriends and chasing skirt," Double Bubble said.

"Okay, see you again soon," DS White said as he left the flat.

The officers passed through the flats quickly and got back into the car.

"The plot thickens," DS White said.

"How so Guv?"

"I saw the look on Kenny's face when that high-priced brief turned up to spring him. He didn't see it coming, which means that he either knows someone with clout that has his back or he's a player himself and unless he's an Oscar winning actor, he just doesn't have the minerals. I want to know who is looking out for him, Bernie, and why," DS White said.

Chapter 11

Ricky was at home in the kitchen when there was a knock at the front door.

"Deano. Hello mate, come in." Ricky said as he showed Deano through to the kitchen where he had just put two pieces of cheddar cheese on bread under the grill. "This is a nice surprise. I don't think you've been to my place before."

"I haven't Ricky, very nice. Very nice indeed, it's definitely a step up from the Milton Road Estate."

"Yeah, I like it and thanks to Doreen it's been fitted out nice too. Do you fancy a bit of cheese on toast and coffee?"

"Hey, don't you go telling Melanie about your place or she'll be on at me," Deano said.

Ricky held up the kettle.

"Yeah, go on then, just a quick one and if you have a slice of that cheese on toast going too, I won't say no."

Ricky poured two cups of percolated coffee and handed Deano a plate with a slice of cheese on toast.

"So, what brings you around Deano?"

"Well we may have to do some running about today, and I'm going to need you as back up. Are you okay with that?" Deano said. He paused momentarily before putting the food in his mouth.

"Yeah, of course. I was going to have a look over the salvage yard for a couple of motors to do up but that can wait."

"Cheers Ricky, I appreciate it."

"How are you feeling Deano? I mean are you fully recovered?"

"Ricky I'm fighting fit."

Ricky put the two empty coffee cups into the sink along with the matching side plates from Knightsbridge.

"Can we take your motor, Ricky? Mine is running a lot better, thanks to you, but I still just don't trust it. Maybe you could sort me out a motor one of these days. Something nice, comfortable and a bit more reliable, but I can't be paying big money. I'll be looking for mate's rates," said Deano.

"No problem," Ricky said as he opened the driver's side door to his Rover P5B. "Do you fancy something like this?"

Deano's eyes lit up.

"This is a very nice motor. If the price is right, then yes, I'd love something like this."

"Leave it with me and I'll see what I can do," Ricky said.

"One minute," Deano said as he opened the door to his PA Cresta, reached over to the passenger side floor well and took out a small black sports bag.

Once inside the car, Ricky turned the ignition key and the three and half litre throaty V8 burst into life.

"Where to," Ricky asked as he slipped the gear shifter into drive.

"The Bedford Working Men's Club," Deano said.

"Okay," Ricky said as he reached over to the glove box and took out the brass knuckle duster that Deano had given him.

"I'm hoping you won't need it, but it's better to be safe than sorry."

Ricky drove across town and stopped at the traffic lights before the turn onto the Bedford Estate.

"What's the plan Deano?"

"I just need you to be back me up. You don't have to say anything, just be my number two and back me up."

"You got it," Ricky said.

Ricky could feel a strong sense of excitement building in the pit of his stomach, mixed with a healthy dose of fear.

"What the fuck is this all about? The club will be filled with people that we kicked the shit out of only a few months back. This is madness," Ricky thought.

Ricky stopped the car outside the club and slipped the knuckle duster into his pocket. The adrenaline began to rush around his body.

"What's about to happen? Are we here to sort out Eddy Boyce? What the hell is going on?" Ricky wondered.

As Ricky and Deano sauntered towards the club entrance in their drainpipe trousers, silk shirts, bootlace ties and brothel creepers, Fat Pat the doorman held out his hand.

Deano looked him up and down. He looked scared, and his left hand was in plaster.

"What the fuck do you want?" Fat Pat growled.

"Less of the attitude. I'm here on business so step away," Deano said.

Fat Pat remained firmly in place.

"I will not ask you again," Deano said with a menacing glare.

Fat Pat stood to one side.

"Thank you," Deano said as he strolled into the heart of the Bedford Estate.

Ricky looked around quickly to assess the situation. There were maybe fifteen or sixteen lads in their age group, and a number of slightly older men who still looked like they were game for a tear up. Deano strolled down between the tables and chairs and then stepped up onto the makeshift six-inch-high wooden stage. The club had been noisy with clinking glasses and loud chatter between friends and neighbours. As Deano fanned away the thick cigarette smoke the noise died away, until there was just silence.

"I think most of you know me. I'm Deano, Deano the Dog from the Milton Road Estate."

"Yeah, we know who you are," one of the Bedford Boot Boys shouted.

"Good," Deano said. "I'm looking for someone."

"Well fuck off back to your own estate," a middle-aged man sitting with two older women yelled.

Deano glared at him.

"You better climb back into your wife's handbag before you get proper hurt," Deano warned.

There was no retort. All eyes from around the working men's club were fixed on Deano. Ricky stood firmly by his side with the knuckle duster armed and ready for whatever was to come. He tingled from head foot with excitement at the prospect of it kicking off.

"Somebody from this estate stabbed me a few months back. Sadly for him, I didn't die, which can only mean that I must come looking for him. Now, you all know who he is and some of you will know where he is. I'm here to tell you that I will find him, and he will pay, and he needs to know that. My number two and second in command, Ricky Turrell, has put up one hundred quid to anyone who makes the call to The Milton Arms with his whereabouts," Deano yelled out.

"No one is going to grass him up Deano," one of the Bedford Boot Boys yelled.

"We'll see," Deano said before stepping off the stage. He walked slowly through the club maintaining unflinching eye contact with anyone looking in his direction. Deano the Dog was utterly fearless.

As they left the pub, Fat Pat the doorman spoke out.

"You will get what's coming to you!"

"Join the queue," Deano hissed.

Ricky looked back at Fat Pat as they got into the car.

"Don't worry about the hundred quid I said that you'd put up in there. You won't ever have to pay it," Deano said.

"Why, because no one will grass him up?"

Deano turned and gave him a manic smile.

"No because I already know where Eddy Boyce is, and when it gets about that I found him, they will start to question who the grass is in their own camp. The staunch solidarity they have for each other becomes questionable, and some will not be so quick to rally around if and when it ever comes to blows again," Deano said.

"You are one extremely smart, devious, man, Deano," Ricky thought.

"So where to?"

"Drive to the end of the road and park up out of sight," Deano said.

"Alright, stop here Ricky," Deano said as he picked up his black sports bag. "Get as close to the entrance to the flats as you can.

Deano took a deep breath and turned Ricky's rear-view mirror towards him, so he could see his own reflection.

"Right, let's do this," Deano said as he opened the car door and began to quickly walk towards the flats. Ricky clambered out of the car with his fist clenched tightly around the brass knuckle duster and followed him.

Deano stopped outside flat number three. He took three steps back and then launched himself forward. His brothel creepers smashed through the door with the lock flying off down the hallway. Deano ran down the hallway and into the living room. Eddy Boyce was startled; he'd been asleep on the couch. He tried to get onto his feet, but Deano fired a punch that sent him sprawling backwards. Eddy Boyce tripped on the coffee table and landed awkwardly, with the corner of the wooden table digging into his ribs. Clutching his side with one hand he tried to pull himself up. Deano fired a second and then a third punch. The sound of his nose shattering echoed around the small room.

"Leave it out Deano!" Eddy Boyce cried, holding his blooded nose.

Deano kicked him in the side he was holding. Eddy yelled out in pain as he fell forwards.

Deano calmly placed the sports bag down on the couch and opened it. He took out a ball of rope and threw it to Ricky.

"Tie his hands," Deano commanded.

Ricky took the rope and raced around to where Eddy Boyce was laying. He grabbed his left arm and placed it under his knee and then grabbed his right arm before tying the rope so his hands and arms couldn't move.

"Get him onto his feet," Deano said.

"I'm sorry Deano, I'm really sorry," Eddy Boyce pleaded.

Deano took a short length of material from the bag. He stared into Eddy's eyes as he wrapped it around his mouth and bound it at the back tightly, before walking back to the bag and producing a thick chrome dog chain that doubled as a collar by sliding the link back and forth. Deano placed it over Eddy's head and then pulled the chain firmly, so it chinked on his neck. Eddy's eyes were wide with fear, his legs shook and only a muffled 'sorry' could be heard. Deano handed the chain to Ricky. He then pulled out a small black hessian sack from the bag. Eddy was shaking his head back and forth as tears streamed down his face. Deano opened the bag, put it over Eddy Boyce's head and pulled it down firmly to his shoulders.

"Give me the chain, Ricky, and go and open the boot to your motor," Deano said.

Ricky hesitated for a second.

"Now Ricky, do it now," Deano said.

Ricky bolted down the hallway and through the front door. He looked from left to right, but the commotion hadn't brought anyone out. Ricky walked over to the car and opened the boot. He looked back towards the flat and there stood Deano and Eddy Boyce with the black hessian bag over his head. Deano edged forward and pulled Eddy to make him follow. Once they were by the car's open boot, Deano shoved him in while Ricky manoeuvred Eddy's body around so that he could close the boot. They both got into the car. Ricky could feel his hands were clammy and his brow was covered in sweat.

"Are you okay Ricky?" Deano asked as he sat back in the leather passenger seat.

"I'm as good as could be expected. What now, Deano?" Ricky said.

"Do you know The Swan & Sugar Loaf pub in Croydon?"

"Yeah," Ricky said.

"Good, we're going to pay Jock Addie a visit," Deano said.

The drive to Croydon was mostly quiet, with Ricky listening out for scuffles from the back of the car but there weren't any. Ricky parked in the pub car park and then followed Deano into the pub. *"The Wanderer'* by Dion and The Belmonts had recently been released into the charts and was pounding out of the Jukebox. Deano spotted Jock sitting amongst several suited-up Teddy Boys. Ricky had seen that smile before. He quickly slipped his hand into his pocket and slid his fingers into the brass knuckle duster. Deano strolled casually through the pub. Teds stood up and acknowledged him with nods as he finally came to a halt by Jock Addie's table.

Jock looked up and smirked. He stood up to face Deano.

"Well fuck my old boots, it's Deano the Dog. You're a long way from home, matey! What, have you come to do the plumbing or something?"

Deano could see that Jock was cautiously reaching for his pint glass. In that second, Deano launched himself forward and head-butted Jock. SMACK! His nose snapped and blood shot out onto the table. The lads around the table winced and pushed their chairs back. Deano leaned back with his clenched fist ready to strike, but Jock just howled as he clutched his broken nose.

"You, Jock Addie, are out of your league, son. I've had brewer's droop harder than you. The King of the Teds hasn't come back, son, he never left. As for the rest of you Croydon Teds. I have the utmost respect for you all. We have stood together in the past and I've no doubt that we will again. Jock is your leader and I'll not take that away from him. He is a good, solid, man and has stood by my side during utter blood and carnage. It is because of that that I'm going to let what has happened go. Let's agree that it was a misunderstanding. Your choice, Jock, is to take my hand and move forward as my friend and ally to the Milton Road Teds, or, well, we don't even want to go there."

Jock held out his right hand while his left hand cupped his broken nose. Deano shook it fiercely and looked around at all those in the pub.

"In the not-too-distant future, I will be bringing the leaders of Teddy Boy gangs right across London together, and as our allies and

Drape wearing Teds, I would expect you all to be there. Are you good with that Jock?" Deano said.

Jock muffled a yes and sat back in his seat.

"Right, now that we're all friends again, who is going to get the beers in?" Deano said.

Ricky threw two ten-pound notes down on the table.

"What the hell is going on here?" Ricky thought. *"I've got Eddy Boyce tied up in the back of the motor and Deano's stamping down his authority here bold as brass, as if it's all just business as usual."*

Deano checked his watch. He had shared three pints with the Croydon Teds, and it was dark outside. Although Jock was still a little upset, all had been put right in Deano's world.

"Drink up Ricky. We've still got one bit of business to finish off," Deano said as he put his empty glass down on the table.

Deano shook Jock's hand again and waved to all those in the pub as he left.

"That could have got nasty," Ricky said.

"Maybe, but my money was on that this was a move by Jock and Jock alone. Today he just discovered that those Teds are not his but mine. If they truly followed him, they would have been all over us. You can believe that anybody trying shit like I've just pulled in the Arms wouldn't leave alive," Deano said.

"It was certainly bold mate. So, what's the plan now, Deano?" Ricky asked as he slowed down to a turning. "We throw Eddy Boyce into the road outside the Bedford Working Men's Club?"

"No, I've not finished with Eddy Boyce yet," Deano said in a soft menacing tone. "Do you know the woods in Addington? There's a car park where blokes take their birds after the pubs close."

"Yeah, I know it," Ricky said.

"Good, drive us there and get a move on," Deano said, looking down at his watch.

Ricky's thoughts were racing with a hundred and one scenarios playing out in his mind. He slowed down and drove into the car park.

"Over there in the corner," Deano said, pointing to the far end.

Ricky stopped the car and two lads got out of the car.

"What now Deano?" Ricky asked.

"Are you still my number two?" Deano asked.

"Teddy Boys Forever – Forever Teddy Boys," Ricky said.

"Let's get this jug headed mug out of the motor," Deano said.

Ricky opened and raised the boot lid. Eddy Boyce was lying still with just the occasional murmur.

"Come along Eddy," Deano said as he pulled on the dog lead. "We're going for a little walk.

Ricky helped Eddy out of the boot and onto his feet.

"Hi Ho, Hi Ho it's off to work we go," Deano sang as he pulled Eddy deeper into the woods. Ricky followed behind, looking left and right. He found it hard to make out anything as it was pitch black, with the only lights being the ones back at the front of the car park.

"Deano," a voice whispered. "Over here."

"What the fuck!" Ricky said, clenching his fists.

"Over here."

Deano tugged at Eddy's chain and led him into a small clearing by a large tree.

"Nice one," Deano said.

Terry and Steve Parker stood by the tree holding shovels with a full moon behind them. They stood over a freshly dug grave.

"What's all this?" Ricky hissed.

"Rightful retribution," Deano said calmly as he slid the black hessian sack off Eddy's head.

Terry Parker came forward and positioned Eddy in front of the grave. Eddy shook his head violently, tears streamed from his eyes and his pleas for forgiveness were muffled by the homemade gag. Steve reached into the inside of jacket and produced a handgun. He handed it to Deano.

"Fuck," Ricky thought. *"This has gone beyond serious."*

"Eddy, mate, my friends here are both ex-army and have seen shit that you would not believe in Northern Ireland. They managed to bring home this shooter as a kind of souvenir. They offered it to me, believing that I might want to shoot you for what you did to me."

Ricky could see the sweat streaming down Eddy's face under the moonlight. His eyes were wide, and the muffled pleas became a little louder.

"I'm not going to shoot you though, Eddy," Deano said as he handed the gun back to Steve. "Instead, I'm going to give you back something that belongs to you." Deano pulled a switchblade out of his pocket. He pressed the button and the blade shot out from the side. Deano took a step closer to Eddy.

"There you go Eddy. I believe this is yours," Deano said with a wild grin as he thrust the blade deep into Eddy's chest. Terry grabbed the dog chain and tugged him so hard that he fell backwards into the open grave.

"I'm no church going man, Eddy, but even the bible says an eye for an eye. Fill it in lads," Deano said.

At the bottom of the grave, Eddy was still wriggling and kicking his legs as both Terry and Steve shovelled damp soil back into the hole. Within a few minutes Eddy's body was covered, but Ricky could still see the parts of the soil moving. Terry and Steve shovelled harder and faster until the grave was full and the ground level. Steve pulled down several old leaf covered branches and laid them over and around the grave.

"No one will ever find him here Deano," Terry said.

Chapter 12

Shortly after Terry and Steve Parker joined the British Armed Forces in 1971, they deployed, along with thousands of British Troops, to Northern Ireland as part of Operation Banner to support the Royal Ulster Constabulary and assert the authority of the British government in Northern Ireland. Both Steve and Terry thrived in their roles and soon found themselves involved with counter-insurgency operations, guarding key points, checkpoints, going on patrols and carrying out raids on suspected terrorists.

The brothers were despatched to Portadown to clear Catholics who were blocking an Orange Order march through their neighbourhood. With tensions running high, violence quickly erupted, and the army used CS Gas and rubber bullets to take back control of the streets. A masked man attempted to attack Steve from behind with a tyre iron, but Private Colin Ramsey took the assailant out with a rubber bullet to the thigh. Control was recovered and the Orangemen marched through the Catholic area escorted by fifty masked and uniformed members of the Ulster Defence Association. From that fateful day in July 1972, the three men became firm friends.

While away from the front line they would talk about life after the British Army. Terry and Steve had tabled going to fight in Africa as mercenaries. The money was good and there was always conflict between those that sought power. Colin had been seeing a pretty young girl in Belfast called Dawn. They had tried to keep the blossoming relationship a secret to avoid local problems, but one small group of lads, Connor, Jack and Seamus had seen them together. Connor waited by Dawn's home and stopped her as she walked through an alleyway at the back of the main road on her way to meet with Colin. Connor grabbed her by the throat with his left hand and pushed her up against the crumbling, graffiti covered, red brick wall. He held a knife to her face and threatened to cut her if she continued to fraternise with the British. Dawn was in fear for her life but was in love with Colin and risked all by meeting with him, where she shared her fears and what had happened. He was angry, and whilst he promised not to take action, the thought of Dawn having a knife held at her throat ate away at him. He shared what had happened with Terry and Steve who immediately volunteered to help take care of business. Colin finished his shift early and had arranged to meet Dawn away from her home. The two lovers had planned to spend the weekend together at a hotel close to the Giant's Causeway. Connor, Jack and Seamus had followed her to where the couple had planned to meet. The three men began to threaten the couple and had been warned. Colin fired a punch that sent Jack sprawling to the floor, Connor produced a knife and began swinging it around wildly. Colin stepped in front of Dawn to protect her, when Connor plunged the blade into the side of his neck. He yelled and grabbed his neck as blood spurted out. He fell to his knees, desperately holding on to his neck to stem the bleeding, when Seamus raced forward and kicked him to the floor. Dawn tried to push Jack away but was knocked to the ground. The three men kicked Colin over and over until he lay motionless in a pool of blood. Dawn was warned that there would be reprisals on her and all her family should she tell the authorities what had happened.

The news reached the Army barracks where Terry and Steve were stationed. The brothers were livid that their friend had been murdered. However, they maintained a cover of indifference to the news and continued to soldier as they always had but secretly planned their revenge.

Colin had taken Terry and Steve to the pub where Dawn told him they drank. The three lads had sat outside in a stolen car. Terry and Steve were armed and ready to fracture and break bones as a clear message not to mess with Colin or his girlfriend, Dawn, when Colin decided to call it off, deciding that it would be better if the couple took greater care where they met. The brothers knew where the future murderers of their friend could be found.

Terry and Steve were both dressed in blue jeans and black leather bomber jackets. They had stolen a transit van and waited outside the pub's entrance. At just after 8.00pm Terry saw the lads approaching the pub in the side mirror. The brothers pulled black balaclavas over their faces and got out of the van. Terry carried a Barrett 'Light' .50 rifle that had been recovered from two killed snipers in South Armagh, and Steve carried a Browning handgun with an extended twenty shot magazine, traditionally used by British Army Intelligence operatives. The lads immediately stopped and held up their hands, unsure if the mask wearing gunmen were IRA. Steve opened the rear doors of the transit and ushered Connor, Jack and Seamus into the back of the van. Connor began to plead that they were IRA sympathisers and would fight for the cause. Steve remained silent, but kept the weapon firmly fixed on them, while Terry ran back to the front of the transit van and drove away. Jack asked over and over what they were supposed to have done but Steve, still masked, moved the gun from Connor's head to his and gently wagged the end of the barrel. Terry drove out through the town, avoiding where they knew the check points were and then drove up towards Giants Causeway.

The van came to a halt in an empty car park where the light from just the one lamp post was still working. Terry opened the rear doors of the van and Steve got out with his gun still firmly fixed on Jack. Seamus had his head in his hands and was mumbling to himself. Both Terry and Steve took off their black balaclava's revealing the traditional short back and side's military haircut. Connor got brave and told them that they were now marked men, unless they took them back immediately. Steve moved the gun to face Connor who yelled defiantly 'Fuck you British!' Steve pulled the trigger 'BANG!' It was a head shot and caused Connor's body to rise and then slump back. Steve lowered the gun's barrel and shot again 'BANG! BANG! BANG!' Jack began to plead for his life, saying over and over how he had nothing to do with anything and that everything was Connor's fault. Terry leaned his rifle against the back of the open transit door. Steve casually passed Terry the handgun. 'BANG! BANG! BANG!' Jack was dead. Seamus, with tears streaming down his face, confessed that he was an informer for the British and he was building up evidence against those that frequented the pub and that hanging around with Connor and Jack was just a cover. Terry and Steve looked each other, neither saying a word. Terry turned back to Seamus and raised the Browning pistol. 'BANG! BANG! BANG!'

The three men who murdered their friend Colin had all been executed.

Terry stopped for a moment to take in what they had done and slowly breathed in the cold night air. In the corner of the car park was a parked Cortina that the brothers had left there earlier that day. Terry threw his balaclava into the back of the van alongside Steve's, before walking over to the Cortina. He opened the boot and put the rifle and handgun inside a black army weapons case. Terry then picked up a homemade car bomb that had been taken during a raid the week before. He took it back to the transit van and handed it to Steve who placed it under the passenger's side seat. Steve armed the device and carefully closed the transit van's door. The two brothers walked back to the Cortina. As they drove slowly away the bomb detonated. The explosion was so fierce that it sent the transit van several feet into the air and into a ball of flames that lit up the night sky.

The word around the barracks the following day was that three terrorists were killed by their own car bomb at a secret meeting. In May 1974 both Terry and Steve Parker were discharged, having served their time in the British Army. They returned to their home in South London on The Milton Road Estate.

Chapter 13

The black Mercedes Benz E320 hearse, carrying Specs' body, drove slowly towards the cemetery in Lower Morden. Deano, Ricky, Kenny, Lee, Terry, and Steve were the pallbearers and were all dressed in dark coloured drape suits and black brothel creepers. They were in the lead car, a Ford Zodiac MK4 limousine with the funeral director and clergyman, followed by the hearse with a wreath spelling out 'SPECS' in white flowers in the side windows and then a second limousine carrying friends and family.

"This isn't right," Lee said.

"Tell me about it," Kenny said.

"I mean all of it isn't right," Lee said. "You should have kept your prick in your pants!"

"You're not yourself today," Kenny said. "Mate, I noticed the improvement immediately."

"Alright that's enough," Deano said. "This is not the time for bickering like school children."

"I was just saying, Deano," Lee said.

"Well keep your thoughts to yourself, and if you really feel like you need a straightener with Kenny, you can both find somewhere to fight out your differences and then put them behind you," Deano said.

The limousine came to a slow stop and the Teds got out of the car.

"How are you feeling mate?" Ricky whispered

"One of my best mates is dead and another is partly responsible. So, other than that, I'm all hunk dory," Deano said.

"Sorry mate," Ricky said.

"No, no it's me," Deano said. "I've known Specs since we were kids, and this is just a lot to take in."

Melanie, dressed in a black knee length skirt, jacket and a black hat with lace over her eyes, stepped forward and put her arm through Deano's.

The couple both lowered their heads and walked into the church for the service. It was a small church with just over thirty family and friends from the Milton Road Estate. Specs' sister, Emma, had made all the arrangements and maintained contact with Melanie as they had been friends at school. The funeral home had carried out the necessary cosmetics, embalming and dressed Specs in his favourite red drape suit with leopard velvet collar, pocket tops and cuffs. The casket was left open inside the church so that Specs' family and friends could face the reality of physical death. The funeral Directors had told them how the last image of the deceased could have a strong psychological effect on the mourners and would help for them to say goodbye.

Once the clergyman had finished the service, he invited Deano, as Specs' oldest friend, to say a few words for his friend. Deano stood and cleared his throat. He walked to the front of the church and stood by Specs' open casket He looked down and put a black boot lace tie threaded through a solid gold razor blade that he had bought in the Kings Road a few years before. Specs had commented on it several times, but he could never find one or anything like it. Deano whispered 'Rest in peace my friend' and then turned to face the congregation. He reached into his inside pocket and pulled out a speech that he had written the night before.

"I stand here today to pay tribute to a Rock n Roller, a Teddy Boy, a loving father and husband. Specs was my good friend - the kind of man most men could only aspire to be.

Specs was a truly extraordinary man that could always be counted on to do the right thing even when it didn't appear right to those around him. We have been friends since junior school and I remember the very first day we met. He looked over at me and smiled and I just thought 'Specs' and that name stuck with him ever since. As we got older, Specs and a few of us would come to my house and we'd play old Rock 'n' Roll records on the record player. He was the first of us all to actually do the bop and still look good. He would smile continuously as we all danced around my front room to Jerry Lee Lewis and Elvis. As we got a little older and became Teddy Boys, I can still see Specs calming down situations or putting a positive spin on what had seemed like a dire situation and tell us all that we had a lot more to be grateful for than to complain about.

While others in the group would hop from one girl to another, that kind of relationship was never for Specs. He was a man that took his responsibilities seriously so when he announced that he would be getting married, we all knew that whilst we would still see Specs, he would be away busy working hard at becoming a good husband and father.

There are times in life when you can do with a gentle nudge to push you in a certain direction and for me that was Specs. A balanced man with reason to underpin his own decisions and the advice he would offer. For as long as I can remember, it was Specs who gave me those gentle nudges. Had it not been for Specs then maybe, just maybe I would never have built up the courage to ask Melanie to go out with me. For that alone Specs, my friend, I am eternally grateful.

Specs was an integral part of the Milton Road Teds, and a dependable voice of reason for us all. He has left behind friends all over London that are truly crushed to the core and his passing has crippled me too. Lives are like records in the music charts. Eventually they pass, but we can look back when we hear them and remember. We will all remember you Specs and embrace your reasoning, compassion and selflessness."

Deano looked up and put his speech into his inside jacket pocket. He gazed out into the mourners and rested his eyes briefly on Kenny and then on Specs' sister Emma, who sat alone with her head down in the back seat.

"Kenny, you must be squirming in your seat after that," Ricky thought.

The funeral director closed the casket and invited the pallbearers to carry the casket out to the cemetery. The Milton Road Teds led the procession to a freshly dug grave. The clergyman performed the committal service at the graveside while the casket was lowered into the ground.

Ricky could feel a lump in his throat and a single tear ran down his cheek. He looked over at Kenny, who was staring down at a framed photograph of Specs that had been placed by the graveside.

Once the service was complete, the small congregation began to break up. They drove back to the Milton Arms where Melanie, with Ronnie's help, had arranged food, and tea and coffee so that friends and family could celebrate Specs' life.

It was just after 1.00pm when the family and friends arrived at the Arms pub. Ronnie had rushed back to help lay out the tasty refreshments buffet style.

"This is a nice spread, Ronnie," Deano said, nodding his head and looking around at the sandwiches, sausage rolls, bowls of crisps and cheese boards. "Thank you."

"No problem," Ronnie said. "It's the least I could do for Specs."

Emma, Specs' sister, walked over to the bar and asked for a large gin and tonic. The barman looked over at Ronnie who gave the nod to go ahead and pour the drink. It had been agreed earlier, as custom dictates, that there were to be only light refreshments. Ricky watched as Emma sank the drink in one and then asked for another.

Kenny and Denise stood alone. Their paper plates had just a single quarter of a sandwich and a few crisps. After the third drink, Emma turned and faced all those standing around the buffet tables.

"Thank you, Melanie, for helping me get through this awful time. I couldn't have done it without you," Emma said, taking several steps towards Deano. She kissed him on the cheeks and smiled. "My brother loved having you as his friend and he lived for Rock n Roll and being a Teddy Boy. For many years that was his life."

Emma turned and walked towards where Kenny and Denise stood.

"That was until he believed he was to become a father with the woman he fell in love with. The family saw less and less of him as did his friends in here, because he was working around the clock to provide a home for his wife and the child he believed was his."

Emma took a step closer and with her right hand, slapped Denise across the face.

"I will never forgive you, Denise, for how you betrayed my brother and I hold you responsible for his death," Emma said and then turned towards Kenny. "Specs was your friend Kenny, and you took away the life he thought he had for what? A girl, like the many you have bedded, and now my brother is dead, he's gone, and never coming back and make no mistake, I will never forgive either of you!"

Emma slapped Kenny across the face.

There were a few gasps amongst the silent guests.

"I hope that you can both live with yourselves!" Emma hissed as she stepped back and looked the couple up and down. She sneered, turned abruptly on her heels and strode back to the bar where she thanked Ronnie and then left the pub.

Ricky poured a cup of coffee and joined Kenny and Denise.

"Kenny, I need to get home for the babysitter. I'll see you later," Denise said, putting the half empty cup of tea on the edge of the table.

It was a little too close to the edge and slipped off, spilling the tea out onto the carpet. Denise looked up, apologised, and then scampered out of the pub.

"Are you alright Kenny?" Ricky said.

"Mate I feel fucking awful. I'm having nightmares with Specs just looking at me though those bloody national Health glasses and shaking his head, and then my mate, Deano today, as good as puts Specs' death at my door in front of everyone at the funeral and then to cap it all I get slapped by his sister Emma. Ricky I've known Specs and Emma all my life. It's killing me mate, and I just don't know what I can do," Kenny said, reaching down and picking up Denise's broken cup.

"I'm not sure you can do anything mate. It'll just be time. I don't know what else to say," Ricky said.

"That's just it, because that's where Specs always came good. You know, any kind of problem you'd have, and he'd give you half a dozen potential solutions. For a bloke that didn't get too many birds he would just have all the answers. I don't know Ricky, I just don't know," Kenny said.

"Mate, if you need me at all then you know where I am," Ricky said, shaking him by the hand. "I'm going in to work to keep my mind off all this, and I'd suggest you do the same."

Ricky wandered around the guests, shook hands and said goodbye.

"Ricky," Deano called.

"Yes mate," Ricky said.

"Thanks for coming today. I know that it would have meant a lot to him, you being here, and… I appreciate your loyalty and support too."

"No problem," Ricky said.

"Are you okay?" Deano asked.

Ricky could feel his stare burning into his flesh.

"I'm fine mate, well as well as could be expected with all things considered," Ricky said, returning Deano's stare.

"Good, I'm going to need my number two, Ricky, because we have business to attend to," Deano said.

"I'm there Deano. Just give me the word," Ricky said, shaking Deano's hand. "I have to crack on, I'll catch you later."

Deano nodded.

"Nice spread Ronnie," Ricky said as he passed the bar and stepped out into the sunshine. He walked over to his Rover, started her up and drove away. *'Only you Can'* by Fox was playing on the radio. Ricky quickly reached over and turned the stereo off.

"You think you're having nightmares Kenny?" Ricky thought. *"Mate, I was party to an execution killing. Deano the fucking Dog stabbed him up, didn't think to tell me the plan. I mean I'm only the number two, but it was alright having Terry and Steve Parker there with a ready dug grave. What the hell was all that about? I'm an accessory to murder, joint bloody venture, and that, Kenny, could be life in prison!"*

Ricky wound the window down to let some fresh air in.

"He should have told me what the score was," Ricky thought. *"Deano should have brought me up to date and given me the choice. I knew that Eddy would be in for one hell of a kicking. Maybe even smash his legs a bit with a hammer because you can't go stabbing the King of the Teds and think that you're going to walk away. That was never going to happen. If Deano hadn't made it, then chances are I would have had to do something myself. Who knows, maybe it would have been me that killed Eddy because I'd look weak and start to lose control if that happened and that could never happen. So, fuck you Eddy Boyce, you stepped up and failed and now you're brown bread. I'll just have to live with it and move on."*

Ricky stopped outside London Tyre Co. Every bay had a customer in it.

"This is coming together nicely," Ricky thought as he watched Justin the tyre delivery driver wheeling off a batch of tyres from the back of his truck.

"Alright Justin, how many have you got for me?" Ricky said with a broad smile.

"I managed to get you fifty tyres," Justin whispered as he looked around him.

"Nice one, but I'll need more," Ricky said as he reached into his pocket and revealed a large wad of bank notes. He peeled off a small wad and handed them over.

"Cheers Ricky," Justin said. "What I said before about taking the whole truck? Well, I did mean it you know. You'll have three hundred tyres in one go and believe me it'll just be filling in a few forms my end and that's about it."

"I am working on that Justin, but in the mean time I want everything you can get. You know that I pay pound notes on the nose every time."

"I'll keep them coming," Justin said, wheeling the last of the tyres off and closing the truck's rear door.

"Doughnut," Ricky called out, "It looks like we're busy. How are you coping?"

"It goes like this every so often, but a little bit of help wouldn't go amiss," Doughnut said.

"It's all in hand, Doughnut," Ricky said as he walked into the office area.

Chapter 14

"I think those upstairs are well pleased with the clean-up, Guv," DC Bernard Jacobs said as he wound up the window of their unmarked police car.

"So, they should be Bernie. We've been down here grafting and putting dodgy villains away," DS Ray White said.

"It was a good move getting Double Bubble to inform Guv," DC Jacobs said.

"Yeah, well, we can keep that one to ourselves Bernie. I want that low life squeezed for every bit of info we can get our hands on, and then when I make Detective Inspector you can be sure I'll be putting in a good word for you," DS White said.

Detective Sergeant Ray White and Detective Constable Bernard Jacobs were driving through the Milton Road Estate. The previous day a dawn raid had been carried out on Scott Jones. Scott had set up a full printing press at his home and was producing counterfeit Giros that were being sold both on the Milton Road Estate and others in South London. The Giros were being sold at twenty percent of the face value. A one-hundred-pound giro would be sold at twenty pounds which gave the buyer of it eighty pounds. The Giros had a one hundred percent record of being cashed without question. Some on the estate had seized the opportunity and were out daily cashing giros while others would buy just the one to help them get through the week. Scott's thriving counterfeit business was beginning to impact Double Bubble's money lending operation. Initially Double Bubble had considered buying everything that Scott could produce, become his one and only customer and build a team of people keen to earn a few quid to cash them for him, but following another visit from Detective Sergeant Ray White, he opted for the easier option of telling him everything he knew about Scott's operation and then just sitting back and waiting for Scott to get nicked so he could get back to lending out cash to hard up and cash-strapped families at his usual one hundred percent per week, mark up. DS White's superiors were thrilled with the arrest and estimated that over two hundred thousand pounds had been fraudulently obtained. He was given the heads up that his recent string of high-profile arrests would earn him a well-deserved promotion before the year was out.

DS White came to a halt outside the Milton Arms.

"Let's take a little look at who is in the bookies," DS White said.

"Okay Guv," DC Jacobs said, reaching for the door handle.

DS White stood on the pavement with his legs apart and looked skywards. He brushed his new suit down and turned to DC Jacobs.

"This is my jungle, Bernie, where discipline and focus are the keys to success. When cops like us go on the hunt we make less noise than the villains and focus in like they're our prey. That way, my friend, we'll always have the element of surprise," DS White said as he strolled off towards the bookies.

"Hello, hello and what have we here?" DS White said.

Deano had just finished writing out a betting slip and handed it to Stan the owner.

"I'm surprised to find you out and about Mr Derenzie, or is it still Deano the Dog?"

"Call me what you like," Deano said.

"Returning to the scene of the crime, are we?" DS White said, slowly turning so he could catch a glimpse of everyone in the bookies.

"No, just placing a bet," Deano said.

"You seem remarkably calm for a man that was stabbed by one of the Bedford Boot Boys," DS White said before scanning the room for any reaction that would give something away.

"I'm fine thank you, and it's like I've told you countless times, Detective Sergeant White, I have no idea who did it," Deano said before looking up at the information on the next race at Newmarket.

"A little birdie whispered in my ear that you do know who did it and that you were dead set on taking care of it yourself," DS White said.

"Only a fool or a man incredibly confident in his abilities would go on the hunt for someone with a knife," Deano said.

"Feeling confident then, are we?" DS White said.

Deano held up his betting slip.

"I've just won twenty pounds," Deano said as he turned his back on DS White and walked over to the window to collect his winnings.

"I want the man who stabbed you, Mr Derenzie. I want him nicked and banged up so don't go on some kind of mission to take care of this yourself or you will have me to contend with!" DS White said firmly.

"I would never do that, you're far too scary," Deano said with a smirk.

Some of the punters in the bookies' let out a chuckle but quickly stopped when DS White swivelled swiftly on his heels to face them.

Ricky pulled up outside in his Rover P5B. He could see the two detectives talking with Deano.

"Shit, what's all this about. What do they know? Why are they here?" Ricky thought. *"Has some one grassed? Have Terry and Steve been boasting about taking care of Eddy Boyce? Hold up a minute. Calm yourself down, Ricky. You know what you have to do, it's what we always do around the gavvers, we front it out. The old bill only knows what you tell them, remember that and pull yourself together!"*

Ricky got out of his car, locked the door and walked towards the bookies. Both DS White and DC Jacobs turned to face him.

"Alright Deano, how's it going mate?" Ricky said.

"And who might you be?" DS White said, looking Ricky up and down.

Deano rolled his eyes.

"I could say the same, but then you both have 'I am a policeman' written all over you," Ricky said.

"So, you're a smart arse, eh?" DS White said.

"No," Ricky said, "just stating a fact."

"Right," DS White said, taking a note pad from his inside pocket. "What's your name?"

"Ricky Turrell, and no, it's not spelt with a silent 'P'" Ricky said.

DC Jacobs sniggered.

"Is that your car outside, the Rover?" DS White said, squinting so he could read the number plate.

"Yep, it is," Ricky said.

"Do you have a full driver's licence?"

"Yep," Ricky said as his folded his arms.

"Insurance?"

Ricky nodded.

"What about road tax?"

"It's in the post," Ricky said before unfolding his arms.

A couple of the bookies' punters chuckled.

"Do you have these details on you?"

"No, but I'm happy to come down to the station and produce them," Ricky said.

"You're both a pair of smart arses in my book and far too cocky for my liking!" DS White said before clamping his note pad closed.

"My friend here was the victim of a vicious knife attack and I'm here to buy him a drink, DS White. Respectfully, we are not the criminals here," Ricky said with a hint of arrogance.

"Mark my words Ricky Turrell, we will catch him because we always get our man," DS White said before turning briskly and swiftly walking back out of the bookies' shop.

"You alright Deano?"

"Yes mate, it's just plod doing their job. Tell you what though; I've had a right result this afternoon with not one but two winners at Newmarket. That's fifty quid! It looks like the pints will be on me."

"Deano, mate, you have more front than Harrods and that's a fact!" Ricky thought.

Chapter 15

"Looking good Ricky," Deano said.

"You're not looking too bad yourself," Ricky said.

The two Teds admired their reflection in the shop window. Ricky had worn his dark blue drape suit with a light blue velvet collar, cuffs with a pale blue silk shirt and bootlace tie. On his feet he wore a new pair of white brothel creepers with decorative black squares on the throat line just below the black laces. He'd greased back his hair and grown and shaped his sideburns. Deano wore a black drape suit with red velvet collar and cuffs, with a red silk shirt. On his chest pocket read 'Deano the Dog' in gold stitching. On his feet he wore Ricky's favourite blue suede shoes with the chrome knuckle dusters as eyelets for the laces. Deano looked every bit the King of the Teds.

Ricky looked at Deano's hand as he ran it through his combed back his greased back hair.

"Deano, have you had a tattoo?" Ricky asked.

Deano turned and faced Ricky. He held up his clenched fists together. The tattoo spelt out 'TEDS RULE'.

"Yeah, I had it done in Croydon a few days back. I thought about 'KING TEDS' and a couple of others but settled on this one. I like the idea of those who fancy their chances getting their faces pounded in by this simple message," Deano said.

"Do you have any others?"

"Nah, never really fancied a tattoo before. What about you?" Deano asked as he looked up and down the road outside The Arms for the taxicab they had booked the night before.

"I did think about it when I was about fourteen, I suppose. I even went as far as going to the Tattoo Studio and taking a look around, but nothing grabbed me, you know. If I was going to have something then it had to be a tattoo that I could look at in the mirror in ten or twenty years' time and still like what I saw. My mate had one. It was a black panther with red claw lines. It did look the business when it was first done, but now it's kind of stretched and looks out of proportion. I suppose that's because he's grown since we were fourteen," Ricky said.

"You're definitely a thinker Ricky. You've never struck me as the kind of bloke that just does things on a whim and thinks, 'Sod the consequences'," Deano said.

"I would say that you're more than a thinker Deano. From what I've seen and learnt about you over the last twenty odd months that we've been friends, I'd say that you were a strategic thinker. I admire your strength, leadership and courage. On top of all that you have an uncanny charm that just gets people to follow you," Ricky said.

"That's a bit too deep for me. I just like a tear up every so often," Deano said.

"Nah, that's more Terry and Steve Parker. There's a lot more to you than that," Ricky said.

"I read this book called 'The Art of War by Sun Tzu' when I was in school. It was given to me by my English teacher. We had always got on well and one day while I was standing outside the headmaster's office waiting for yet another caning, she handed it to me and suggested that I read it while stuck in detention. I have to say that it was a little hard going to start with but increasingly it made sense and the principles were as relevant today as they were in Sun Tzu's time. I can tell you this, Ricky, because I know that you don't go blurting stuff about. Besides I wouldn't want every Skinhead, Boot Boy or Ted that fancies their chances getting hold of a copy," Deano said.

A green Cortina MK3 pulled up and beeped his hooter.

"That's our taxi," Ricky said.

The two Teds got into the car. Deano took the front seat next to the driver.

"Morden Underground Station please mate," Deano said.

The driver nodded and took off at speed.

"What, are you lads in a Rock n Roll band or something?" the driver asked.

"No mate," Deano said.

"It was just the Drape suits. You both look well smart," the driver said.

"Yeah, cheers," Deano said.

"I was a Ted back in the day," the driver said.

"Really," Deano said, before turning away and looking out of the side window.

"Yeah, back in the 50s I was part of a gang of Teddy Boys. We called ourselves the City Centre Teds because that's where we used to hang out on a Friday and Saturday night.

"City Centre Teds? I think I may have heard of them," Deano said, still looking out of the window.

"Those days have long gone now but back then, being a Ted was something really special. We were so much more than just a fashion statement. That's not to say that we didn't look pretty damn sharp, but we belonged to something much bigger than that. Before the Yanks gave us Jerry Lee Lewis, Elvis and Eddy Cochran, we danced about to jazz and skiffle music. It was the love and passion for Rock 'n Roll that really brought us all together. We would go out to a dance hall on a Saturday night in our best gear and the girls, damn those girls were sizzling hot, and game too for the right Teddy Boy," the driver said.

Deano turned back to the driver.

"What else did you do?" Deano asked.

"I can remember when the movie *'Blackboard Jungle'* came out at The Trocadero on the New Kent Road. It had songs by Bill Haley and The Comets. It was bloody manic. Teds ripped up seats and tore up chairs while others danced in the aisles with their girlfriends. I can remember never feeling so alive and free. We were a force, and those that governed feared us. On one Saturday night a minor fight broke out in the town centre. It was all over in minutes and nothing more than a few scrapes and bruises. The newspapers made it out to be some kind of riot and likened us to mobsters, saying that no self-respecting teenager should aspire to become a Ted. My old man went up the wall when he read that. He believed it word for word no matter what I said. It was shortly after that when I met Peggy and that was that. No more Teddy Boys, no more freedom just responsibilities what with the rent, electric, gas, water, food, nappies, clothes and so on. Twenty years later and my daughter is probably your age but if she came home with a Teddy Boy then I'd probably see it completely different from my old man," the driver said.

"Not if his name was Kenny," Ricky chuckled.

"Sorry, what's that?" asked the driver.

"Oh, it's just a private joke," Ricky said.

The driver stopped outside Morden Tube Station.

"What's your name?" Deano asked.

"Freddie," the driver said.

"I'm Deano and it's good to meet you, Freddie. Stick some Rock n Roll on your stereo, mate, and let your mind take you back to better days. Once a Ted always a Ted," Deano said, shaking him warmly by the hand.

The two Teds strolled over to the tube station and bought return tickets to Elephant and Castle. Morden was on the Northern Line which was just ten short stops to Elephant and Castle.

"What time are others turning up?" Ricky asked as he brushed the seat with his hand and sat down.

"The bands start at 7.30 so they should be there about seven-ish," Deano said.

Deano and Ricky strolled out of the tube station and into the Elephant and Castle pub just twenty-five minutes later. In the far corner of the mini hall was an extended table with a large crowd of Teds sat around it.

"Landlord, I'll have two pints of pints of bitter mate, and can you send over whatever they're having?" Deano said.

"Yes mate," said the landlord as he poured out two pint mugs of bitter.

"Hello Deano," one Ted said as they approached the table

"Alright Deano," another said.

"How's it going Deano?" a third said.

Deano took his seat at the head of the table.

"Here you go lads," the barmaid said.

"I'm Suzie and if you need anything just call for me."

Everyone around the table, including Deano, turned to see Suzie dressed as an original teddy girl. She wore a yellow drape jacket with black velvet collars and cuffs. Her open neck white silk shirt exposed part of her ample cleavage. She wore tight black drainpipe trousers that fell short of her ankles with stiletto heels. Suzie was a mousy blonde with a side parting and had her hair brushed back, cascading over her shoulders.

"When you've all finished gawping at the blonde," Deano said.

The lads around the table laughed and reached for their drinks.

"I'm pleased to see so many of you here today. This here is Ricky Turrell, my loyal and trusted second in command," Deano said.

The gang leaders nodded to acknowledge him.

 "I've asked for this meeting between the leaders of Teddy Boy gangs across London for a reason, but before we talk about that I want to tell you about the significance of this place. This place here, the Elephant and Castle, was the birthplace of the Teddy Boys as we know them. That's right, our movement was started here by strong, powerful working-class lads, and now, twenty years later with the Rock 'n Roll revival, supported by bands like Showaddywaddy, Crazy Cavan and The Rhythm Rockers, Mud and many others, the Teddy Boys are back with a vengeance. When I look around at you all here, I see good size gangs, but we're fragmented as a movement."

Deano paused and took a sip from his pint.

"Over there you have Andy Fransham from the Lewisham Teds who regularly has problems with Skinheads from The Excalibur Estate and Barry Pearson from the Stockwell Teds who has similar problems with lads from the Brandon Estate in Kennington. What I'm trying to say here is that together we have the numbers, but alone we're fragmented and therefore weaker than some of our individual enemies."

Deano paused and looked around the table.

"Last year the Milton Road Teds came under attack from three estates that mobbed up together in a bid to bring us down. These boys brokered a deal with Skinheads, Boot Boys, Glam Rockers, you name it. We didn't have none of it and with our friends here, Jock Addie from the Croydon Teds and our allies in Clapham and Wandsworth we beat the living shit out of each and every one of them. As one we became a Ted army and everything in our path just melted away. We watched as so-called hardened Nazi Skinheads had it on their toes and ran for the hills when we came into view. Together, as a force, we became unstoppable."

Deano took another sip of his drink.

"What I'm proposing is that we form an unbreakable alliance between all of us around this table. There are sixteen leaders here, with maybe thirty members in each gang. That's almost five hundred Teds if you count the hangers-on. Now include us and some of the smaller gangs around Sutton, Mitcham, Wimbledon and Tooting and you have, well, almost seven hundred hardcore Teddy Boys. That, my friends is power. Imagine now, just for one moment, that if any one of the gangs around this table was to come under attack from Skinheads, Suedeheads or Boot Boys and you can make a phone call and have almost fifteen hundred fists and brothel creepers at your disposal to reign unimaginable carnage and terror."

"I like it Deano but how will it work?" Jock asked.

Ricky smiled wryly at Jock as he still had two black eyes and a swollen nose.

"Everybody here continues to be the leader of their own gang. That doesn't change, but you also become a member of the board representing your Teds and the area you live in. We will meet once every three months formally, here at the Elephant and Castle, to share information about what is happening and where necessary agree to take decisive action.

"And what, you'll be Chairman of the board?" Jock asked.

"You all know me or know of my reputation. I'm Deano the Dog and King of the Teds but that doesn't mean that I will force you all to accept me as what Jock Addie describes as Chairman of the Board. Becoming an alliance, a Ted Army if you like, is bigger than any one man, so I would suggest that at the end of each year we take a vote, and the right man has the role of holding the alliance together and building on it further. There are thousands of Teds right across London and we should look to build on our numbers and extend our reach to other areas of the country too."

Deano stopped to let his words sink in. He could see the excitement around the table as each of the gang leaders saw the endless possibilities and potential as a unified Ted Army.

"We're with you Deano," Jock Addie said.

"Yeah, we are too," Andy Fransham said.

"And us," Barry Pearson said.

One by one each of the gang leaders signed up to Deano's vision.

"To a united Ted Army!" Jock said, standing up and raising his glass.

"TED ARMY!" they all yelled out together

"And to Deano the Dog, the rightful King of the Teds!" Jock said.

"KING OF THE TEDS!" the leaders of each of the Teds called out. They stood up and raised their glasses.

"TED ARMY…TED ARMY…TED ARMY!"

***

The beer flowed and the afternoon passed by quickly.

"Jock, I appreciate your support," Deano said.

"No problem, Deano. I can see what you're trying to do and yeah, we're all in," Jock said.

"So, are we good?" Deano asked softly.

"Yeah, look, I tried it on and got a slap. I'm not going to bitch about it. As far as I'm concerned, it's yesterday's news and I've moved on. We don't have any issues Deano," Jock said as he shrugged his shoulders.

"Good. I'm pleased, because I like you guys," Deano said.

"You may want to look over your shoulder though as the word is out there that some old-school enforcer called Fat Pat is looking to do you. Also, Clifford Tate is back from his place of hiding and looking to settle a score," Jock said. "All this is second hand news from my sister who is still seeing that twat on Bedford Estate."

"I couldn't give a rat's arse Jock. I'll batter each and every one of them if they show their faces around me," Deano said.

"I'm just keeping you in the picture on what I've heard, that's all," Jock said.

"What else have you heard?" Deano asked.

"The rumour mill about what happened to Eddy Boyce, the Skinhead who stabbed you, is working overtime. Some say that after you called into the Working Men's club to let them know you were looking for him, he had it on his toes and did a bunk," Jock said.

Deano shrugged his shoulders.

"There are others that say his front door was smashed in and there were signs of a struggle. Those same people think that he's either been battered senseless and is in a hospital somewhere with no recollection of where or who is. Then there are a few who think that he's paid the price of going up against you with his life," Jock said.

"What do you think Jock?" Deano said.

"I think that you're an extremely dangerous enemy to have," Jock said.

Deano smiled.

"What are you drinking?" Deano said before motioning Suzie over. "Ricky, over here, do you want a drink?"

"I'll have a pint, cheers. I'll tell you what Deano, I wouldn't mind some of that," Jock said, looking directly at Suzie. "She looks the dog's nuts!"

"Oi! I heard that," Suzie chuckled.

"Sweetheart, you were meant to," Jock said.

"Alright Deano, I was chatting with a few of the lads," Ricky said.

"What about you handsome, what are you drinking?" Suzie asked, gazing directly into Ricky's eyes.

"What would you suggest Suzie?" Ricky said, holding her gaze.

"This bitter stuff is for old men," Suzie chuckled. "Everyone is moving to lager these days. Try a pint of Carling Black Label on me."

"How could I refuse?" Ricky said with a broad smile.

"Have a word will yer! Is there anything you Milton Road lot can't do?" Jock said with a feigned laugh.

Deano leaned forward and whispered in Ricky's ear.

"She is one very tasty bird mate. I'd get right in there if I were you."

"Deano, Jock, guys, she's only bought me a drink," Ricky said winking.

"There you go," Suzie said, placing the tray of drinks on the table. "Come on then, take a sip and tell me what you think."

Ricky raised the glass slowly, took a sip of the golden fluid and smiled.

"You know what? I like that," Ricky said. "Cheers Suzie you may just have converted me to becoming a lager drinker. Here Deano have you tried this?"

"Nah, mate I like bitter," Deano said.

"I'll give it a go," Jock said.

Ricky handed him the glass and Jock took a large gulp.

"That is alright ain't it? Tell you what, I'm sacking bitter after this pint and going on to a drop of this Carling," Jock said.

"Go on then, give it here," Deano said.

Jock handed him the glass, now half empty, and he took a long sip followed by a large gulp.

"Can't believe I'm saying this, but that is one nice drop of gear," Deano said.

"I told you, didn't I," Suzie said.

"I'm Ricky, cheers for the drink Suzie," Ricky said as he sank the last of the pint. "Tell you what," Ricky reached into his pocket, pulled out a wad of notes and peeled off two ten-pound notes, "Get all the Teds in here a pint of Carling on me and Deano. Oh, and Suzie… have one yourself."

Suzie grinned as she caught Ricky running his eyes over her slender, athletic figure.

"Here Ricky, with me," Deano said.

"Back in a minute Jock," Ricky said.

Ricky followed Deano over to the large stage area at the end of the pub. A couple of guys were laying out instruments and equipment.

"Les?" Deano said.

The man, wearing blue jeans and a white T-Shirt looked up.

"Hello Les," Deano said.

"Hello mate. How are you?" Les said.

"Yeah, good Les, good. This is a good mate of mine, Ricky," Deano said.

Ricky reached out and shook his hand.

"Hang on a minute," Ricky said. "You're Les Gray. Good to meet you."

"Yeah, but don't go telling everyone that we're still putting up our own gear," Les said, rolling his eyes and smiling.

"I've met you before," Ricky said. "Well not really met you, but me and a few mates used to watch you rehearse."

"Get out of here," Les said with a wry smile

"No really," Ricky said.

"Alright then, where did we rehearse?"

"At the All Saints Church Hall in Hackbridge," Ricky said.

"Yeah, that's right," Les said as he put a large black amplifier at the end of the stage. You must have been the kids up at the church windows."

"Yeah, we were," Ricky said. "Saying it like this sounds kind of stupid now."

"No, of course not mate. Me and the lads appreciate the support of all our fans, Ricky, and any friend of the King of the Teds is a friend of Mud," Les said.

"Can I ask a quick question?" Ricky asked.

"Sure, fire away," Les said as he placed a second amplifier on the stage.

"I've read about this fierce rivalry between you and Showaddywaddy. How true is it?" Ricky asked.

"Ricky it's all just show business. Is there rivalry between us and Showaddywaddy for the Top of the Pops number one slot then…? Absolutely! We want it as much as they do, but away from all that, both me and Ray are great mates with Dave Bartram. We've had many a pint together and I know we have the utmost respect for each other as artists. But if journalists writing a load of tosh in the magazines helps to sell our records, then neither one of us are likely to come forward and put the record straight, if you'll excuse the pun," Les chuckled. "Look we've got a gig to do so I have to crack on, but if you're about later, Deano, we can have a pint and a catch up."

"Yeah, catch you later Les," Deano said.

"Bloody hell, Deano, how did you meet Les Gray?" Ricky asked.

"I was watching them in pubs and clubs long before they got signed to Mickie Most's Rak label. Les, Rob and Dave are all nice fellas; local lads that have made it big. Great band, they deserve all the success that comes their way," Deano said. "I'll tell you what though, back in September 1973, me and a few of the Milton Road Teds took a train down to Margate where we watched Showaddywaddy perform their first professional gig at Dreamland Ballroom. We'd been hearing about these lively Rock 'n' Roll bands Choice and the Golden Hammers up in the Midlands and me, Mick, Kenny and Specs went to see them perform at the Fosse Way Pub in Leicester. Up until that time it was probably one of the best gigs we'd ever been to. So, once they were Showaddywaddy we just had to get ourselves down to Margate."

Suzie brought two pints of Carling Black label in straight glasses over to their table.

"Cheers Suzie," Ricky said.

"Yeah, cheers," Deano said.

"In your own time," Ricky said before handing over a five-pound note, "Can you take a tray of drinks around for Les and the band."

"You're flashing the cash about Ricky. What, are you a pools winner or something?" Suzie said.

"Yeah, I wish," Ricky said as he admired her flawless, bronzed complexion and vivacious blue eyes. "I work hard, and I like to share a bit with friends when I can."

"Yeah, he does," Deano said. "This fella had my car completely overhauled while I was ill in hospital."

"Aww, that was nice," Suzie said.

"I'm curious," Ricky said. "Do you have a boyfriend?"

"Would that make any difference?" Suzie said, fluttering her eyelashes, turning away slowly and walking back to the bar.

"I'm not sure that Suzie cares much for rules or customs Ricky," Deano said. "A girl with a passion for life and freedom like that can make or break a man. In many ways she's not unlike my Melanie. She can be one hell of a bitch or the cutest thing you've ever seen. Between you and me, Ricky, I'm thinking about asking Melanie to marry me."

"Bloody hell mate, that's great news," Ricky said, raising his glass.

"Yeah, don't go saying anything alright," Deano said.

"No mate, of course not," Ricky said.

"I'm only toying with it at the moment. If and when the moment is right, then I'll ask her," Deano said.

"Mate, what brought this on?"

"Before being stabbed and at death's door, I hadn't given stuff like marriage any real thought but as I lay in that hospital bed thinking about my life and having Melanie visit me every day without fail, I suppose I knew it was the right thing to do, when the time was right, to ask her to be my wife. Fuck me, Ricky, that doesn't half sound strange. Me, Deano the Dog, a married man. What the hell?"

"I suppose you know when it's the right one," Ricky said.

"Yeah, and Melanie would never try to change me. Not that she could, mate, because the other thing I got from laying in that hospital bed was focus and a vision that I must turn into a reality. Today, here at the birthplace of the Teddy Boy movement, we made history. Mark my words Ricky, we will be a thousand Teds strong within eighteen months. I'll be meeting with Teds from Hackney right through to Wembley and if they don't roll with it then mate, we'll rock n roll right over them. They'll be given twenty-four hours to remove the drape, disband, and lose the name. Any failure to comply will result in, well, you know Ricky. We do not take prisoners."

"Fuck me Deano, you weren't too quick to share that part of your vision with the other gang leaders," Ricky thought. *"I don't see you giving up running the Ted Army no matter what the outcome of any annual vote."*

It was just after 7.00pm when Kenny, Lee, Terry and Steve Parker and the rest of the Milton Road Teds arrived at the Castle pub. Shortly after that the Croydon Teds turned up and were quickly followed by Teds from all the other gangs. Ricky convinced them all to try the Carling Black label, much to Suzie's delight. Ricky noticed that Kenny had seemed a little distant and took him to one side just before Mud was due to come on and perform.

"Kenny are you alright?" Ricky asked.

"I don't know, mate. I mean I'm having bloody nightmares every night so sleeping isn't the bed. Little Tommy is teething so that's not helping much either," Kenny said.

"You're just going to have to give it time Kenny," Ricky said.

"Do you know that sometimes I can be walking along, just minding my own business, and from the corner of my eye I catch a glimpse of Specs. It's like he's haunting me mate, and believe me after the slap I got from his sister at the funeral, I'm already feeling bloody guilty," Kenny said.

"I know it can't be easy. How is Denise coping?" Ricky said.

"The hard-nosed, self-centred, bitch!" Ricky thought.

"She's just carrying on like nothing has happened. I did try to talk to her about it one night, but she just changed the subject. Denise was having none of it. I suppose I'm grateful that she isn't feeling like I am. She's a lot stronger than me, that's for sure," Kenny said.

"That's because she's a mercenary, egotistical, nasty piece of work," Ricky thought.

Suzie brought two pints of Carling Black Label Lager down to the end of the bar where the lads were chatting.

"There you go lads," Suzie said with a chuckle. "Courtesy of Jock."

Both Ricky and Kenny raised their glasses towards Jock who was standing with his inner circle by the stage.

"Did Deano get what he wanted?" Kenny asked.

"How do you mean?" Ricky said.

"Come off it, Ricky. If Deano was pulling the leaders of all this lot together then he wanted something. Don't forget, mate, I've known him a hell of a lot longer than you have," Kenny said.

"I'm sure he'll fill everyone in as and when he's ready," Ricky said.

"Spoken like a true number two," Kenny said. "Forgive me, mate, but I've heard stuff like that from Mick many times before."

"Have you heard anything about Mick?" Ricky asked.

"I was thinking about going to visit him in the nick. Lee said that he's at Brixton so he's not a million miles way. I'm not sure that he would want us to see him in that shitty prison gear and caged up. Besides, what do I tell him? Deano got stabbed and nearly croaked it, the person that he hates most, you, is now Deano's number two, and his mate since junior school, Specs, has jumped off the roof because his wife is now with me. Not exactly good news, is it?" Kenny said.

"Well mate, when you put it like that…" Ricky said.

"Mick's only got another sixteen months to do, providing he keeps his nose clean and doesn't go around bashing up too many people. What are you going to do when he gets out, Ricky?"

"I'm second in command now, Kenny. I'm the right hand to Deano and I was his choice. Now, if Deano decides to fuck me off in favour of Mick when he gets out, I suppose I'll have to deal with it. However, if he doesn't and Mick can't accept his new place in the scheme of things then we'll have to find somewhere and have an all-out straightener. He doesn't concern me at all," Ricky said.

"It will come to that. You do know that don't you?" Kenny said.

"Like I said Kenny, I am not concerned in the slightest," Ricky said.

"Here Ricky," Suzie called. "Are you going to take me out for a drink later or what?"

Ricky beamed.

"Absolutely!"

The lights around the pub went dim as the evening's compère came on stage.

"Good evening, ladies, gentlemen and Teddy Boys of London," the compère said.

The three hundred plus Teds attending the pub gig all cheered.

"Feel better for that do you? My name is George and I'm your compère this evening. Now, not a lot of people know this, but many years ago I thought about starting my own rock and roll band. I thought about calling it the 'rubber band' but thought it might be a bit of a stretch."

The crowd laughed and cheered.

"I feel proud and honoured to be standing on the same stage Buddy Holly and the Crickets did in the 1950s, and I would like to thank all those Teds back then who threw coins at Cliff Richard. I mean have you heard that song he did last year *'We Don't Talk Anymore'*? What was that all about? Cliff, it's because you're boring! Do you know that when he was performing in Japan the audience went wild when he asked them what song they would like him to sing. Funny lot these Japanese… Anyway, the crowd is screaming out 'Tits and Fanny'. So Cliff said he couldn't sing that because he was a devout Christian. 'Tits and Fanny' the crowd screamed again. Oh come on, really? Cliff said, shaking his head at the crowd. 'Tits and Fanny' the crowd persisted. Okay, okay, Cliff finally said, but I don't know how it goes.

'Tits and Fanny' … the crowd sung together in unison… 'We don't talk anymore!'"

The crowd of Teds cheered.

"You're a great audience, thank you. So now I need you to put your hands together for one of London's very own Rock 'n' Roll bands … MUD!"

Everybody in the pub cheered as Les Gray and the band bounded on to the stage and took up their instruments. Les Gray wore a bright red drape suit with red silk collar, a black shirt, blue socks and black brothel creepers. The other band members wore similar outfits in the same bright red. As the crowd calmed down, Les counted the band in and began to perform *'Tiger Feet'*. Teds all over began to bop around while others stood opposite each other and mimicked the band rocking from side to side and back and forth with their thumbs in their trousers belt loops.

Chapter 16

Deano and the Milton Road Teds left just after 11.30pm to catch one of the last trains of the night. Ricky had opted to stay and go out for a drink with Suzie.

"Do you know of a lock in somewhere?" Ricky said as he helped Suzie put her coat on.

"I've got somewhere special in mind," Suzie said.

"Ricky, my old son, you are so in here," Ricky thought.

Suzie took Ricky by the hand and led him out of the pub. She held up her hand and within a few seconds a black taxi pulled over. Ricky held the door open, and Suzie clambered in and sat back in the seat.

"Where to love?" the taxi driver asked.

"The Speak," Suzie said.

"The Speak? Where's that darling?" the taxi driver asked.

"Sorry, can you take us to the Speakeasy Club near Oxford Circus," Suzie said and then turned to Ricky. "Everyone who goes there just calls it the 'Speak'. I think you'll like it, Ricky."

"I'm sure I will," Ricky said as he held her gaze.

Four minutes later the taxi driver stopped outside The Speakeasy Club in Margaret Street. Ricky reached over and paid the fare.

"You didn't have to do that," Suzie said.

"I know, but I wanted to," Ricky said as he looked himself over and brushed himself down by the reflection of the shop next door to the club.

"Don't worry, you look… delicious," Suzie said with a giggle.

"Delicious. I don't think anyone's ever described me as delicious. I like it…. I really like it." Ricky thought.

"That must make us dinner and dessert then," Ricky said, returning her smile.

There was a doorman outside the club dressed in a black suit with a black bow tie. He looked the size of Double Bubble. Ricky looked at the sign by the entrance it read: Strictly Members Only.

"Good evening," the doorman greeted them.

"Hello Archie, how are you today?" Suzie said.

"Another day, another dollar Miss Suzie," the doorman said as he stood to one side to allow them both to pass. "Have a good evening, Mr Bartram."

"What? Did he just call me Mr Bartram?" Ricky thought. *"Does he think I'm Dave Bartram, the lead singer of Showwaddywaddy?"*

"Did you hear what he called me?" Ricky whispered.

"It doesn't matter. I'm a member here," Suzie said.

As they entered Ricky stopped to look around the club. It had been decorated like an American Speakeasy from the prohibition era.

"This place is cool, really bloody cool," Ricky thought.

"Good evening, Suzie, good to see you," a smartly dressed man in a navy-blue three-piece suit, white shirt and a royal blue Crimplene knitted neck tie said. He leaned forward and pecked Suzie on the cheek.

Suzie turned to Ricky. "This is Laurie 'O' Leary. He manages the club."

"Nice to meet you David," Laurie said.

"I'm not Dave Bartram," Ricky said. "I'm Ricky, Ricky Turrell."

"This is a private member's only club so you can be whoever you want. Enjoy your evening," Laurie said. "Suzie, I'll send over a waitress."

"Thanks," Suzie said as she led Ricky over to a corner table with a large poster of Al Capone on the wall to their left.

"This is a great club, Suzie. I'm not sure about all this Dave Bartram business but what a place. Is this a regular for you?" Ricky said as he sat back in the leather chair. "A guy could get really used to this."

"I've been coming here a while now," Suzie said. "This place is big with the music industry. You'll find all sorts in here from artists to producers and everyone in between. That's probably why you're being mistaken for Dave Bartram. I mean, you do look like him, what with the drape suit, brothel creepers and, well, that smile of yours. It just lights up the room," Suzie said.

"This bird is dishing out one compliment after another," Ricky thought.

"Hi Suzie, you're in earlier than I thought," the waitress said. "Hello Mr Bartram, or can I call you Dave?"

Ricky sighed and looked up to see a beautiful curvaceous, hour-glass figure and perfectly formed, berry-red, lips. The waitress had locks of chestnut brown hair that curtained over her oval face.

"I know you're not Dave Bartram," the waitress said with a cheeky grin. "I'm just kidding. Can I get you guys a drink?"

"You know me, Lilly, I'll have a scotch on the rocks," Suzie said.

"You certainly had me going," Ricky said. "I'm Ricky. Do you have malt whiskey?"

"We certainly do," Lilly said.

"Then I'll have a large malt whiskey please and have one yourself," Ricky said.

"Hmm, malt whiskey. That sounds good, and perfect for a speakeasy. I'll have the same please Lilly," Suzie said.

"Coming up," Lilly said as she whisked off towards the bar.

"You can get all sorts in here," Suzie said. "Before my time Roger Daltrey drank here and the Monkees had a big party, which was, by all accounts, legendary. I've seen David Bowie here. We've not met, but just exchanged nods as private members do," Suzie said.

"I'm sure this place has a tale or two to tell," Ricky said.

"A lot of up and coming bands from all over the world will gig here in the hope of getting noticed by the big wigs that control the music industry," Suzie said.

"What about you Suzie, how did you end up becoming a member?" Ricky said.

"Oh, I was a member of Sibylla's nightclub in Piccadilly Circus when Laurie ran that, and when I heard he was moving a number of us moved too," Suzie said.

"So you've been friends for a while," Ricky said.

"We don't have any history, if that's what you mean. Laurie runs a good club and always manages to stay at the forefront of whatever's going on. There have been some incredible nights here," Suzie said.

"Damn, put my foot in it there," Ricky thought.

"There you go," Lilly said as she put the tray of drinks on the table. She leaned forward and kissed Suzie gently on the lips. "I'm on my break in half an hour. I'll join you then."

"What the… did she just kiss her or what?!" Ricky thought. *"That was a proper full on kiss, smack bang on the lips! Way beyond friends!"*

"I'll run a tab for you Ricky," Lilly said.

"Did I just see that or am I imagining things?" Ricky wondered.

"Yeah, cheers. I'm good for it," Ricky chuckled.

"She's just wonderful," Suzie said turning to watch Lilly walk back to the bar.

"You've known each other a while then?" Ricky said before reaching for his drink.

"Since school days really," Suzie said.

"So, it's been a while then," Ricky said.

"Yes, Lilly was my first crush and," Suzie said, lowering her voice, "My first kiss with another girl. We would both work with horses, we'd muck them out, groom them together and I just developed this almighty crush on her, and then one afternoon we had finished all our chores early and were just lying on the straw in the sun. We were laughing and joking around and then the laughter just kind of trailed off and we were just looking into each other's eyes. I was smitten by the way her eyes glittered when the sunlight caught them. Lilly would always wear this amazing French perfume and I'd find myself being drawn closer to her so that I could bask in her aroma. As we lay on that straw I felt as though our bodies were magnetised, being drawn closer and closer together. Lilly's voice became lighter, then she just leaned forward slowly and kissed my lips. Oh my God, Ricky that kiss was thrilling, scary and a major discovery of who I am."

"So, you like girls," Ricky said.

"It's not as simple as that. I'm not attracted to a person's sexual organs. That's way too shallow for me. I fall for the person and that can be a boy or a girl," Suzie said before taking a long sip of her drink.

"I ain't so sure I could just reach down into someone's pants and be happy with whatever I found down there," Ricky thought.

"Does that shock you?" Suzie asked as she put her glass back on the table and sat back in her chair.

"I can understand having a good friend and I mean a really good friend of the same sex, but the thoughts of anything else have never entered my head. Don't get me wrong, I do not judge anyone's choices. I mean we're all here just the once so it's important to live your life by your own rules," Ricky said.

"That's okay. It just means that you're heterosexual. I dare say that given the right situation, who knows, maybe you'd discover more about yourself," Suzie said.

"I'm not sure what you mean," Ricky said.

"Okay," said Suzie, "so imagine that you find yourself at a swinger's party, and everyone is naked, free of inhibitions and just enjoying themselves. Then, while you're engaged in some sexual act with someone's wife, the husband wants to watch you play with his wife, maybe he wants to physically help you enter her or pleasure her with his mouth while you're making love. Now, would that be a problem for you if it was in a bedroom with the door closed and just three, adventurous, consenting adults?"

Ricky thought about it for a few seconds.

"Probably not," Ricky said.

"How did it make you feel when you saw Lilly and I kiss? Were you disgusted or shocked?"

"Actually I found it quite exciting, if I'm honest," Ricky said.

"So, your mind is open to situations beyond what society would like to consider being normal?" Suzie said.

Ricky found himself feeling a little hot under the collar. He reached up and undid his top button.

Ricky nodded.

"I melted after that first kiss with Lilly. It was pure ecstasy; she was fiery but sweet and I could happily enjoy her company for hours. Lilly touched my soul and opened my eyes and my heart. In fact, my first sexual experience was with a girl. It was Lilly; we became lovers, sweethearts. After making love we would lay on the bed for hours just talking and talking and we both realised that while we loved being together, we were both open to adventures and relationships with boys too. I can remember how she would return to school and tell me about some boy that she had met and what they had got up to together, and I found it a real turn on. I would hang on her every word and then we would have the most amazing sex together. There were times when I would tell her about my adventures too and she felt exactly the same. We are like those two proverbial peas in a pod."

"I think it's nice, no not nice, bloody fabulous that you've found someone that you can truly share your deepest, inner feelings, hopes and desires with," Ricky said.

"I knew that there was more to you," Suzie said.

"You mean more than the Teddy Boy look," Ricky said before finishing his drink.

"I thought you were more than the latest cliché. I see guys come and go at the Elephant and after a while it's very easy to put them into boxes. Your friend, Deano, for example. I suspect he'd much rather be out fighting with some group somewhere on a Saturday night than say stay at home and ask what his girlfriend's deepest and most personal fantasies were and then make it happen," Suzie said.

"I think you may be right. Deano loves a good tear up," Ricky said.

"The other guy, Kenny, now he's your Saturday night special type. I'm sure his good looks get him plenty of action with the girls, but it's all just mono-level sex. I doubt that he even remembers their names in the morning, and in truth the girls probably found him to be a disappointment too," Suzie said.

"I wouldn't know," Ricky said.

"Okay, we're getting a little defensive which makes you a solid, good and loyal friend to those guys. That's a good thing," Suzie said.

"I've brought you some refills," Lilly said putting a tray on the table. "Was that okay?"

"Yeah, sure. Thank you," Ricky said.

"Hey Dave, good to see you," said an older guy in a brown and cream chequered suit as he passed the table.

"Yeah, good to see you too," Ricky said.

Both the girls laughed.

"I got myself a malt whiskey too," Lilly said. "I hope that was okay?"

"Absolutely," Ricky said. "That one was on Dave Bartram!"

"Good," Lilly said. "I'll get us all another round and stick it on his bill. He can settle the bill the next time he visits."

Lilly slid in beside Suzie. She put her hand on Suzie's and squeezed it.

"Hey you look great," Lilly said.

"So do you," Suzie replied in a sultry voice, "And Ricky looks delicious don't you think?"

Lilly turned to face Ricky with a smile that got broader by the second.

"I think he looks… succulent," Lilly said.

"Now you're embarrassing me," Ricky chuckled.

"You're a good-looking guy, take the compliment," Lilly said.

Ricky raised his glass. "Here's to new friends."

"That will work," Suzie said, raising her glass.

"And lovers," Lilly said.

Ricky swallowed a little too much and began to choke. Suzie reached over and patted him on the back while Lilly chuckled to herself.

"Sorry about that," Ricky said.

"What is going on here? There's a lot of flirting going on and I'm not sure if they're just on a wind up or taking the piss," Ricky thought.

"Do you know what, Ricky?" Lilly whispered. "I've had this big problem watching you chatting away with my girlfriend all night."

"Really," Ricky said with a shocked expression.

"Yes, I've been wondering what you would look like out of that drape suit," Lilly said.

Ricky took a large gulp. He didn't know what to say.

"I've been wondering the same thing about you," Suzie said. "In fact, I've been wondering what colour panties you're wearing."

Lilly beamed and turned slightly to her left so she faced both Suzie and Ricky head on. She gently hitched up her black skirt and parted her legs. Ricky's eyes almost sprung out when he caught sight of the little red triangle at the top of her shapely legs. Suzie reached over and squeezed Ricky's thigh. Ricky could feel the adrenaline racing through his body and his heart thumping so hard and fast that he thought his chest would tear open and his beating heart would land on the table alongside the drinks.

"You are getting me very excited," Suzie said to Lilly.

"Would you like to touch?" Lilly whispered.

Suzie closed her eyes and looked up towards the ceiling and then slowly lowered her head and smiled.

"Oh yes please, but with my lips," Suzie whispered.

"You, Suzie, are just wonderfully naughty," Lilly said.

"What is going on here?" Ricky thought. *"Am I on with Suzie, Lilly or both of them? Maybe I'm just blown out because they look pretty taken with each other!"*

"I'm owed an early finish," Lilly said. "We could leave if you like?"

"That sounds like a plan," Suzie said. "Would you like to come to our place for a night cap or coffee?"

"Either one sounds great," Ricky said.

Lilly went to the bar and spoke to Laurie briefly before returning with her coat.

"I'm ready when you are," Lilly said before handing the bar bill to Ricky.

Ricky reached into his pocket and left a small pile of notes on the tray.

"Good night, Mr Bartram, or was it Ricky Turrell?" Laurie said.

"Good night Laurie. You have a fabulous club. I hope to visit you again," Ricky said.

Suzie leaned in and kissed him on the cheek. "See you soon Laurie," Suzie said.

As they walked out into the road the cold night air hit Ricky. He closed his eyes and took several deep breaths.

"Are you okay?" Suzie said.

"Yeah, I'm fine. I just love that feeling of walking out into the night when the cold air fills your lungs," Ricky said.

"I know what you mean," Lilly said. "When I was younger and living at my parent's home, I would always leave my bedroom window open so my room would fill with that clean air."

Suzie flagged down a taxicab and the three of them got into the car.

"Hello darling, where to, treacle?" the taxi driver said.

"Harrington Gardens, Kensington please," Suzie said.

"Kensington!" Ricky thought, *"How the hell do you girls afford a place in swanky Kensington when you're working in pubs and clubs?"*

With empty roads the taxi passed Hyde Park and arrived at the Kensington address in just over fifteen minutes. Ricky couldn't help but notice that Suzie had been running her hand up and down Lilly's thigh and disappearing beneath her skirt. Lilly caught his gaze. He looked away for a second and turned back to see that she was still maintaining eye contact. The sexual tension between the three of them was electric.

Ricky tried to pay the fare, but Suzie insisted on paying. He looked up at the five-storey terraced building.

"This is class, real class," Ricky thought.

"Come on up," Suzie said, racing ahead and opening the black main entrance door to the building. Lilly took Ricky by the hand and led him in. Suzie opened the door to her immediate right on the ground floor. The door swung open, and Ricky was ushered into the apartment.

"This is really nice," Ricky said as he looked around at the period furniture. It was old but classy and timeless. The ceilings were almost ten feet high, and the curtains fell from ceiling to floor. Ricky caught a glimpse out of the window before Lilly had completely closed them. There was a large green outside, with trees and a seat under a lamp post. Ricky shivered with excitement. He couldn't believe that he was in the company of two beautiful, adventurous and sexy, girls.

Lilly sat on the sofa while Suzie brought over three large glasses of white wine on a tray. Ricky was still standing by the window. When Suzie sat next to Lilly, he walked over to the chair opposite them and sat down.

"I bought this wine earlier. I hope it's okay. I've wanted to try this for ages but can't guarantee you'll like it," Suzie said.

"I'm sure it'll be fine, thank you," Ricky said.

"You know that Suzie and I are together," Lilly said.

Ricky nodded.

"I hadn't had many boyfriends and had never even thought about being with a girl," Lilly said. "I knew that I liked Suzie and that we had become close friends and our relationship had been quite physical in as much as we would hug each other when we met or hold hands. It always felt special and became an integral part of our earlier friendship. Neither of us felt strange about kissing each other on the cheek but the more time we spent together the more I knew that I wanted and needed more."

Ricky took a sip of his wine and watched as Suzie gave Lilly a reassuring squeeze on her bare knee.

"It was after our first kiss that I invited Suzie for a sleep over at my parent's home. I knew that they were going away so we could be alone and allow destiny to play out. I had been nervous and excited all day, which only became heightened when my parents finally left. When Suzie arrived at my home, she looked amazing, absolutely stunning. She appeared so cool and calm while I felt so nervous about how the evening would pan out. I remember how we both raced up the stairs and jumped on my bed, laughing. I played some music on my tape recorder, and we just chatted. Suzie suggested that we get into our nightwear, and I remember vividly watching Suzie take off her dress. I couldn't take my eyes off her body, and she caught me. I felt so guilty but Suzie, the sweetheart that she is, just smiled. We both lay on my bed in our bra and panties and then there was a silence that could have gone two ways. Suzie leaned in and kissed me, and that was the start of our relationship, our adventure together and here we are, five years later and still exploring our sexuality both together and apart. It's pretty damn near perfect," Lilly said.

Lilly turned to face Suzie. They smiled and began to kiss, each of them running their hands over each other's bodies, exploring each of the curves while kissing with increasing passion. Ricky sat back and watched as Suzie ran her hand along the inside of Lilly's thigh.

Suzie began to kiss her ears and neck while Lilly took deep breaths and moaned with pleasure. The two girls stopped and stood up. Lilly held out her hand for Ricky and the three went through to the bedroom.

Ricky was woken up with a cup of coffee. Both Suzie and Lilly were out of bed and dressed.

"Ricky you'll need to drink this quickly because we have to leave soon," Suzie said.

"Yeah, cheers," Ricky said, before pulling himself up and taking a sip of the coffee.

Both the girls were dressed, and Ricky noticed how Lilly kept on looking at her watch. So he slipped out of bed and pulled on his trousers. He picked up his clothes and went through to the bathroom where he quickly got dressed and cleaned his teeth by putting toothpaste on his finger and rubbing it around his mouth. Ricky brushed his hair. He wanted a shower and to dress properly but felt that he needed to leave.

"Sorry for ushering you out, Ricky, but we are pressed for time," Suzie said.

"No problem," Ricky said. "Do you both fancy meeting up later for a drink or something?"

Suzie shook her head and smiled awkwardly.

"I don't think that's a good idea," Suzie said.

"Really, why? I thought we were all friends," Ricky said.

"You were a fantasy Ricky," Lilly said. "I've indulged another of Suzie's threesome fantasies."

"Oh, right," Ricky said.

"It's not personal Ricky. You are a nice guy and we all had fun, but that was it," Suzie said.

"I'm not sure what to say," Ricky said.

"What about goodbye and have a nice life," Lilly said.

"Have I upset you Lilly? I'm at a bit of a loss here." Ricky said.

"The night is over Ricky; the deed has been done and the box has been ticked for Suzie and I, so that's it. This is goodbye and thank you for the memory."

Ricky smiled. "Well in that case, thank you for the experience of a lifetime. You can be sure I'll never forget either of you," Ricky said as he headed towards the front door. "Take care."

Ricky took a taxi back across London to his home in Carshalton Beeches where he pondered on the night's events and how strange the conversation had been that morning.

Chapter 17

Neil drove down the quiet tree lined avenue in the Cortina he had stolen just half an hour before as transport to get him to the address of a Jaguar XJ6 he had earmarked as part of the next export order of prestigious cars to Africa. He watched as the owner pulled up outside his detached home and strolled up the driveway. He got out of the Cortina, looked up and down the road and then quickly walked towards the Burgundy short wheel base Jaguar XJ6. The registration number plate ended with an 'M', meaning that the car was less than twelve months old. Neil concluded that this would be the perfect car to complete the next batch. He stopped by the car and looked through the open driver's side window at the maroon leather trim. To his surprise, the owner had left the car keys in the ignition. He quickly opened the car door and slid into the driver's seat. On the passenger seat was a black briefcase. Neil turned the ignition key and the 4.2 litre straight six engine fired up.

"Hey you!"

Neil turned quickly to see a red faced, irate, balding middle-aged man bounding down the driveway towards the car. With his left foot, Neil quickly covered the brake pedal and jolted the automatic transmission lever down into drive.

"Got you, you thieving little bastard!"

The car owner's hand shot through the window and grabbed Neil's shirt collar. He gripped it tightly and dragged him towards the window.

"Get out of my car!"

Instinctively, with the car now in drive, Neil floored the accelerator pedal and the Jaguar leapt forward with a slight screech from the rear tyres. The Jaguar lurched forward at speed, with the owner still hanging onto Neil's collar tightly.

"Stop my car!" the owner yelled.

The automatic gearbox slipped into second gear. Neil looked down at the speedo as he fought with the steering wheel and saw he was doing nearly thirty-five miles an hour. The car's owner slipped and dragged Neil's head, by the collar, down to the bottom of the side window. As the car touched on forty-five miles an hour, the car owner let go. Neil shot up and looked into his rear-view mirror. The car's owner bounced twice and then rolled along the hard tarmac road behind him. Neil was rapidly approaching the end of the avenue and so had to slam on the brakes. The car screeched to a halt. Neil quickly looked in his rear-view mirror. The owner came to a stop by the kerbside, but he wasn't moving. Neil put the left indicator on and drove away. At the end of the road he spotted a red public telephone box. He stopped the car, raced inside and called 999 and requested an ambulance for an accident he had just witnessed. With sweat pouring from his brow and clammy hands, he got back into the Jaguar and drove it back across London to the garages where they were storing cars ready for export.

The black briefcase had fallen into the passenger side foot well. Neil reached down and picked it up. He pressed the clips and opened it to find a masonic apron, white gloves and a small blue book. Neil then checked the mileage. It had less than one thousand miles on the odometer.

Neil left the keys in the car and locked the garages. He was shaken by the incident but still a little high on the excitement of stealing yet another high-end motor car and the large pay day he knew he would be due from Ricky within the next few days.

Neil got into his Metallic brown 1972 Datsun 240Z. He had treated himself to the sports car after his last pay day from Ricky. Neil had taken Jackie down to the Datsun dealership with him and bought the car in the showroom at full list price. The car had covered less than ten thousand miles and had been fitted out with every extra. Neil paid cash for the car and celebrated its purchase with a bottle of champagne at a restaurant they had begun to use regularly in Wimbledon Village. It was just a short drive to the flats where Doreen lived. Neil had arranged to meet Jackie there at 7.00pm.

Knock… Knock!

"Hi Doreen, is Jackie back?" Neil said.

"Come in Neil, I've just put the kettle on. Would you like a cup of tea?"

"Yeah, sure, thank you," Neil said.

***

Neil sat on the chair he always sat on when he babysat for her. He looked over at the record player and spotted the Simon and Art Garfunkel album which had led to their discussion over the movie 'The Graduate' with Dustin Hoffman. That was the first time that they had slept together. As Doreen bent down to put the mug of tea on the table, he looked at her curves and found himself thinking back to when he first saw her clothes come off. Neil pulled the cushion from his side and put it on his lap.

"So, is business good?" Neil asked as he reached for the tea.

"Business is booming." Doreen beamed. "It's never been better. I've picked up a lot of work from the Bedford Estate as two of the regular shoplifters went and got involved in cashing post office books with some postman that was nicking bundles of them from the sorting offices. I heard they were doing so well that they started letting down punters, so I stepped in and took the work. Unfortunately for them the police were on to them. One of the girls, Shirley, went and bought herself a bright red Jaguar. I mean, if there was anything that screamed out from the roof tops saying 'look at me living in a council flat and driving a motor that cost more than some people homes' then a bright red Jag is going to do it. Needless to say, the gavvers swooped in and she was done for fraud. I know that Shirley was hoisting gear right up until they banged her up for thirty-six months at the Old Bailey. I was lucky, because I know people on the estate and so after a few introductions, all that work has come my way. If anything, I could do with another couple of girls."

"I'm pleased for you," Neil said. "Do you know what time you're expecting Jackie?"

"She called me earlier and said that she was going to stay at a local hotel overnight as she hadn't been able to fulfil all the orders I gave her. She wanted me to tell you and to say that she'll be back here at my place around seven tomorrow night if you could pick her up. Something about her car going in for a service," Doreen said.

"Oh, right okay. Yeah, because her motor is quite new, we wanted to keep it maintained at the dealership so it could be sold eventually for top money with a proper service history," Neil said.

"Well that makes sense. It looks like you two are getting quite serious? I mean you've moved in together," Doreen said as she leaned forward.

Neil caught a glimpse of flesh at the top of her black stockings and quickly turned away.

"Yeah, we do get along well. I'd like to buy a place eventually like Ricky has," Neil said.

"Property is probably one of the best investments you can have," Doreen said. "Between you and me, I have four flats and a house which I let out."

"Bloody hell Doreen, you own five properties, but you still live here on the estate?"

"Yeah, of course. This where my customers live. It's none of my business, but from the looks of you, in all your trendy gear and that new sports car outside, you and Ricky must be doing alright," Doreen said.

"We're doing alright. I mean the cash is tumbling in and Ricky got us some regular work from a trusted source," Neil said.

"I know," Doreen said, as she stood up. "It's well past seven now so I'm going to fix myself a nice gin and tonic. What can I get you?"

"Err, I'm okay thanks Doreen," Neil said.

"Oh, come on. I've got a nice malt whiskey if you fancy it. I know that's what Ricky drinks when he meets with Frank," Doreen said.

"You know about Frank," Neil gasped.

"Oh Neil, Frank and I go way back. In truth it was him that helped me with my very first start, back, well let's just say some time ago," Doreen chuckled as she poured a large tumbler of malt whiskey and handed it to Neil. "I was about sixteen when I first started hoisting for Margaret Crumb. What a name eh, it always made us girls laugh

'Marge Crumb'. It was her that introduced me to making proper money out of shoplifting. Like our Jackie, I was the best of the bunch. I rarely got caught and when I did, I just kept my mouth shut, did my paltry four weeks, got out and went straight back to work. Marge loved me but I had bigger plans. I wanted my own girls and the freedom to operate and do whatever I wanted, when I wanted. It was in the Cadillac Club that I met Frank. We chatted and I opened up to him about what I did and what my plans were. The following week Frank introduced me to a few people who told me what they wanted on an on-going basis, and I made my start. Within a few weeks I had made more money on my own that I earned with Marge in a month. So that was the beginning of my career in hoisting. Don't get me wrong, Marge was pissed with me and I mean she wanted blood, but I had Frank's protection and she knew it. With that in mind, I talked each and every one of those girls into coming to work with me on a more even split. I played to their greed. Like us all Neil, we all want more, and I offered them the chance to carry on as they had, but put more money into their pockets."

"Why didn't we ever talk like this when we were together Doreen?" Neil said. "I have learnt more about you, the person, in the last half hour, than I did in the three and half months we were together."

"I don't know Neil. I can be quite a selfish person sometimes. But you must know that I always liked you and enjoyed our time together," Doreen said as she refilled his glass.

"I always felt that we had a connection, but I suppose I just wanted more than you could comfortably give me at that time," Neil said.

Doreen shrugged her shoulders and took a sip of her gin and tonic.

"If it's any consolation, Neil, I did regret calling it to an end and, well, I'm not sure I should be telling you this," Doreen said.

"That's okay," Neil said, "We're just good friends chatting about old times."

"Well I started seeing this guy, Craig, I think that's what his name was. Nice guy but a bit dim if you know what I mean. Anyway, when we got around to… you know what, I just found him, well, boring, whereas you had just been so damn enthusiastic. If he was fish fingers, chips and peas then you were like the Sunday roast with all the trimmings and so, and this is the naughty part," Doreen said before sitting right back in her chair. "I would take a deep breath, close my eyes and fantasise that Craig was you, Neil. In all honesty it was the only thing that could bring me to climax because he was all fingers and thumbs and none of it in the right place. Oh, I'm sorry Neil. I really shouldn't have shared that with you," Doreen said.

Neil had become increasingly excited and had to reposition the cushion because his manhood was trying to force its way to freedom.

"No," Neil coughed to clear his dry throat, "That's okay, in fact it's more than okay. It's quite the compliment. Thank you, Doreen."

Doreen smiled.

"What about you, have you ever thought about us?" Doreen said as she topped up his glass.

Neil reached into the top of his shirt collar and loosened it.

"Our time together was the best and most exciting thing that had ever happened to me. I had fantasised about you for a good few years. I think I was still at school when I first started admiring the way you looked and moved. That was one of the reasons I always volunteered to help out with baby-sitting. I just loved being around you. I do remember once, and this is a little pervy, but you were in the front room wearing a pale blue dressing gown and I can remember that it rode up when you sat down and on this one occasion I swear I saw right up between your legs. You dominated my thoughts for months after that. No need for dirty mags as I had that image stored up for every time I, well you know," Neil said. He was now feeling warm all over and a little merry.

"Oh how lovely that I was your fantasy for so long," Doreen said, her eyes wide with excitement. "That explains all that enthusiasm you had in the bedroom."

"You were amazing Doreen," Neil slurred.

"Have you…?"

"What?" Neil asked.

"Have you thought about me or us since we separated?"

"I'm not sure I should say," Neil said.

"Oh come on, it's just two good friends chatting about old times," Doreen said. "I won't say anything if you don't."

"You promise?" Neil said.

"Cross my heart," Doreen whispered.

"Well there are times when I'm with Jackie that I imagine it's you," Neil said.

"Does it help? Does it make your climax more intense? It did when I thought of you with Craig," Doreen said.

Neil nodded and downed the last of his whiskey in one gulp. Doreen got up and walked over to where Neil sat. Whilst maintaining eye contact, she slowly lowered herself down so that she kneeled at the base of his chair.

"I've missed you Neil," Doreen whispered as she reached over and removed the cushion that covered his constrained, rampant, swollen, manhood. "It looks like you missed me too."

Doreen slowly undid his trouser button and pulled down his zipper, maintaining constant eye contact. She reached up with both hands and slowly tugged at his trousers and underwear. Instinctively Neil raised himself so his garments could be brought down below his knees. He looked down and took several short breaths as Doreen planted small kisses on the inside of his thighs.

"Hello again," Doreen purred, as she ran her tongue suggestively around the base of his manhood.

***

It was well after midnight when Doreen lay back in her bed and lit a Dunhill International cigarette.

"Would you like one?" Doreen said as she inhaled the smoke.

"No, I'm okay, thanks," Neil said.

"Are you sure?" Doreen said turning towards him.

"That was everything I fantasised it would be if we were ever to, well you know," Neil said.

"So, no regrets," Doreen said.

"No regrets but…"

"But you're thinking about Jackie, right?"

"Yes, I am," Neil said.

"I'm a big girl Neil, and I understand that you're not ready to split with Jackie. Am I right?"

Neil nodded.

"So, what you'd like then is to have your cake and eat it," Doreen said.

"What do you mean?" Neil said, sitting bolt upright.

"What I mean, Neil, is that despite sharing a home with Jackie you wanted to come around here and bed me but, now don't go getting silly because... that is okay. You and I have a connection that many just wouldn't understand. I have my needs and you have yours."

"So, you're not going to tell Jackie," Neil said.

"I wouldn't dream of breaking my best worker's heart Neil, but this is where you come in."

"How do you mean?"

"I need you to make sure that Jackie continues to be my best worker, my number one shoplifter," Doreen said sternly.

"I don't understand," Neil said.

"Let me spell it out for you. Sooner or later Jackie will start to have thoughts about going alone, just as I did when I was with Marge Crumb. Now, what I want you to do, as my friend and secret lover, is to make sure she doesn't actually do it. I want you to use any influence you have to keep her from going alone and in return, Jackie will never hear about what happened here tonight, or should we decide that it should happen again. Because Neil, I would like it to happen again, and I think you would too. There is no need for Jackie to be hurt, so you will have a once in a lifetime opportunity to have your cake and eat it," Doreen said as she reached down below the bed covers and slowly, but firmly, took Neil in hand.

Chapter 18

Ricky reached for his 'That'll Be the Day' double album. He pulled out the vinyl record and placed side three on the turn table of his stereo system. When *'That'll Be the Day'* by Bobby Vee and The Crickets played, he turned up the volume. Ricky had stayed in the office an extra hour to create more fictitious invoices for puncture repairs, wheel balancing and wheel alignment so he could launder more cash through his business.

"Sweet," Ricky thought, *"My new business is coming on a treat with over a grand a week in cash washing through the books and more to come. If this keeps up, then it might be time to start looking for another tyre bay."*

Ricky had just had a shower and was choosing something to wear when he heard a knock at the front door. He slipped on a pair of jeans and a white t-shirt and ran, barefoot, down the hallway to open the door.

"Jackie," Ricky said, leaning out of the front door and looking for Neil. "What are doing here?"

"Well, is that any way to greet an old friend," Jackie said as she pushed past him and walked into his apartment.

Ricky closed the door and turned to face her.

"Damn Jackie," Ricky thought, *"you look stunning!"*

Jackie stood in her black high heel shoes, black knee length skirt and matching jacket. She could have passed for a senior partner in a firm of solicitors.

"Are you putting the kettle on or have you got something stronger?" Jackie said as she sauntered down the hallway and into the living room. *'Book of Love'* by the Monotones was blaring out of the speakers.

Ricky watched her hips sway from side to side and was transfixed by how the material clung to her curves.

"Yeah sure," Ricky said as he raced past her and turned down the volume. "What do you fancy to drink?"

"Gin and tonic would be nice, if you have it," Jackie said as she sat down on the chair closest to the window.

Ricky was a little flustered. Jackie was the last person he was expecting to see. He opened his drinks cabinet and poured a Gordon's Gin with Schweppes Tonic water for Jackie and a small malt whiskey for himself. Having shared the malt with Frank Allen at the Cadillac Club, he had bought a couple of bottles for his drinks' cabinet.

"There you go," Ricky said as he handed Jackie the crystal cut tumbler he'd bought from Doreen.

"Nice glasses," Jackie chuckled. "These might have come from me."

"Is everything alright with Neil?" Ricky said.

"Neil is fine Ricky. I've been thinking about you a lot during the last couple of months and it really wasn't right how we ended our friendship," Jackie said.

"Yeah, I know, and look, I'm really sorry. I would never want to hurt you, Jackie. We've been friends since, well forever," Ricky said.

"It's me that owes you the apology," Jackie said as she took a sip of her drink. "Hmm, perfect. Just as I like it."

"Maybe we're both at fault in some way," Ricky said.

Jackie smiled.

"I've missed being around you Ricky. We have a lot of history, and I couldn't stay mad at you forever."

"I've missed you too, Jackie. I'm pleased that you took up with Neil though, he's a good mate and you guys seem happy together," Ricky said.

"We are," Jackie said. "Have you got something else to play in the background other than this Rock 'n' Roll stuff? It makes it difficult to think with all that fast drumming."

"Sure," Ricky said as he ran his fingers through his album collection and pulled out the 'Al Green Is Love' album. "I've just bought this - not that I'd want Deano or the rest of the lads to know."

"I like Al Green, Ricky, he's always been one of my favourites," Jackie said. "We used to listen to 'Green is Blues back in… blimey Ricky, that must have been in 1970."

"I remember that, Jackie. Your mum and dad would go out to work in the summer holidays and we'd stick Al Green on and just drink coffee and smoke whatever cigarettes we could get our hands on while putting the world to rights," Ricky said as he poured Jackie another large gin and tonic.

"They were good times," Jackie said. "We used to talk for hours and hours about, well everything and nothing. I would tell you that I'd like to work in an office when we left school and you said that you wanted to make enough money to just do whatever you wanted."

"It seems like a lifetime ago now," Ricky said.

"Well in our own ways we've both been successful Ricky. The best thing I ever did was to leave working at the Arms pub and go shoplifting with Doreen. I didn't and still don't care what people think of it. To me it's a job and I'm bloody good at it."

"I think you would have been good at whatever you turned your hand to," Ricky said.

"Last week I made over twelve hundred pounds, a grand the week before, and this week looks like another thousand-pound week. The money has put good clothes on my back and gave me a choice as to where I wanted to live. Neil and I have a little flat at the top of Wallington. It's good for now, but I want our own place. Something like this," Jackie said, looking around the room. "This is very nice Ricky, and I'm pleased that things have worked out for you too."

"Jackie you're hoisting from shops and I'm having motors stolen, broken up, rung and sold while others are shipped off to Africa. We use whatever opportunities come our way to stay ahead of the game and give us a life other than what we're expected to make do with. I don't think either one of us would have settled for a flat on Milton Road Estate."

Jackie shook her head adamantly.

"Absolutely not!" Jackie said. "We both deserved so much more than that. Neither of us were about to follow our parents into a lifetime of slavery to debt. I watched as week in and week out people from the estate, my mum included, lined up outside the community centre to borrow money from Double Bubble so they could put food on the table and clothes on our backs. That was never going to be a life for me, and I know it was never for you."

"Jackie, are you expecting Neil?"

Jackie shook her head.

"No, Neil thinks that I'm staying over in London to make an early start to catch up on some outstanding orders. That was my plan, but then I thought it was probably about time that you and I talked, you know, to get our friendship back on track so there was no animosity or complications between us. I wasn't sure how to explain that to Neil or even if I had to. I mean we are together, but it's not like I have a ring on my finger and have to explain where I go or what I do," Jackie said.

"Yeah, I can see that would be difficult and to be honest I'm really pleased that you have," Ricky said.

"Yeah, me too. Look, I'm starving. I haven't had anything to eat since breakfast. How about you and I go out and have something to eat like old times. That's only if you're not seeing someone tonight," Jackie said.

"No, I'm fine. I thought about having a drink at the Arms, but didn't make any firm plans," Ricky said.

"So, there's no special girl to meet then?"

"If you mean Michelle, well, that ended after that massive tear up we had with the Bedford Boot Boys. Once it got plastered all over the newspapers not only did my old man want me out of the house, but Michelle's old man put a stop to me seeing her and sent her packing back to university to finish her degree. There's been a couple of girls but nothing serious. I did meet a girl at the Elephant and Castle, she was kind of special, but she was a bit on the wild side. I mean she would just as easily made a play for you as she would me," Ricky said.

"Oh my Ricky, you have been around some adventurous, free spirited young ladies," Jackie said as she put her glass on the coffee table.

"Yeah, but it wasn't going to go anywhere. I think I might have been just her bit of rough," Ricky said.

"Well that would have been her loss then," Jackie said. "Anyway, are we going to eat or what?"

"Yeah, okay, let me just go and get dressed," Ricky said.

"Wait," Jackie said.

"What?" Ricky said.

"Look neither of us wants to cause any problems and you know people will talk if they see us together," Jackie said.

"Oh yeah, what they don't know they'd make up. Do you want to give it a miss then?"

"No, but what about you not wearing any of your Teddy Boy gear just for tonight? I mean it will attract attention wherever we go. Would that be okay?"

"My wardrobe is full of Teddy Boy gear, but I do have a pair of blue flares and a black leather box jacket. I normally wear them when I visit the bank manager. I could stick them on," Ricky said.

"I'm sure you'll look great," Jackie said.

"Give me a minute then," Ricky said as he hurried out of the living room.

Jackie sat back in the armchair and closed her eyes as *'What am I going to do with Myself'* by Al Green played in the background.

Ricky stood in the doorway in his trendy slacks, white Ben Sherman shirt and black leather box jacket.

"You, Ricky Turrell, look wonderful," Jackie said.

"I have to tell you, it don't half feel strange not wearing drain pipes and my creepers," Ricky said.

"You'll get used to it," Jackie said. "This is a great album, Ricky. I'm going to get myself a copy. It'll make a nice change from *'Night at the Opera'* by Queen. I'm not kidding when I say that Neil plays it constantly. It's like every time I get home I walk into the sound of *'Bohemian Rhapsody'* or *'I'm in Love with my Car'*. The other night I walked into the bedroom, and he's standing in front of the mirror in his underpants, arms spread apart and singing *'Death on Two Legs'* at the top of his voice. I don't think he was expecting me home that early," Jackie chuckled.

"Can't say I blame him," Ricky said, pulling out the *'A Night at the Opera'*, album from his collection. "It's a bloody great album."

"Well, some hardcore Ted you turned out to be," Jackie said as she stood up. "I might have expected it from Neil, but not from you."

"Good music is good music," Ricky said.

"I'd bet you a hundred pounds here and now that Deano doesn't have a copy of it," Jackie said.

"Nah, I can't take that bet," Ricky said.

"I'm getting a bit peckish myself," Ricky said as he walked down the hallway to the front door.

The two friends walked down the two stories and out of the main entrance.

"I've got the Rover parked up around the back in the garage," Ricky said.

"We are most definitely not going in that," Jackie said. "Come on we'll go in mine."

"What a minute, is that yours?" Ricky said as he looked at a brand new, signal red, Jaguar XJS V12.

"It is. They're not even supposed to be on sale yet, but I took my Stag into the garage for a service this morning, saw this in the showroom and fell in love with it. So, I traded in the Stag and bought it. I picked it up at 5.30pm this evening. She doesn't even have twenty-five miles on the clock."

"Jackie, she's beautiful. I just love the lines, the curves, and a V12 you say?"

"She drives like a princess, so smooth and quiet, and yet you know that it'll rocket up to 150mph without any effort if you want it to," Jackie said.

"I just might have to get myself one of these and keep the Zodiac for weekends," Ricky said.

Jackie opened the car with the central locking and Ricky peeked inside and smelt the new, biscuit coloured, leather.

"Don't you just love the smell of new leather," Ricky said.

"Whatever turns you on," Jackie laughed.

Ricky got into the car and pulled his seat belt across and clipped it in. Jackie turned the ignition key and the car started. The radio was on and playing *'The Hustle'* by Van McCoy. Jackie reached forward and turned it down.

"Now I know this lovely little Italian restaurant in New Malden. Do you like Italian?"

"Sound great," Ricky said as he looked around the Jaguar's interior.

Jackie drove over to New Malden and parked outside Il Padrino on the High Street. They were shown through to a private table in the corner where they enjoyed a traditional Italian three course meal with a bottle of Montepulciano d'Abruzzo, a medium bodied red wine. The time passed quickly as they joked, laughed and reminisced about old times. Ricky had to insist on paying the bill as Jackie wanted it to be her treat.

Ricky held the door open for Jackie and stepped out into the cool night air.

"That was fun, Jackie. Thank you for a truly fabulous evening. It's really good to be back to where we were," Ricky said.

"It is Ricky, and the food is to die for here. And I've developed quite a taste for red wine," Jackie said.

"Tell me about it," Ricky laughed, "Are you okay to drive?"

"Yeah, I'm fine," Jackie chuckled.

Ricky watched three lads pass by. They wore blue faded Brutus Jeans, leather bomber jackets and Doctor Marten Boots. Ricky overheard one of the lads.

"I bet that posh sort has got a minge like a ripped bus seat."

Both the lad's mates burst out laughing. Ricky looked at Jackie, she had heard it too.

"Oi, you!" Ricky called out.

The three lads stopped and turned to face him.

"Yeah, you," Ricky said to the lad who passed the comment.

"Leave it Ricky," Jackie said.

"No, Jackie, I'm not letting that go," Ricky said.

"You better do as your posh bird says, matey, or you might end up getting hurt," the largest of the three lads said.

"Yeah, go on, fuck off you mug," a second lad said.

Ricky stepped forward.

"I want an apology for my friend," Ricky said.

"Go on Clive, give the twat a good hiding," the second lad said. "Then that posh little number could come with me."

As the larger of the Boot Boys stepped forward, Ricky's right arm shot out and smacked him clean on the nose. Ricky fired his foot straight between the lad's legs. As he buckled over, Ricky sent his knee up at full force. The lad's head jerked back, blood spurted from his split lip as he shot backwards and landed on the kerb. The second mouthy lad raced forward with his arms and fists shooting off in all directions. Ricky stood back, holding his fists up to protect his chin. He waited until the lad was in striking distance and then let him have a left jab, quickly followed by a powerful uppercut that lifted the lad an inch or so off the block paving. Ricky looked at the two lads out on the ground and then turned to the third.

"Do you want to try your luck as well?" Ricky said calmly.

"No mate, sorry, I didn't say anything."

"My friend here needs an apology, and she needs it now," Ricky said.

"Yeah, lady, we're sorry alright? We didn't mean any disrespect, okay? We had a few drinks and just got a bit out of order."

Jackie looked at the two lads on the ground and the third lad pleading for forgiveness.

"You and your friends might want to think about what you're saying and to who next time," Jackie said. "Shall we get out of here?"

Jackie stepped over the lad by the kerb as he held his bleeding mouth and opened the Jaguar's driver's side door. Ricky and Jackie sat inside for a couple of seconds as she looked through a bunch of cassettes in a plastic carrier bag on the back seat. She produced a Harold Melvin & the Blue Notes cassette, and slid it into the cassette player. *'The Love I Lost'* pounded out of the speakers.

"I love this track," Jackie said.

"Yeah, me too," Ricky said.

Jackie slid the gear shifter down into drive and the V12 Jaguar edged slowly away from the carnage Ricky had left behind.

"Sorry about that, Jackie, but you just can't let people take liberties like that. If I had been wearing my drape suit, chances are it'd never have happened, but they just saw an average Joe out with his bird and started mouthing off," Ricky said.

"You were like my knight in shining armour racing to my rescue," Jackie laughed. "No, but really. That was a nice thing to do. There are a lot of guys that would have let that slide, but then again, you're not just some boring, run of the mill, everyday guy."

"I'm not sure about that Jackie, but hey, if there's a compliment about, I'll take it," Ricky said.

***

As Jackie turned into Ricky's road, *'If You Don't Know Me by Now'* by Harold Melvin & The Blue Notes began to play.

"Would you like a night cap or a coffee, Jackie?" Ricky asked.

"Yeah, that would be nice," Jackie said as she stopped the Jaguar and turned off the ignition.

Ricky got out of the car, raced around and opened the driver's door for Jackie.

"A girl could get used to this," Jackie said. "You're always the gentleman, eh Ricky?"

"One tries," Ricky said, before taking a deep breath of the clean night air. He closed his eyes and took a second breath.

"Are you okay?" Jackie asked.

"Yeah, you know when you've had just enough to drink that it just feels, well calm and nice and there's a slight tingle that spirals down your neck and spine every so often."

"Yeah," Jackie said. "I like that feeling. It's then that you know just a few more drinks and you'll be into the silly stage when two headlights become four and you start repeating everything you've been saying."

Jackie followed Ricky up the stairs and into his flat. She sat on the settee while Ricky poured her a gin and tonic and himself a neat malt whiskey.

"Hey, do you remember that time when I took that half bottle of Bells Whiskey from my Nan's?" Jackie said.

"Bloody right I do," Ricky said. "We couldn't have been more than about ten years old."

"We were eleven and had just started secondary school and you thought it would be a good idea to bunk off during the games lesson and I, like a fool, just went along with it," Jackie said before taking a big sip of her drink.

"All I remember was you producing this bottle of whiskey and we just started necking it back," Ricky said. "I was as a sick as a dog!"

"I think I must have come out in sympathy with you because I was throwing up too. What a pair we must have looked like," Jackie said.

"I think we were both lucky to never have been caught. I know that after you left, I slept like a log," Ricky said.

"I staggered home and just made straight for my bedroom, pretending that I had an upset stomach. Do you know I hated the smell of whiskey for years after that?" Jackie said.

"Yeah, me too. One whiff and I thought I'd heave, and yet here I am now thoroughly enjoying a good malt whiskey," Ricky said.

"They were good times Ricky. We made some memories," Jackie said before drinking the last of her drink.

"I'm not sure that you should be driving," Ricky said.

"Yeah, I might have been pushing it earlier, but now I think I'm well and truly over the limit. I don't want to go getting a ban when I've just treated myself to a new car," Jackie said.

"I could get you a taxi," Ricky said.

Jackie looked at her watch. It was almost midnight.

"I'm not booked into a hotel, and it might take another half hour if not forty-five minutes to get me to one, and then there's no guarantee of a room. I might have shot myself in the foot," Jackie said with a snigger. "Because I can't exactly go home either now, can I? I mean explaining this would be, well, difficult to say the least."

Ricky paused for a few seconds.

"Look, I have two bedrooms here and you're very welcome to stay," Ricky said.

"Are you sure? I don't want to cause you any bother," Jackie said.

"Really it's no problem," Ricky said, as he stood and then shot off down the hallway.

He returned a few minutes later.

"I've put a couple of towels on the end of the bed. It's brand new and never been slept in, so it should be comfortable," Ricky said. "Feel free to use the bathroom. I've put out a spare toothbrush and all the other stuff. I have an en-suite, so you'll be fine."

"You are so domesticated Mr Turrell, who would ever have thought it," Jackie said as she leant on the couch arm and stood up.

Ricky led her down the hallway and showed her to the bedroom. It had a large double bed with matching duvet cover, pillows and cushions. There were bedside cabinets on either side with matching lamps.

"This is very nice, thank you," Jackie said.

"No problem. Mostly courtesy of Doreen," Ricky said. "My bedroom is just over there, but feel free to help yourself to anything you need."

Ricky found that he looked into Jackie's eyes a few moments longer than he should have.

"What an absolutely brilliant night," Ricky thought. *"I forgot just how much fun Jackie could be."*

Ricky took his clothes off and hung them over the chair by the wardrobe. He stripped off his underwear and put it in the washing basket he kept in the en-suite. Ricky squeezed the Colgate toothpaste onto his toothbrush and began to clean his teeth. He leant in and turned the shower on and then took a pee while it warmed up. He shook himself several times and then got into the warm shower.

"I wonder if Jackie's taking a shower," Ricky thought.

Ricky dried himself and then climbed into bed. He listened out for any movement from Jackie's bedroom. There was silence.

"She must have fallen asleep," Ricky thought. *"That's a good thing, because, well, just because!"*

Ricky reached over and turned out the bedside lamp. His eyes quickly adjusted to the dark. The moonlight lit up part of the wardrobe. He lay on his back and thought about the evening. Several minutes later he turned over to face the window. This was the position that he liked to sleep in. It was an almost nightly ritual that he would toss and turn several times before settling on facing the window. He closed his eyes and began to allow his mind to wander. Then he heard movement in the hallway. Ricky could feel his heart pumping. He stayed still. He sensed that someone was in his room. The bedside cover was pulled back and Jackie slipped in beside him. Ricky's heart was pounding as Jackie snuggled her warm, naked body, against his.

"Don't say anything," Jackie whispered as she reached out and turned him towards her.

***

Ricky had been awake since 5.30 am. He looked over at Jackie sleeping beside him and an overwhelming feeling of guilt washed over him.

"What the hell have I done?" Ricky thought. *"How could I have done this to one of my best mates? Damn Ricky, you've known Neil for almost as long as you have Jackie. This is bad, man, really bad. You are one downright nasty piece of shit to do this. But it wasn't me. It was Jackie that made all the moves. Don't try and kid yourself it was Jackie because you bloody well know, Ricky Turrell, that you've been thinking non-stop about her for months now. All of a sudden when she's out of your reach you want some forbidden fruit. You wanted your mate's girl. That, Ricky Turrell, is bloody unforgiveable, and you know it. When he finds out that will be it. You can kiss working together goodbye and that will bloody well cost you, and as for being mates, you'll be lucky if he ever speaks to you again. You're a shit Ricky Turrell and you know it!"*

Jackie stirred.

"What the hell were you thinking?" Ricky thought. *"Why didn't you just do the right thing and tell her to go back to her room. You could have said it in a way that wouldn't have cost your friendship or put everything you've been working and scheming towards at risk. Don't go blaming the drink, you knew what you were doing and so*

did Jackie. You have got to find a way to make this work now. You have to try and save your friendships with both Jackie and Neil!"

Ricky slid out of bed carefully so as not to wake Jackie up. He slipped on his trousers and the white T-shirt he'd worn the day before when Jackie arrived unexpectedly and wandered down to the kitchen and put the kettle on."

"You are going to have to box clever here," Ricky thought. *"This could easily go tits up and you'll have everyone turn on you. Just look at what happened to Kenny. One minute he's Mr Popular with birds throwing their drawers and at him and now Specs, one of his best mates, is dead and he's shacked up with a no-good heartless bitch and Deano has all but removed him from the inner circle."*

Ricky took two cups of tea through to the bedroom. Jackie was awake and sitting up in the bed.

"Good morning," Ricky said. "I've made you a cup of tea."

"Hmm, that's nice," Jackie said. "Why don't you slide back in here and we'll drink it together?"

Ricky put the cup on the bedside cabinet and sat on the edge of the bed.

"Are you okay?" Jackie asked, reaching for the tea.

Ricky hesitated and then nodded.

"Alright," Jackie said, putting the cup back on the bedside table. "What's up?"

"It's this," Ricky said. "It just feels wrong."

"Wrong, what do you mean wrong? How can what we have and what we've done be wrong? I'm in love with you Ricky and you must have known that."

Ricky found himself shaking his head.

"What the hell are you shaking your head for?"

"I'm sorry Jackie. You know how I feel about you, but I just can't help thinking about Neil. He's my friend and your boyfriend and we've betrayed him," Ricky said.

"If we love each other Ricky, then we'll find a way, and if Neil gets hurt, well I'm sorry, but I don't believe that either of us should live a lie," Jackie said.

"Love? What's all this love stuff?" Ricky thought. *"We had sex, that's all."*

"I just feel so guilty Jackie, don't you?" Ricky said.

"I like Neil, we were right for each other at that moment in time, but I've always thought that it would be you and I Ricky, you must have known that," Jackie said.

"I don't know what I thought Jackie. We had a brilliant night out and it was great to relive some of those special times, but I didn't think we'd end up in bed together," Ricky said.

"You're a bloody liar Ricky Turrell," Ricky thought, *"You hoped, no you bloody wished that she would come into your bedroom and slide into bed with you."*

"What, are you saying that you regret it?" Jackie said, sitting forward.

"I'm just not sure that either of us have thought this through," Ricky said.

"You mean you're trying to save your own arse," Ricky thought.

Jackie pulled the sheets back and got out of bed. She was naked.

"Do you mind!" Jackie said.

Ricky turned away.

"Yeah, I'm sorry."

Jackie began to put on her clothes.

Ricky thought of a hundred and one things that he could say, but none of them would have saved the situation, so he remained silent.

Jackie put her jacket on and stood by the doorway.

"I gave myself to you Ricky because I'm in love with you and now you're treating me like some one night stand you'll never see again," Jackie said.

"Please, Jackie," Ricky said.

"Please Jackie what, Ricky? Please don't say anything to Neil, don't tell anyone what an absolute shit you've been to your best mate? You're a bastard, Ricky, and once again I've allowed you to break my bloody heart!"

"I'm sorry Jackie, please can we talk about this," Ricky said.

"We're done this time Ricky," Jackie said as tears streamed down her face. "I don't know what I ever saw in you!"

Jackie stomped out of the bedroom, opened the front door and slammed it shut behind her.

"This is one hell of a mess," Ricky thought, *"And it's all my fault."*

Chapter 19

Deano had a call from the leader of a small of gang of sixteen teds known as the Clem Attlee Teds in Fulham. The Teds had been having a drink outside the Clem Attlee Pub when The North End Boot Boys started trouble. Two of the Teds had been so badly beaten that they had to be taken to hospital for treatment. It had been the first call asking for help since Deano forged the alliance. He promised the allies that the problem would be taken care of. Deano called over two hundred Teds from Croydon, Streatham, Tooting, Balham, Lewisham, Battersea and Kingston together.

The Clem Attlee council estate had nineteen low and high-rise blocks of flats with views over Chelsea Football Stadium and Battersea Power Station, and was considered by many as one of the roughest areas in South West London. The residents were mainly wannabe gangsters eagerly looking for a way to make a name for themselves, former or aspiring boxers and market traders. From the information Deano had managed to pull together, Garry Dutton was the leader of the fifty plus North End Boot Boys and Martin Barracliff was his number two. The lads were all loyal Chelsea supporters and regularly attended home games.

The Milton Road Teds had taken taxis up to Wimbledon train station at Fulham Broadway.

"What kind of numbers are we looking at?" Ricky asked as he slipped his fingers in and out of his brass knuckle duster.

"I've been told there's a good fifty or sixty lads, and by all accounts they're pretty game," Deano said. "It's a shame that a place as big as Clem Attlee has only sixteen Teds. Those lads need to get recruiting. There's got to be plenty of lads out there that would love to wear a drape suit."

"So, it should be a proper tear up then," Kenny said.

"We'll see," Deano said.

The train pulled into the station and the doors opened, revealing a horde of Teddy Boys standing at the top stairs.

"I'm bloody buzzing," Ricky thought, clutching his knuckleduster.

Deano led the thirty strong Milton Road Ted lads out of the carriages onto the platform. Ricky, Kenny, Lee, Terry and Steve Parker surrounded Deano.

Jock Addie, leader of the Croydon Teds, stood at the top of the stairs and yelled "TED ARMY!"

"TED ARMY… TED ARMY… TED ARMY!" shouted the alliance as they punched the air together.

"Let's fucking do this," Deano said before turning to Ricky. "I want you to shine tonight mate, let everyone know who the fuck Ricky Turrell is."

"I'm on it," Ricky sneered as he clenched his fists.

All the Teds shook each other's hands and patted each other on the back as they mingled and slowly edged out of the train station and out onto the Broadway.

"Deano, mate I can't believe that you brought so many Teds," Jimmy, the leader of the Clem Attlee Teds said.

"You lads are all part of the alliance, the Ted Army, and when I say we will do something then we will. Have you been in the pub?"

"Yeah, I stuck my head in there earlier and its ram packed. It always is on a Friday night. The North End Boot Boys are all psyching themselves up for tomorrow's game against Millwall."

Deano smiled wryly.

"It looks like they're going to lose on and off the pitch then." Deano said before racing forward to lead the lads along the Broadway.

"Are they expecting us Deano?" Jock said.

"I doubt it. This lot think they're a bit tasty and invincible. Apparently this Garry Dutton geezer is a 'someone' amongst all the Chelsea football lads. He's just skin and bone. He'll bleed like every other mug that gets in our way," Deano said.

"I love this Deano, pulling all these Teds together like this," Jock said excitedly. "Nothing and no one can stand in our way!"

"That was always the plan," Deano said firmly. "The Teds will dominate every council estate in London supported by the alliance, the united Ted Army."

Deano led the lads the short walk down the Broadway to the Clem Attlee pub.

"What a shit hole," Kenny said as they approached the pub.

"I'm sure people say that about the Milton Arms," Ricky said.

"Yeah, I suppose so," Kenny said, laughing nervously.

Deano stopped and turned and faced the army of Teds. He looked at their faces. He was confident that he had two hundred lads who could deliver utter chaos and severe punishment to everything that moved.

"Right, we go in bold as brass, right, and I don't want anyone lipping off or lashing out just yet. You guys are to follow my lead, alright?" Deano said calmly.

The Teds were bouncing from one brothel creeper to another clenching and unclenching their fists. Deano knew his Army was ready.

The door of the Clem Attlee pub opened, and Deano strutted in, surrounded by his inner circle and the leaders of the other Teddy Boy gangs. *'Barbados'* by Typically Tropical was playing in the busy cigarette smoke filled bar. As more and more Teds entered the bar, the drinkers put their drinks down. The sound of voices competing to be heard died away as they faced row after row of Teds in their smart, brightly coloured, drape suits, greased back hair and brothel creeper shoes.

Deano surveyed the room and finally rested his gaze on a group of lads in patch pocket trousers with three-button waistband, short sleeved shirts and Ox-Blood Doctor Marten boots.

"Garry Dutton. I'm looking for Garry Dutton," Deano called out with the authority of a general.

There was a few moment's silence when a voice spoke out.

"That would be me, who's asking?"

Deano fixed his eyes on the lad. He stood a little over six foot and had a centre hair parting with his long brown hair brushed back. On his right forearm he had a Chelsea Football Club tattoo.

"Deano, Deano the Dog. You may of heard of me. I'm told that you and a few of your lads got all big and brave and set about some friends of mine," Deano said firmly.

Garry didn't respond.

"Now, what you don't know is that Jimmy and the Clem Attlee Teds are part of an alliance and we don't take too kindly to people taking liberties."

"Why don't you fuck off!" shouted one lad standing by the bar.

Within seconds Terry Parker had bounded over with his cosh and smacked the loudmouth around the head. Terry grabbed him by the hair as his legs buckled and began to slowly but systematically smack him, again and again and then again, until his face was covered in blood. Terry let go of the lad's hair and allowed him to slump to the floor of the pub. Terry nodded back to Deano.

"Thank you, Terry. Now, as I was saying before I was rudely interrupted, we don't take kindly to people taking liberties with our own. I've brought with me today two hundred Teds. My initial thoughts were that we would hit your pub and beat everyone in here to a pulp but then that wouldn't have been fair to the other five hundred battle ready Teds in the alliance, because believe me, Garry fucking Dutton, we all love a right good tear up."

Deano took a couple of steps forward. The dozen lads around Garry Dutton stood up.

"Have you got anything to say for yourself?" Deano said.

"What can I say, it happened," Garry Dutton said, shrugging his shoulders. "I can't turn the clock back now."

"No you can't," Deano said with a smirk. "So here is what we're going to do. Rather than inflict pain and hospitalise the innocents around you, we're going to do this the old-school way. You are going to have a one-on-one straightener."

"What, with you?" Garry Dutton said as he looked Deano up and down.

"Oh no, matey. I am well and truly out of your league," Deano said as he turned to Ricky. This is Ricky Turrell my number two. You are going to have a one-on-one with him."

"Fuck, I didn't see that coming," Ricky thought. *"Yeah, too right, I'll have some!"*

Garry lifted his pint of lager, took a long gulp and then put it back on the table.

"Fuck it, ready when you are," Garry said as he pushed past the table and stood, chest out, just a few feet away from Ricky. He clenched and raised his fists.

"Oh, so you've done a bit of boxing," Ricky thought.

"Go on Garry, fucking do him!" one of his lads yelled.

Suddenly Garry launched himself forward and threw a right-handed punch. Ricky arched his back as the punch passed just inches away from his face. With his fist firmly inside the knuckle duster, Ricky fired a left jab and then a right uppercut that connected and sent Garry sprawling over the table. Ricky wasn't waiting for him to get up, there were no Queensbury rules to abide by here. This was street fighting and winning was all that counted. Ricky pushed the table to one side and kicked Garry in the stomach. His body lifted off the ground and crashed back down again in time for the second and third kick. Garry was curled up on the pub floor gasping for breath. Ricky stood over his victim with a leg either side of his beaten body. He dropped down and turned Garry over and pinned his shoulders down with his knees and then grabbed Garry by his hair. Ricky smashed his head against the floor again and again and then again until his hands were covered in fresh blood.

"Alright that's enough," one of Garry's lads shouted.

"Enough is it?" Ricky said, and grabbed Garry around the throat with his left hand. "What about this then," Ricky said and he smashed Garry repeatedly in the face. The sickening crack of broken bone could be heard right across the pub along with several sharp intakes of breath. Garry cried out in pain.

"Maybe this is enough," Ricky said as he fired another right hander. The force of his punch broke two of Garry's teeth. They were sent hurtling across the pub floor.

Ricky pulled his arm right back ready to deliver the final knockout punch when Deano spoke.

"That'll do Ricky, he's done."

Ricky stood up with blood dripping off his fist.

"Is there anyone else?" Ricky said with his heart beating wildly as the adrenaline raced through his veins.

"What about you?" Ricky said to a large well-built lad that had sat next to Garry Dutton. The lad looked down at the ground, avoiding Ricky's intense stare. "Or you?" Ricky hissed through gritted teeth to another lad.

With no takers, Ricky backed off and stood with his fists tightly clenched, by Deano's side.

"Let me be very clear. The Clem Attlee Teds are part of a seven hundred strong Ted alliance. When you mess with any one of us, you have to deal with seven hundred, psychopathic, blood hungry

Teds. Greetings, North End Boot Boys, you've just met the Ted Army!" Deano said as he scanned the pub.

"TED ARMY... TED ARMY... TED ARMY!" all the Teds belted out as they slowly filed out of the pub and strutted victoriously, punching the warm night air, along the Broadway.

"Well done, Ricky. That was a job well done. You've not only cemented your position in the MRT as my number two, but also in the newly formed Ted alliance. You, my friend, can be one very nasty piece of work. Offering them all out like that was the stuff of legends. They'll be talking about that performance for years, trust me." Deano said as he patted his friend on the back.

Chapter 20

"Doughnut, I've got to slip out for a few hours, can you man the fort?" Ricky said.

"Yeah, of course. No problem, Ricky. Should I be expecting anyone?"

"I don't think so," Ricky said, "but if Justin drops by with a delivery, tell him to leave the tyres here and I'll sort him out either later today or the next time he's passing."

Doughnut nodded.

Ricky drove his Rover P5B through the industrial estate and out onto the main road which lead down to the usual salvage yard for written off motor cars he used for ringing. The road was packed with parked cars, so he had to leave his car in the next road and walk back. He waved to the guy on the gate who now knew him as Ricky and a regular customer.

"Hi Ricky, we've got a couple of Ford Granada's around the back and a Capri that's only six months old. They're a bit knocked about, but we'll do a deal for a regular like," Bert, the owner's son said.

"Cheers Bert. I'll have all three of them. What else have you got? You know the kind of thing I look for. It has to be a maximum of two years old and ideally Ford or something else that moves quickly once they've been sorted," Ricky said.

"I know Dad's got two Cortina Mk3's coming in that fit the bill and there's a couple of Ford Escorts. One's an RS2000 and the other is a Mexico," Bert said.

"I'll have all six motors and ask your dad to sort me out a good price. I'm thinking about something for myself, so I'll take a look about," Ricky said.

"No problem Ricky, the motors are yours. What kind of thing are you looking for?" Bert said.

"I really don't know mate. I've got a good friend who would like the Rover, and I'm thinking maybe something a bit sporty. I've not made my mind up yet, but I'll know it when I see it," Ricky said.

"Go take a look Ricky and I'll have 'Sold' notices stuck inside your motors."

"Cheers Bert."

Ricky wandered up the yard. He looked at a variety of accident damaged cars, but nothing jumped out at him.

"I fancy something comfortable, throaty and yet reliable. The kind of motor you could park up in a five-star hotel and it'd fit right in," Ricky thought. *"Maybe a Porsche or something like it. I did like Neil's Datsun 240Z, good looking car, but I can't have the same motor as him. It wouldn't feel right."*

Ricky heard a woman's voice he thought he recognised.

"What sort of thing are you looking for, Neil?"

It was Jackie.

Ricky felt his heart leap into his mouth.

"What the hell are they doing here?" Ricky thought. *"Shit, I hope she hasn't said anything to Neil."*

Ricky took a deep breath and then looked over to where they were checking out at a Cortina with extensive side damage.

"This is too old," Neil said.

"What difference does that make?" Jackie said.

"Alright Neil, Jackie," Ricky said.

They both turned and faced him. Neil looked guilty, as if he had just been caught with his hands in the cookie jar.

"Alright Ricky," Neil said awkwardly.

"Yes mate, what are you guys doing here?"

"We're looking for a car," Jackie said curtly. "What do you think we're doing in a salvage yard?"

"Alright Jackie, there's need for that," Neil said.

"Tell him, Neil. Tell him what we've been talking about," Jackie said.

"Can't we do this another time?" Neil said with a half awkward looking smile.

"No Neil, we've talked about this, and now is as good a time as any," Jackie said, folding her arms and staring at Ricky.

"We've been talking about me going on my own, Ricky. I mean it's me that takes most of the risk, so Jackie, quite rightly, thinks that I should just do it for myself and make the money for myself."

"I don't know what to say Neil. I'm a bit surprised mate, as we had a good thing going. We've both made good money and that other bit of business with you know who is solid and unlikely to end anytime soon," Ricky said.

"You'll have to get your own cars," Jackie said bluntly. "Neil is going alone so you'll have to find another lackey to run around after you and take all the risks."

"I'm sorry you feel that way Jackie, but Neil and I do have obligations that we have to meet so if we're going to go our separate ways, we need to work through what we are already committed to," Ricky said.

"No, that's not Neil's problem.

"Really, you're just going to drop me like that?" Ricky said.

"No, of course not," Neil said. "We'll meet up and have a chat about what's in the pipeline. I won't leave you in the shit."

"It's about time you grew a pair, Neil! We talked about this and decided that you were going alone, so all business with Ricky would stop," Jackie yelled as she pushed his shoulder with her open hand.

"I know, I know, but I can't just drop my mate in it, alright? I will be going on my own just as we agreed, but I'm not burning my bridges with Ricky just to make a few extra quid," Neil said.

"You really get on my tits sometimes Neil! I'll be in the car when you're done here!" Jackie said before stomping off down the yard.

"Sorry about that mate," Neil said.

"Bloody hell mate, Jackie is really on one," Ricky said.

"Mate she's been like it for a few days now. I'm not sure what's pissed her off, but It's been relentless - just going on and on about what we should and shouldn't be doing. I'm struggling to get a word in edgeways," Neil said, shrugging his shoulders.

"Neil, mate I understand that things change, but I would really appreciate you working out some kind of notice. Neither one of us can be letting Frank Allen down," Ricky said.

"Yeah, I know that. Look I'll drop by your tyre shop in a couple of days, and we'll get stuff worked out and sorted," Neil said.

"Cheers Neil, I really appreciate that mate," Ricky said. "Have you seen anything you liked here?"

"I did fancy those two Granadas, but the geezer's just put sold in the windows," Neil said.

"Bloody hell," Ricky thought, *"Lucky I got in there a bit lively."*

"I'll take a drive down to Mitcham and see what they have in there," Neil said.

"Alright mate. I'll catch you later," Ricky said.

Ricky watched as his friend sauntered off down the yard still looking at the rows of accident damaged cars.

"I am such a shit doing the dirty to Neil," Ricky thought. *"Well fuck you Jackie if you want to be like that. Don't kid yourself Ricky, you know that you're riddled with guilt and would do anything to turn the clock back and have both your old friends back just as they were before all this car ringing, Milton Road Ted stuff, and running around bashing up Skinheads and Boot Boys from other estates."*

Ricky heard the sound of a highly tuned American V8. He looked over at the gate and the Red Zodiac MK1 he'd seen at the Acid bath with Michelle drove into the yard. A big fella wearing jeans and a white T-Shirt got out. He had his hair greased back like a Ted and sported sideburns. It was Jeff Harris.

Ricky continued to look at the row upon row of accident damaged cars and then once Jeff Harris had finished his conversation with Bert, he approached him.

"It's Jeff Harris, isn't it?" Ricky said.

"Yes mate, who wants to know?" Jeff said gruffly.

"Ricky, Ricky Turrell. I've seen your Zodiac about. Nice motor," Ricky said.

"Cheers," Jeff said. "Is that Ricky Turrell from The Arms? You're mates with Deano?"

"That's me," Ricky said.

Jeff held out his hand and Ricky took it.

"I heard what you lads did up on the Bedford Estate," Jeff said.

"I'd love something like that," Ricky said, pointing to Jeff's MK1.

"How serious are you?" Jeff said.

"How do you mean?" Ricky said.

"I mean are you dreaming about it or are you looking for something?" Jeff said.

"Why, do you have a MK1 for sale?" Ricky asked, his eyes lighting up.

"Not exactly, but my dad, Ron, has a really sweet Zodiac MK2 that he's just decided to sell. It's been properly sorted with a rebuilt 302ci Mustang V8 engine and gearbox. It has five spoke racing wheels and a new set of tyres. It's a proper sorted motor and all Harris built," Jeff said.

"Sounds wicked Jeff, what kind of money is he after?"

"Dad was talking about five grand, but it's like everything. If you turn up with cash and dad likes you then he'll probably do a deal."

"I've got over fifteen grand at home," Ricky thought. "Why not, treat myself."

"I'm interested Jeff," Ricky said.

"Alright Ricky, give me few minutes. I've got a list of bits and pieces I need Bert to sort out for me then we'll take a drive over to Dad's," Jeff said.

Once Jeff had sorted his business with Bert, Ricky followed the powerful red Zodiac back from Mitcham and down through Beddington Lane. They came to a halt in a cul-de-sac. Outside a semi-detached house on the corner were three MK1 Zodiacs, including Jeff's, a two-tone grey MK2 Zodiac and a lowered red Anglia 105E on Lotus steel wheels.

"These are some nice motors," Ricky said.

"It's what we do," Jeff said proudly. "We stuff V8's into old Fords for racing about on the streets."

The front door to the house opened and two men walked down the pathway.

"This is my dad, Ron, and my brother Andy," Jeff said.

Ricky reached out and shook their hands.

Ron was an older man with a full head of hair and a warm, trusting, smile.

"This is Ricky Turrell, he's interested in the MK2 Dad," Jeff said.

"Is that interested to buy it or kick the tyres and dream about it?" Andy said.

"I won't waste your time, Andy. If she drives as well as she looks and the price is right, we'll do a deal," Ricky said.

Ron walked over to the Zodiac and lifted the bonnet. The four men looked down at the red painted mustang V8 engine with chrome rocker covers and air filter.

"It looks good Ron. How did she run in traffic?" Ricky asked.

"It did run a little hot, so I've fitted an electric fan," Ron said, pointing to the fan.

"Jeff said that the engine has been rebuilt. Did you do it, Ron?" Ricky said as Ron closed the bonnet.

"No I didn't rebuild this motor, but I bought it from a friend, who rebuilt it for another motor. He ran out of money, so I bought and installed it in the Zodiac. I did, however, take the heads and sump off to take a good look inside, and I'm happy with it," Ron said.

"That's good enough for me," Ricky said.

"Do you want a test run?" Andy said.

Ricky nodded.

"I'll drive," Andy said. "This can be a bit of animal and no disrespect, mate, but you wouldn't have driven anything like this before."

Andy opened the driver's side door and got into the car. Ricky raced around to the passenger side and slid onto the bench seat.

"There's no seat belts here Ricky," Andy said. "You might want to hold on to something."

Andy turned the ignition key and the throaty V8 burst into life. Andy gave her a slight blip on the throttle, and she grumbled like a caged lion. Andy slipped the shifter down into 'Drive' and the car lurched forward slightly.

"We reckon she's good for about three hundred brake horse power," Andy said as the Zodiac burbled slowly away from the house and then stopped on the corner of Beddington Lane. Andy looked from left to right. The road was clear so he arched his right foot over the accelerator and brake and the car lurched forward. Andy increased the revs, and the rear tyres began to spin while the engine purred. He then took his foot off the brake and punched the throttle down hard. The engine roared as the car slid away sideways with tyre smoke belching out of the rear arches. Andy, with one arm resting on the side window, steered the car back into shape. With the car straight and tyres no longer spinning, Ricky looked behind to see two thick black tyre lines on the road. Andy unleashed the full power of the drive train and Ricky was thrown back into his seat as the Zodiac sped along. Ricky looked over at the speedo, it read 50,60,70,80 and the car in front was looming up fast. With just a slight movement of the steering wheel Andy veered right and passed the car on the other side of the road. Ricky looked over at the speedo and it read 90 and was still accelerating.

"She's quick, Ricky, not as quick as my MK1 but still very quick," Andy said.

Ricky found himself sitting slightly sideways with his hand resting against the dashboard. Andy slowed the car down as they approached the traffic lights. When the lights turned green Andy pulled away slowly and allowed the Zodiac to just move along with the traffic.

"This is the business!" Ricky thought.

Andy drove the car to the Harris house and the two men got out of the car.

"So, what did you think?" Ron said.

"I like it Ron, she's a beauty," Ricky said.

Ricky and Ron walked back to the parked Anglia where they talked and agreed on a price that they were both happy with. Ricky gave Ron five hundred pounds as a deposit and said that he would be back later that day with the balance. He took one last look at his 'Harris' built Zodiac MK2 and grinned as he drove away.

Chapter 21

Ricky stood back and looked at how he had transformed the run-down tyre bay. The new signage, written in royal blue and gold had been positioned over the outside of the building. He had invested in new trolley jacks, a modern compressor to cope with the additional work he planned on generating, and a second wheel balancing machine. The old office furniture had been thrown away and replaced with a new modern desk. The walls had been painted and were decorated with images of race cars promoting tyres. Ricky had bought a settee and four matching chairs for customers to relax in while their cars were being worked on, and in the corner he'd put a vending machine for hot and cold beverages.

"It's looking good Ricky," Doughnut said.

"It's definitely coming along, but we have a way to go yet," Ricky said. "I've been out visiting potential trade customers which might make a lot of money and will add volume and keep us busy during the leaner times.

"Do you think we'll cope with all the new business? I mean it's just me and Harvey and he… well, he's old as the hills," Doughnut said with a chuckle.

"That's a good point. I was going to ask if you knew anybody over at National Tyres?" Ricky asked.

"Sure, I know everyone. We've all worked together before, both here and at another tyre bay in Sutton," Doughnut said.

"So you know who the good ones are? The, well, the skivers?" Ricky said.

"Oh, yeah. They've got three good lads and the assistant manager, Barry, is a right good bloke. The customers love him. He asked me a couple of times to join them, but I suppose I was just being loyal," Doughnut said.

"Good. Right, this is what I want you to do. Tell Barry that there's a position here for a manager, reporting directly to me. Tell him the wages are better than he's getting and there's a brilliant bonus system coming into place which should make every fitter another fifty if not sixty pounds a week. I want the three good lads as well. If Barry joins me and brings them with him, I'll pay him another grand a year on top of what I was going to pay him. I'm going to be in all day today so if you could see them at lunch time. Here," Ricky said, handing Doughnut two ten-pound notes, "Make sure that neither Barry nor the lads pay for their lunch today, okay?"

"Sure, Ricky. This is pretty exciting stuff. I hope you don't mind me asking, but what about me?" Doughnut asked.

"I've got bigger plans for you Doughnut. Once the new team are all in place and we're selling tyres hand over fist, I want you to go out and visit new trade customers. We'll find some sales course for you to attend, and I'll put packages together that will bring us the new business," Ricky said.

"Really?" Doughnut said.

"Yes, of course. The business is out there, Doughnut, all we have to do is go out and get it. I'll sort you out a car and then we'll agree to some sales targets, and you'll be away. Now don't worry, because if I didn't think that you could do it, I wouldn't be putting this opportunity on the table. I have big plans, Doughnut, and this is only the first of many depots I plan to open over the next few years, but first things first, we have to make London Tyre Co here successful," Ricky said.

"I won't let you down, Ricky," Doughnut said. "I really appreciate you giving me this opportunity."

"Right, now if you go into the office, you'll find a box of blue overalls with London Tyre Co. written on the back and there's another box with white T-Shirts that also carry the company logo. Go and help yourself. You'll need three sets of overalls and five T-shirts. Oh, and here's another twenty quid. When you can, go and get some safety boots. We don't want any accidents."

"Will do Ricky. I'm pretty certain Barry will join you now. He's been waiting on being given his own branch to run for months. It's been one broken promise after another and this is what might just sway him," Doughnut said.

"Good, I'm sure he could probably bring some business with him," Ricky said.

"That's a definite," Doughnut said. "That's what happened when he joined NTS. The trade customers just love him, and as long as he gave them the same deal, same service and they only dealt with him, then they were happy."

"Alright, so you crack on and see Barry and the lads at lunch time and tell Barry that I'll be here until about seven tonight and that I'm looking forward to meeting him," Ricky said.

"Will do, Ricky."

There was hoot from a distribution truck as it came to a halt. Justin, the driver, climbed out and was beaming.

"Hello Justin," Ricky said shaking his hand. "How are you?"

"I'm good Ricky. I've got your usual delivery, plus I've managed to swing fifty tyres. They're a good mix of sizes. I just had to take what I could comfortably get my hands on," Justin said.

"Nice one Justin, well done," Ricky said, handing him a wad of notes.

Justin winked and put the money into his pocket.

"Have you thought any more about taking the truck? It is still possible, you know. I stop off at the same café most days and I've already had a spare set of keys cut," Justin said.

"Yes mate, it will happen. I've just got to see some people, so leave it with me for the time being. In the meantime, I'll take everything you have, so if you have family or friends you can cut a side deal with, do it, because we are going to be selling shed loads and I need the low cost stock to take market share," Ricky said.

"I've mentioned it to my brother-in-law. He covers part of North London and Hertfordshire. We could have a meet up and transfer whatever he's got onto my truck. I'll iron out some details and try to have your first lot by the end of next week."

"I'd appreciate it if you can try to get the popular sizes," Ricky said.

"I'll do my best, but it really is grabbing whatever you can. I'd love to get my hands on the articulated trucks that make the deliveries to us direct from the manufacturers. Now there are bloody hundreds of tyres. Those trucks are packed from top to bottom," Justin said, "And we get five or six of those every day."

"That is interesting, Justin. One step at a time, but yes, I'm interested in whatever you can bring and as you know I always pay cash straight away, no messing about," Ricky said.

"I know mate, which is why you're my only customer now," Justin said.

"Doughnut," Ricky called. "Can you help Justin unload this lot?"

Doughnut smiled, nodded and bounded over to the back of the truck.

Ricky walked through the tyre bay and into the offices. He was happy and proud of what he'd achieved. He sat down at his desk and looked over the quotes he'd been getting for advertising in the local newspapers. He had a marketing plan, but needed volumes of tyres and knocked off prices to get customers through the door and starve his competitors of sales.

The door to the office opened and Neil stepped inside.

"You alright Ricky?" Neil said.

"Well mate I was flying up until you dropped me in it, to be honest," Ricky said.

"Look I know, and I'm sorry, but Jackie is really on one right now. I don't know what's pissed her off, but she's not only been pushing for me to go alone but she's talking about dropping Doreen and that, mate, could be really bad news," Neil said as he pulled out a chair and sat down opposite Ricky.

"What, you mean worse than failing to deliver promised cars for Mr Frank Allen when he has containers waiting to be shipped to customers in Africa?" Ricky said with a hint of sarcasm.

"I know mate, but look, I'm not going to drop you in it. I'm going to keep getting you motors, alright? I'll make sure that we have everything Frank wants plus I'll keep our own ringers coming through, just don't say anything to Jackie," Neil said.

"Neil that's a weight off my mind and I appreciate you sticking it out. Has Jackie said what's pissing her off?"

"Not a word mate. I'm not kidding she's been walking around like a bear with a sore head for a few weeks now. I thought it was me to start with but then she just announced that we were going to work together as our own bosses. I think she's bloody mad. I mean you and I are making a fair few quid and she's got money rolling in week after week hoisting for Doreen. Why rock the boat?" Neil said, shrugging his shoulders.

"I can only imagine that Doreen isn't going to be happy," Ricky said, slowly shaking his head.

"Tell me about it, mate and I really can't have her unhappy," Neil replied softly.

"Why, what's up?" Ricky said.

"Look I know you'll keep this to yourself, but I went round to pick up Jackie after getting that Jag. Bloody hell mate, I never told you about that did I?"

"No," Ricky said.

"Well, this geezer has only gone and left his keys in it so I just waltzed over. As I'm about to bugger off, this geezer legged it down his drive and grabbed me through the window. I just floored the motor and this plonker is hanging for dear life calling me all the names under the sun. Finally he lets go and bounces off down the road. He ain't dead or nothing or it would have been in the papers. There was this briefcase in the motor, and it had some kind of apron in it. It was like cream and blue and had chrome bits on it. There were also these white gloves and a blue book. I think the bloke must have been one of these Freemasons," Neil said.

"Fuck me," Ricky thought, *"That could be Michelle's dad. He's a freemason and he drives a Jaguar."*

"That ain't funny mate," Ricky said.

"Tell me about it," Neil said. "Anyway, once I parked the motor in the garages I went around to Doreen's to pick up Jackie as her car was in the garage. Well, she was staying in London to get an early start and I had a drink with Doreen. We kind of talked about old times, you know?"

"Sounds very friendly," Ricky said.

"Well one thing led another and... Well, I ended up shagging Doreen again," Neil said.

"You're joking," Ricky said.

"Wish I was mate. I just couldn't help myself and then once the deed was done, she said that providing I made sure that Jackie kept hoisting for her then our little secret was safe," Neil said.

"Bloody hell Neil, you've been right turned over, and all for a bit of the other," Ricky said.

"You can imagine once Jackie started acting up and getting pissed with you, Doreen and life in general, I thought maybe she suspected something," Neil said.

"I can't believe this," Ricky thought. *"While you're having it away with Doreen, I've done the same bloody thing with Jackie."*

"What are you going to do?" Ricky asked.

"I'm taking one day at a time. The first thing I wanted to do was to let you know that I'm still game and will keep at it, mate. Then I'll try and talk Jackie around to keep working with Doreen and not be so greedy," Neil said.

"What about Doreen? Can you trust her to keep her mouth shut?"

Neil was silent and looked down at the table.

"You've been back and done the business again, haven't you?" Ricky said.

"I couldn't help myself Ricky. Mate, she is the fuck of the century, and it was just there, stockings, suspenders and heels mate. What is a red-blooded bloke supposed to do?"

"This can only go wrong," Ricky said as he leaned back in his chair, "And there will be a fall out. You do know that, don't you?"

"I thought about dumping Jackie, you know give her the sack. I like her, but in a different way to Doreen. I mean Jackie is lovely and all that, but Doreen is, well, Doreen is just…"

"Yeah, yeah, I'm getting the picture Neil. You don't have to give me the details," Ricky said. "It looks like taking one day at a time is your best option for right now. Who would have thought, eh Neil? A year ago you would have been happy with anything with a smile and a short skirt and wet dreams over Doreen and now, well, now you're balls deep in trouble with two, powerful and volatile, women. Rather you than me mate," Ricky said.

"I ain't exactly on solid ground here either," Ricky thought. *"But I feel slightly better knowing that you've been playing away."*

"Have you got a list of what motors we need?" Neil asked.

"I like the way you changed the subject there Neil, nice one. Yes, I do have a list," Ricky said, reaching into his desk drawer and handing Neil an A3 sized piece of paper with what cars were required. "I'm due to see Frank shortly so I'll have some money for you. So, just so we're both clear mate, will you be fulfilling all these orders for Frank and the motors I've bought for us?" Ricky said.

"Unless I'm struck down by a lightning bolt then yes, I'm on it," Neil said.

"That's good to know," Ricky thought, *"but I'll have to put something else in place just in case this goes tits up at short notice. There are far too many variables, and I cannot afford to let Frank down, plus I have plans, big plans, and I need the money to keep rolling in to make them happen."*

"So we're good then?" Neil said.

"Of course we are," Ricky said as he stood up and shook Neil's hand.

"Right, I'll get back to work. I've got a sweet Granada outside, so that's one straight off our own list," Neil said. "See you later."

"Yeah, I suppose a drink at the Arms is probably not a good idea at the moment," Ricky said.

"It won't be forever," Neil said, before getting up and leaving the shop.

Ricky sat back in his chair.

"What a bloody mess this is," Ricky thought. *"Women, bloody women. Nah, who am I kidding, I could have and should have said no. Unfortunately the deed is done now. I just hope I don't lose a mate over it."*

"Ricky, I've seen Barry and he is well interested. He said he'll pop by after work, about six-ish," Doughnut said as he leaned against the door frame.

"Great news, well done," Ricky said.

"Here's your change," Doughnut said as held out his hand with several one-pound notes and change.

"Stick it in your pocket," Ricky said.

"Cheers," Doughnut looked down at the cash and beamed.

The door opened and young Terry from the estate walked in.

"Hello Terry. Doughnut can you give us a few minutes please?" Ricky said.

"Yeah, of course," Doughnut said as he turned and closed the door to the tyre bay behind him.

"Thanks for popping in Terry," Ricky said.

"This is a nice place you've got here," Terry said as he looked around the office.

"We're getting there," said Ricky.

"What can I help you with?" Terry said.

Ricky chuckled.

"No, I didn't ask you in so that you can do something for me. You know that bit of jewellery you had away?" Ricky said.

"Was it alright? I've already spent that money you gave me," Terry said.

"It was good. In fact, it was better than good. Here, this is yours," Ricky said, handing him an envelope stuffed with notes. "I passed it on to a contact who got it sold on and it fetched quite a bit more than either of us thought it was worth. So, mate, there's five hundred quid in there. It's yours."

Terry looked at him wide eyed and speechless.

"There's no catch," Ricky said, shaking his head.

"You're a top bloke Ricky, thank you. I never saw that coming," Terry said with a broad smile.

"Are you working?" Ricky said.

"What, you mean a proper nine till five job?" Terry said.

"Yes?"

"No, I duck and dive a bit but don't have anything fixed," Terry said.

"Well I have a bit of part time of work, to start with," Ricky said, "If you fancy it."

"Yeah, sure. I mean, what is it?"

"All I need is for you write out invoices for me. This is an ask no questions kind of a deal and I'll pay you cash in hand," Ricky said. "You can get in here for 9.00 and all you have to do is go through this phone book putting names and addresses on these invoices and then filling them out as puncture repairs, wheel balancing and tracking. Can you do that?" Ricky said.

"Yeah, of course and thanks Ricky," Terry said.

"Good, well you can make a start on Monday, if that's alright. I should be in but if I'm not then have a chat with Doughnut, that's the lad you saw me talking with when you came in," Ricky said.

"Great, will do. I'll get myself off then," Terry said.

"If I don't see you before, I'll see you on Monday," Ricky said.

***

It was just after 6.00pm when Barry, the assistant manager from Ricky's competitor, arrived. Ricky kept their meeting informal. He liked him straight away and could see why the customers trusted him. A deal was struck, and Barry was appointed Branch Manager with a salary that matched his new position. Barry had spoken with the three tyre fitters that Doughnut said were good workers and they had all agreed to join him at London Tyre Co if he was to leave. Ricky asked that Barry made the appointments as they were his team. He also asked that he spend the first week calling his customers and confirming by letter that he was now the Branch Manager of London's fastest growing company and that their special price agreements would be honoured. Ricky left the office just after 7.30pm, feeling extremely pleased with his day. It was all coming together.

Chapter 22

"We haven't had a Saturday at the Arms in ages," Kenny said.

"Yeah, I know but Deano seemed keen that we showed up," Ricky said.

"How have you been Kenny?" Ricky said quietly.

Kenny took a swig from his pint and looked around him.

"Mate I'm riddled with guilt over Specs, and living with Denise and playing the dutiful dad isn't all it's cracked up to be. Just look around here," Kenny said, pointing to a bunch of young girls chatting by the Juke box. To be honest Ricky, I'm bored with the mundane, dull life of going to work and just paying bills. You know she even caused grief over me coming in here tonight for a few pints with my mates. It's not like I'm down the Cadillac Club giving it the large one and pulling some cracking little sort. It seems like those days are over. No more of the chasing, no more adventurous sex with some completely unknown girl that leaves you with a memory for life. No, it's shitty nappies and an attitude. I tried to have a conversation with Denise about Specs. I needed to air some stuff and thought she might have also been having issues with guilt and stuff, but no she just closed that conversation down. As far as she was concerned Specs made his choices and that was it. That seems kind of heartless to me, doesn't it to you?" Kenny said as he reached for his pint.

"Look mate, I think the whole thing is a bit of a mess, and made worse by Specs committing suicide. I'm not Denise's biggest fan to be honest, but she's your bird and you have a kiddie together, so you're just going to have to front it out and do the right thing," Ricky said.

"What is the right thing then, Ricky? Stay bored and miserable for the rest of my life or do I look about for something with no strings to ease the boredom?" Kenny said.

"No strings? You must be joking or just kidding yourself mate. There are always attachments. Birds think differently to us blokes. They get sentimental and all emotional over something that we might just see as nothing more than a one-night stand, a release and that's it. The only no strings sex you'll get, mate, is with Trudy, and you'll have to pay for that," Ricky said.

"I ain't paying for it, Ricky, no way," Kenny said.

"One way or another you always pay for it. A clever man about town like you must know that," Ricky said. "Besides, I'm not saying that you should do that. Why don't you just try and table all this stuff with Denise. It wasn't that long ago that you were both super keen to make it work."

"I know, I know, and at the time I did, Ricky. I mean I really wanted it. Maybe if I didn't feel so bloody guilty it'd feel different," Kenny said.

"It's just time mate, and what will be, will be," Ricky said. "Now, do you want another pint or what?"

"Yeah go on," Kenny said.

"Two pints of Carlsberg please Ronnie," Ricky said, putting a pound note down on the bar.

"It's not like you lot to be in here on a Saturday night," Ronnie said. "Have you been banned from somewhere?" Ronnie chuckled.

"Nah, Deano just called us all together," Kenny said.

"Are we expecting trouble?" Ronnie said.

"Give over," Ricky said. "I can't see anybody mad enough to try anything on at The Arms on a Saturday night.

"Good, because I don't need any reasons for the pub to be splashed all over the front of some newspapers. If you think that something is going down, I'd expect you to give me the wink, the heads up, alright?" Ronnie said.

"Yeah, course," Ricky said.

When *'Bye Bye Baby'* by the Bay City Rollers played, the two lads looked over at the juke box. Melanie, Kaz and Donna were dressed up in their short white skirts, heels and Bay City Roller tops with red tartan down the short sleeve.

"I've always fancied a crack at that," Kenny said.

"What, Melanie?"

"Leave it out! I ain't got a death wish. Mate, if she stood in front of me and played peek-a-boo with that short little skirt of hers, I'd run for the mountains as fast as my legs would carry me. No, I meant Kaz. She has a cracking little shape on her and none of the drama that goes with a bird like Melanie," Kenny said.

***

The girls danced merrily to their favourite band.

"Did you tell Deano about it?" Kaz said.

"Keep it down will yer," Melanie whispered.

"I'll take that as a no," Kaz said.

"Look it's no big deal," Melanie said.

"Melanie, you were nicked for shoplifting," Donna said. "You might go down."

"Yeah, yeah I know, but Doreen said that it's a first offence and it'll probably be a stiff telling off," Melanie said.

"The key word there, Melanie, is probably," Donna said.

"Kaz, how much did you make last week?" Melanie said.

"Why?"

"Just answer the question!" Melanie said abruptly.

"Just over three hundred quid," Kaz said.

"What about you Donna?" Melanie asked.

"About the same."

"Exactly, and I've been making that kind of money week in and week out, just like you, and now I've been caught. If you remember, Doreen said that this can and will happen. If we are out hitting the shops day in and day out, sooner or later we'll get caught. What I should have done was decked the silly old bint and made a run for it but instead I tried talking my out of it. My mistake, I'll know better next time," Melanie said.

"What will Deano say?" Kaz said as she handed Melanie a fresh gin and tonic.

"I won't tell him, simple as that. I'll go to court and if they lock me a way for a month or so I'll deal with it then," Melanie said. "The last thing I need right now is grief from him too. I've been saving my money because I want to get a place like Jackie and Neil's. Don't you want to be off this estate?"

"We've been saving our money too," Kaz said. "We're going to take a look about next year. Maybe even get a mortgage on a place."

"Ricky is probably the best person to talk to about that," Melanie said. "Deano said his place is really smart, you know, proper upmarket."

"I do like Ricky," Kaz said.

"Oh really," Melanie chuckled, "Now tell us something we don't know."

Kaz blushed.

"He's just a nice guy. I think he'd make good boyfriend material," Kaz said.

"I always had a thing for Kenny," Donna said.

"What? He was a right playboy," Melanie said.

"Yeah, I know but he just has this smile, you know, the kind of smile that…"

"Makes you drop your drawers?" Melanie said with a raucous laugh.

"Maybe," Donna chuckled, "But he's off the market now."

"That was a nasty business with Specs," Kaz said.

"That wasn't Kenny's fault," Melanie said. "He must be right cut up about it, no matter how he looks on the outside."

"That's what I think," Donna said.

"Do you think he'll stay with Denise?" Kaz asked.

"I don't know," Melanie said.

"I hope he does what makes him happy. It's not like life is a practice run, so you've got to be happy even if it upsets other people," Donna said.

"Hello girls," Doreen said as she approached them.

"Alright Doreen?" Melanie said.

"You're all looking good tonight," Doreen said with a broad grin.

"You too," Melanie said, stepping back and looking Doreen up and down. "Nice outfit, are you off to the Cadillac Club?"

"No, I just popped in for a quick one and to give you girls these," Doreen said as reached into her handbag and brought out three envelopes. "I don't like to talk shop in here, but we've had a good month, so there's a little extra for you."

Kaz opened the envelope and looked in at the wad of notes.

"There's got to be two hundred quid in here," Kaz whispered.

"Like I said we had a good month, so you girls deserved a little extra," Doreen said.

"Thanks Doreen," Kaz and Donna said together.

"Yeah, thanks Doreen," Melanie said. "Can I have a quick word, in private?"

"Yeah of course," Doreen said before leading her away to an empty table and two chairs.

Kaz put a coin into the juke box and *'Sky High'* by Jigsaw began to play.

"What's up Melanie?" Doreen asked as she sat down.

"Are you sure that I'll just get a good telling off in court?" Melanie said.

"Look, you walk into that court with your head down and tell them how sorry you are and that it'll never happen again, okay, and the chances are the judge will either let you off or if you have a bastard of a judge you'll get two months," Doreen said.

"Two months!" Melanie said.

"Yes, two months, but you'll do four weeks and then straight back to work. You have to trust me on this Melanie. If the worst comes to the worst, doing four weeks in Holloway is a doddle. I've been there, done it and it's nothing. The time will pass quickly, and you'll be out and earning again," Doreen said.

"Okay," Melanie muttered.

"Melanie you're a talented operator, and you're making good money. And with all the new work I've got coming in, you could easily be making five hundred quid a week. That, Melanie is life changing money. That's a nice fully furnished home, good clothes on your back and a nice motor outside. The kind of things most of the people in here will never see in their lifetime, but for you it's all there for the taking," Doreen said.

"Yeah, I know. I've just never been nicked before. Let alone gone to court," Melanie said.

"Well next time if it looks like it's all going pear shaped, you crack the shop assistant one and run for your life. Right?" Doreen said.

"Yeah, yeah, I know you're right. Let's just hope there isn't a next time," Melanie said.

Doreen finished her drink.

"Would you like another?" Melanie asked as she finished her drink too.

"No, no thank you. I have other plans this evening," Doreen said with a smile.

"Now that sounds promising. Anyone I know?" Melanie asked.

"Now that would be telling," Doreen said with a wink.

"Well, have fun," Melanie said.

"Oh, I will," Doreen chuckled as she waved and walked back across the bar.

Melanie joined her friends at the juke box where *'I Wanna Dance Wit'choo'* by Disco Tex and the Sex-O-Lettes was playing.

"There you go," Ricky said, putting a full tray of drinks on the table.

"Cheers," Deano said.

"Yeah cheers Ricky," Lee said.

Terry and Steve Parker raised their glasses.

"What is all that crap the girls are playing?" Deano asked.

"I don't mind it," Ricky said.

"Next you'll be telling me you like the Rubettes," Deano said.

"Actually, I do. Have you heard their latest record, *I Can Do It*, Deano?" Ricky said, raising his glass to Melanie, Kaz and Donna when the barman informed them that Ricky had already paid for their drinks.

"No and I can't say I'm in any rush to listen to it either," Deano said firmly.

"Mate, it's a good rock 'n' roll track," Ricky said.

"I'll take your word for it," Deano replied.

"Here, have you seen that bloke over in the corner?" Deano said, pointing.

The lads followed the direction of his finger.

"Do any of you know him?" Deano said.

The lads all took a second look and one by one shook their heads.

"I think he's filth, old bill sent in to spy on us," Deano said.

"Really, you think?" Ricky said, taking another look.

"He's got plod written all over him," Deano said.

"Yeah, look at the short back and sides plus he's wearing shiny shoes with jeans. What's that all about?" Lee said.

"Ricky, go and have a quick word with Ronnie. If he's been drinking shandy, then he's definitely old bill," Deano said, "And we don't tolerate old bill in the Arms."

Ricky stood up and sauntered over to the bar.

"Here Ronnie, there's a bloke in the corner by the window, that Deano thinks is old bill," Ricky said.

"I was thinking that myself," Ronnie said. "He's had the same pint of shandy all night and he doesn't look familiar."

"Alright, cheers Ronnie," Ricky said before returning to Deano's table.

"Looks like you could be right," Ricky said.

"I told you, didn't I?" Deano said.

"What do you want to do?" Ricky said.

"This could be a nice little intimidation job for you," Deano said, looking at Terry and Steve.

The two brothers looked each at other and grinned.

"It'll be sorted Deano," Terry said.

A few minutes passed and the guy got up and walked over to the bar.

"Take a look at him," Deano said with a sneer, "Is he plod or what?"

"Yeah, he's plod alright," Lee said.

Terry and Steve got up from the table and walked over to the bar. Steve stood to the right of the suspected officer and Terry to his left.

"Hello mate," Terry said.

"Err hello."

"You live around here?" Steve said.

"Err no."

"So, what are you doing in here then?" Terry said bluntly.

"I'm just having a pint, if you don't mind."

"Well that's just it. We do mind… officer," Terry said. "This is a pig free zone."

"I don't know what you mean."

"Yes, yes, you do," Steve said as he put his left foot on the officer's and pressed down hard.

"Owww, that hurt."

"So does a right good kicking. Are you getting the picture, plod?" Terry said.

"Look, I'm not what you think I am. I'm just out having a pint. I say, landlord… landlord… these two gentlemen are harassing me."

Ronnie walked over to the man and looked him up and down. His lip curled as he shook his head slowly.

"Go on fuck off, you're barred!" Ronnie said.

"Barred? Barred?"

Steve raised his leg and stamped it down hard, crushing the officer's foot.

"Owwww that really hurt!"

"Fuck off mate, while you still can," Terry said.

"Go on then, on your bike, plod," Steve said.

"I told you, you're barred," Ronnie said sternly.

"Well I never," the suspected police officer said.

"Don't show your face in here again," Ronnie said firmly. "You and your lot are not welcome."

Terry leaned forward and whispered in his ear "If I ever see you in here again, I will fucking hurt you so bad neither your mum nor your filthy mates back at the station will even recognise you."

"Okay, I'm leaving."

"Well fuck off then," Steve muttered.

Terry, Steve and Ronnie watched as the suspected police officer hobbled off towards the exit.

"Well done, lads," Ronnie said. "We can't be having the gavvers in here."

"Right, I think I'm just about ready," Deano said.

"Are you alright?" Ricky said.

"Yeah, I think so," Deano said before standing up and nodding to Ronnie.

The lights around the pub went dim and suddenly the 1957 version of 'The *Stripper*' by David Rose and his orchestra played through the pub's speakers. Everyone in the pub looked around expecting to see a girl prancing about taking off her clothes when Deano walked out from behind his table and began to move his hips back and forth slowly.

After a few second's hesitation everyone in the pub began to cheer him. Deano reached up slowly and removed his black drape jacket with the gold 'King of the Teds' stitching on the breast pocket. Kenny wolf-whistled. Deano threw the jacket back to his table. The stunned looking Melanie, Kaz and Donna slowly stepped forward and watched as Deano slipped off his bootlace tie and then began to undo his shirt buttons in time to the music. When the final button was undone, he stuck out his chest and pulled his silk shirt wide open exposing a black T-shirt with 'WILL YOU MARRY ME?' written in white.

The music stopped and everyone in the pub cheered. Melanie looked startled as Deano reached into his pocket and produced a small red velvet box. He slowly dropped down onto one knee and opened the small box, revealing a diamond engagement ring. The cheering subsided until there was just silence.

"Melanie, you are the most important person in the world to me and I love you. Will you do me the great honour of becoming my wife?" Deano said, offering the ring to Melanie.

Melanie looked like she had been caught in the headlights of an oncoming, speeding car.

"Deano! Yes! Yes, I will marry you!"

The pub erupted with cheers as the lights were turned back up. Deano stood up and walked over to Melanie. He looked into her eyes as he put the engagement ring on her finger. The cheers turned to clapping with congratulations being shouted out from every corner of the pub.

"You never said a word," Melanie whispered.

"I wanted it to be a surprise," Deano said before slowly leaning forward and kissing her on the lips.

"I love you Deano," Melanie said.

"Right then," Ronnie called out from the bar. "Bubbly for the happy couple!"

The barman carried over a black plastic ice bucket with a bottle of champagne and two crystal cut flute glasses.

"Now that was class," Kenny said.

"You have to hand it to Deano. That was top notch. I mean if you're going to propose to a bird then you're right Kenny, that was pure class," Ricky said.

Chapter 23

"Are you sure about this Guv?" DC Bernard Jacobs said.

"It's time for us to shake things up a bit," DS Ray White said.

"But do you trust what Double Bubble tells you Guv?"

"Double Bubble is a no-good slag, Bernie. He will have his reasons for pointing the finger at Deano Derenzie and Ricky Turrell. Maybe they owe him money or maybe he just doesn't like them, but I'm sure he has his reasons for saying they murdered Eddy Boyce. We're going to pull them in and shake the bloody tree to see what falls out," DS White said.

"We don't have a body Guv, in fact we have nothing," DC Jacobs said.

"What we have is good old-fashioned police instinct and that gut feeling when you just know someone is up to no good. My sniffer tells me there's something," DS White said.

The unmarked police car stopped outside Ricky's home. They looked up at the window and saw that the light on the top floor was on.

"This is a nice place," DS White said. "What was it he said he did again?"

DC Jacobs rifled through a folder on his lap.

"He owns a tyre bay, London Tyre Co, Guv," DC Jacobs said.

"What, do they sell Rolls Royce tyres or something? This is better than my place and I'm twenty years into the job," DS White said.

"Mine too Guv. Maybe we should knock it on the head and open a tyre bay?"

DS White got out of the car and walked towards the main doors. They had issued instructions for uniformed officers to bring Deano Derenzie in, saying that there had been new information in relation to the stabbing.

"Look at this Bernie. He has an intercom," DS said White pointing to the consol. DS White pressed the button with 'Ricky Turrell' written above it.

"Hello," Ricky said through the intercom.

"Good evening. It's Detective Sergeant Ray White. We have a couple of questions."

Ricky buzzed them in.

"Come on up," Ricky said.

DS White and DC Jacobs walked up to the third floor.

"This is nice Bernie, too nice," DS White said.

When they reached the top floor, they could hear *"Three Steps to Heaven'* by Showaddywaddy on low volume. The front door was ajar. As it opened and the officers let themselves in, Ricky called out.

"Come on through. I'm in the kitchen."

The policemen walked down the hallway. DS White stopped by the living room and looked in. He shook his head in disbelief when he spotted the Bang and Olufsen sound system and the twenty-six-inch television in the corner of the room. The crimson velvet curtains were fashioned into swags and tails.

The officers entered the kitchen where they saw Ricky holding a sharp knife. He had been cutting Spanish onions, mushrooms, garlic and fresh tomatoes.

"You'll have to excuse me," Ricky said, wiping tears from his eyes. "These onions are really strong."

"That smells nice, what are you cooking?" DC Jacobs said.

"Spaghetti Bolognaise," Ricky said. "I have come up with this recipe which really just hits the spot. There's a secret ingredient."

"What that?" DC Jacobs asked.

Ricky lifted an open bottle of red wine.

"A good healthy splosh of Italian Rioja," Ricky said as he walked over to the sink to wash his hands.

"Right, when you two have finished playing Fanny Craddock we have some police business," DS White said.

"How can I help you?" Ricky asked as he began to dry his hands on a hand towel.

"We need you to come down to the police station to answer some questions," DS White said.

"As much as I'd like to help, I'm in the middle of cooking my dinner. Can we do this another time?" Ricky said.

"No, Ricky Turrell, we want to talk to you about the murder of Eddy Boyce. Cuff him Bernie," DS White ordered.

"I've no idea what you're talking about," Ricky said.

DC Jacobs took out a set of handcuffs and put them on Ricky's wrists.

DS White turned the cooker off and moved the saucepan off the heat.

"You'll not be seeing this for a while," DS White said. "I'd like to know whose gaff got screwed for you to have this lot!"

"I'm a hard-working business owner and I resent your accusations Detective Sergeant White," said Ricky.

"Of course you are," DS White said sarcastically.

Ricky was led through the hallway.

"I'm going to need my keys," Ricky said nodding towards a hook by the front door. "Would you mind?"

DC Jacobs took them off the hook and pushed them into Ricky's trouser pocket. Ricky was led down the stairway and placed in the back of their plain police car.

On the estate, Deano had been collected by uniformed police officers, taken back to the police station and put in an interview room.

At the police station Ricky was taken through to the interview rooms where DS White made a point of stopping him outside a closed door. He opened it and immediately Ricky spotted Deano. The two men exchanged glances.

"Everything alright in here?" DS White said to the officer sitting opposite Dean. "Is he being co-operative?"

"Yes sir," the officer said. "Extremely helpful."

DS White quickly closed the door and led Ricky through to an empty interview room two doors down from Deano.

"What the fuck!" Ricky thought. *"Deano what are you saying?"*

Ricky was shown to a seat and DC Jacobs removed his hand cuffs.

"Was that really necessary?" Ricky said, rubbing his wrists.

"Keep your hair on Ricky. It's just protocol," DS White said.

"I've got no idea why you've brought me in, and I'd like to see my brief," Ricky said.

"You will, in time," DS White said. "Bernie go and get us a couple of cups of tea, would you? This is going to be a long night."

"Yes Guv. How do you take it Ricky?" DC Jacobs asked.

"Strong, no sugar, please," Ricky said.

"Now, Ricky Turrell, you have probably noticed that bit by bit we're cleaning up the Milton Road Estate. Villains are being plucked from their homes, having their ill-gotten gains taken away and getting banged up. Some are away and doing pretty serious time. Now under normal circumstances a bunch of rowdy young lads playing gangs wouldn't be of any interest to us but when one of your lot, Michael Deacon, decided to, what was it again? Call out "Fight the Filth', well, that was when you lot stepped into the limelight and became of interest to people like me. You and your friends overstepped the mark because no one takes a pop at one of us and gets away with it, and that Ricky Turrell, is never."

"I wouldn't know, I wasn't there," Ricky said.

"Well, that's what you say Ricky, but that's not what we know. You see, I know that you and Deano Derenzie have been pretty active after his stabbing, building some kind of Ted Army with lads from all over London. What's all that about Ricky?"

"I've never heard anything about a Ted Army, but there's a lot of guys out there with a love for Rock 'n' Roll," Ricky said.

"So you lot didn't go to Fulham then?"

"How the hell does he know about that," Ricky thought.

"I heard that you lot bashed up one of their main men," DS White said. "There's no need to deny it, because we know, Ricky Turrell. We know a lot more than you think. So, tell me, how many does it take to make up a Ted Army?"

Ricky shrugged his shoulders and remained silent.

"What does a Ted Army do, Ricky Turrell and who is the leader of this illustrious gang? Is it you Ricky, are you the main man?"

Ricky remained silent.

"The judges don't like gangs Ricky. You must have heard what they did to the Krays and the Richardsons. Those boys are never coming home. Like I said, judges don't like gangs and they come down very hard on murderers who belong to gangs."

Ricky remained silent.

"We have had word from several sources, that you and Deano Derenzie murdered Eddy Boyce. Deano is in the other room right now, singing like a lark. He doesn't want to join the rest of his neighbours in Brixton and is probably putting you in the frame as we speak."

"I have nothing to say other than I'd like to see my solicitor," Ricky said.

"You could be looking at a thirty stretch Ricky. Is keeping your mouth shut really worth thirty years of your life rotting away in a cell?"

Ricky remained silent.

"That's a nice place you have Ricky. Lots of nice stuff you have. I wonder how much of it is knocked off? I suppose a warrant would allow us to check it all out but then a few bits of stolen gear compared to a murder charge is nothing," DS White said.

Ricky remained silent.

"Do you have a girlfriend, Ricky? I would have thought that a man about town like you would probably have some nice little sort. I mean you have a nice car, a beautiful home and your own business. Yeah, I can imagine that this girlfriend of yours must be quite something," DS White said.

Ricky remained silent.

"I can tell you one thing that I know for absolute certainty and that is when you are banged away in a cell for the rest of your life, you'll be yesterday's news in days. Take a look at old Ronnie Biggs' wife. Within a few months she was shacked up with another geezer and rumour had it she was up the duff when he escaped. If you have a bird and she means anything to you Ricky, then just tell us your side of the story and we'll put in a good word for you with the judge.

Who knows, you may even be able to walk away if we've got Deano bang to rights."

Ricky remained silent.

"I'm not going to give you too many chances to tell your side of the story Ricky," DS White said. "Do you have anything that you'd like to tell me?"

"I'd like to tell you to go fuck yourself," Ricky thought.

"I'd like to see my solicitor," Ricky said.

DC Jacobs entered the room carrying a tray with three cups of tea. He put them on the table. DS White spooned in three sugars and used the spoon to stir his tea.

"Did you take one in for Deano Derenzie?" DS White said.

"Yes Guv," DC Jacobs said.

"Was he being helpful?"

"Yes Guv, he's busy giving names and places. He's been talking about you too Ricky," DC Jacobs said, shaking his head slowly.

"It sounds to me like your mate has flipped in there in a bid to save himself Ricky. Sounds like you're bang in trouble now," DS White said. "I wonder how long a pretty boy like you would last inside?"

Ricky reached for his cup of tea.

"Bernie, keep an eye on Ricky here while I go and listen to what Deano Derenzie has got to say," DS White said.

DS White left the interview room; he paused for a moment and then smiled as he closed the door.

"What the hell does he know?" Ricky thought.

***

"Good evening, Deano Derenzie. You may remember me, Detective Sergeant Ray White. We spoke briefly after you were viciously stabbed on the Milton Road Estate. I think you must have been suffering with amnesia at the time as you couldn't remember anything," DS White said.

"Yeah, I remember you," Deano said. "What's all this about? I don't remember anything new."

"Is it Deano Derenzie or Deano the Dog, King of the Teds and leader of London's Ted Army?"

"No comment," Deano said bluntly.

"I've been told that you and your Ted Army like bashing up Skinheads and Boot Boys. In fact, I was told that you visited Fulham and smashed someone's head in quite recently," DS White said. "Do you have anything to say about that?"

"I'd like to see a solicitor," Deano said.

"Of course you would. Do you know Eddy Boyce?"

Deano remained silent.

"He knows you. Well at least he did until you murdered him, Deano. Now if someone was to stab me then I'd most probably want some kind of revenge too. Maybe you went too far Is that what happened Deano? Did a little slap end up getting out of hand?"

Deano remained silent.

"Your friend in there, Ricky Turrell, said that it all just got out of hand and was never meant to happen. Is that what happened Deano?"

"I'd like to see my solicitor," Deano said.

"Ricky is helping us with all our enquiries, and he's got plenty to say about you Deano. I have this theory though; would you like to hear it?" DS White said.

Deano remained silent.

"I think Ricky Turrell is responsible for taking care of Eddy Boyce and he's trying to save his own skin by placing all the blame at your doorstep. Murder isn't your game, Deano. You're just a bloke who likes rock 'n' roll and hanging out with your mates, but Ricky Turrell wants more. I think it's him behind building this Ted Army with some kind of criminal enterprise in mind."

Deano chuckled and shook his head.

"We've spoken to your friend Micky Deacon in Wormwood Scrubs and he tells us that you wouldn't kill someone, but he wouldn't put it past Ricky Turrell. Is that what happened Deano? Did Ricky Turrell get carried away and kill Eddy Boyce?"

Deano remained silent.

"I admire your loyalty, I really do, but it's misplaced because Ricky Turrell is making a statement right now naming you as the killer of Eddy Boyce. All I want is the truth. I want the right person to go away for Eddy Boyce's murder and my cop instincts tell me it wasn't you despite what Ricky Turrell is saying in there."

"I want to see my solicitor," Deano said firmly.

"That girl of yours Deano, what's her name again? Oh that's it... Melanie. She a pretty little sort, isn't she?" DS White said before leaning back in his chair.

"Choose your words very carefully," Deano said with a menacing glare.

"I was just wondering who she'd take up with after you've been locked up. I suppose Ricky Turrell is the logical choice. I mean he's good looking, has a nice motor, money and a lovely home. That can't be a nice thought can it, Deano? What with you being banged up for the rest of your natural and Ricky Turrell smashing the granny out of her night after night," DS White said.

Deano composed himself, closed his eyes momentarily and took a deep breath.

"I would very much like to see my solicitor," Deano said.

"I'm going to see how Ricky Turrell is coming along with that statement naming you as Eddy Boyce's killer," DS White said.

***

Detective Sergeant White returned to the interview room where Ricky was being held. He entered the room, looked at Ricky and slowly shook his head.

"What a waste of a life Ricky. Okay son it's all over now. Just tell us where the body is. Eddy Boyce's family are fraught with worry. Do the right thing and let these people say a proper goodbye to their son. We know you did it, Ricky. Deano Derenzie's statement is being typed up right now. We have you, son, but if you want us to take it easy it's not too late to tell us where Eddy's buried. I can give you my personal word that we will put a good word in to the judge for you. You know, ask him to go easy on you," DS White said.

There were several loud bangs on the door. It opened and a man in a black suit carrying a briefcase stood in the doorway.

"Detective White?" the man said.

"Yes, who wants to know?"

"My name is Gerald Hart and I'm Ricky Turrell's solicitor. Are you charging my client?"

"We are interviewing your client in relation to a murder," DS White said.

"Really, and you didn't give him the option of legal representation?"

"It was an informal conversation," DS White said.

"If you have no evidence and don't plan to charge my client, we're leaving," Gerald Hart said, motioning Ricky to stand up.

"They're holding a friend of mine too, Deano Derenzie," Ricky said.

"Detective Sergeant White I am going to have to speak with the Chief Inspector. I want Mr Deano Derenzie released now!" Gerald Hart said, motioning Ricky to leave the room.

"Bernie, show them out, DS White said.

Ricky followed DC Bernard Jacobs to the interview room where Deano was being questioned.

"Deano mate, this is Gerald Hart, my solicitor. They have nothing." Ricky said.

Deano smiled and got up from the table. The three men walked through the hallway and out of the police station into the cold night air.

"How did you know we had been pulled in?" Ricky asked.

"Our mutual friend, Frank Allen, has eyes and ears everywhere Ricky. This is my card. If there's a next time, you insist on calling me first before say anything, okay?" Gerald Hart said.

"We know the rules Gerald," Ricky said. "We don't say anything, ever, to the old bill. Ain't that right Deano?"

Deano nodded.

"You learn that kind of stuff before you even start school," Deano said.

"I have Santa to thank for that," Ricky said.

"Nice old fella Santa, full of wisdom before those bastards fitted him up," Deano said.

All the youngsters on the Milton Road Estate learnt from an early age that when they are told by police officers that they have the right to remain silent, then that was exactly what they did. Then if they are prosecuted, they cannot force you to give evidence at your trial. Santa would tell the youngsters on the Estate how the police would always resort to intimidation, lying or tricking you into a confession. He told the youngsters how the police were free to and encouraged to lie during an interrogation. The most common ruse would be that they had signed witnessed statements. Santa told them not to wait for the words 'anything you say will be used against you' because everything you say is potential evidence. Santa would repeatedly say that they should never tell them anything but their name. The police are liars, he would tell them, when they offer deals. Ignore the promises of putting in a good word in exchange for co-operation because it was all nonsense. The police have no authority, he would say, to make any kind of deals regarding the outcome of any criminal case.

Ricky flagged down a passing taxi which took them both back to their homes.

***

Back in the police station, DS White was livid.

"We've been grassed up by our own," DS White said. "One of our fucking own!"

"Keep it down Guv or we'll have the Super down here," DC Jacobs said.

"What kind of slag puts on a police uniform and then grasses on their own. We would have had them, Bernie. Sooner or later one of them would have slipped up and then we would have had them!" DS White said.

"Guv, we don't even know if Eddy Boyce is dead. There is no body, just the word of a grass and you said yourself that you can't trust Double Bubble," DC Jacobs said.

"Don't be a smart arse, Bernie. It doesn't suit you. I'm bloody pissed off and you know what this means don't you?"

"What Guv?"

"That Ricky Turrell is bloody connected. He's in with Frank Allen which would explain the business and the flash flat. They're up to something and we're going to find out what," DS White said.

"What and talk to Double Bubble again?"

"No, no I'll deal with him when the time is right. I want to know why Ricky Turrell is important to a criminal king pin like Frank Allen," DS White said.

Chapter 24

"Whose idea was it to meet at the Blind Beggar Pub?" Ricky asked.

"Mine actually," Deano said. "I thought it was appropriate, being that its London's East End and the Kray Twins association.

"What do you think of the Krays, Deano?" Ricky said as he slowed for the traffic lights.

"I suppose back in the sixties, they were it. You can't take anything away from them. From humble beginnings the Twins created a firm of very handy and extremely capable villains and then went on to expand their empire out of East London and into the West End. You know Ronnie, the landlord, did a bit of business with the Krays. I'm sure he said that he did a bit of work with Alfie Kray while he was running Esmeralda's Barn in Knightsbridge," Deano said.

"I agree mate. You can't take anything away from them, but for me the smartest of all the old-school, villains was Charlie Richardson. He had no interest in making a name for himself with the show business types, just grafting and making a few quid. I had a chat with Ronnie some time ago and he did say that he worked with the Krays, Richardsons and the Nash's in North London. It sounds like he was a bit lively back in the day. I like Ronnie, he's a good bloke," Ricky said.

"Yeah, Ronnie is the right man for the Milton Arms for sure."

As Ricky turned onto Whitechapel Road, he blipped the throttle of his high-performance Mustang V8 powered Zodiac MK2. The engine roared like a raging prehistoric monster from the Jurassic period. The oversized rear tyres spun as the car slid slowly sideways with thick grey tyre smoke belching out of the rear arches. Pedestrians stopped on the pavement to watch as Ricky controlled the slow rolling burnout before straightening the two-tone Zodiac out and slipping her smoothly into second gear and coming off the throttle.

"This motor is a bloody animal," Deano said. "What's the chances of me getting a V8 motor like this fitted in my PA Cresta?"

"If anyone can do it, Deano, it'll be the Harris family. There's plenty of room under your bonnet to fit either a Rover V8 or even something like mine, a small block, five litre, pony motor. I can get you a Rover V8 engine and gearbox, then all you'll have to do is pay Ron, Jeff or Andy to install it," Ricky said.

"I might just do that you know," Deano said. "There's the Blind Beggar."

Ricky cruised past the pub and found a place to park.

"Right, let's get the last piece of the puzzle in place," Deano said as he got out of the Zodiac, brushed himself down, stood upright and inhaled deeply.

The two Teds sauntered towards the pub like two powerful CEOs of a large corporation. Ricky looked at the 'Blind Beggar' green and gold sign and 'Watney Combe & Reid' written over the arch entrance.

At the far end of the pub sat over a dozen Teddy Boys. They turned as one as Deano and Ricky entered the pub. Ricky had bought another made to measure drape suit for the occasion. It was black with a gold velvet collar, cuffs and pocket tops. He had been tempted to have Ricky Turrell or Ted Army stitched into the gold velvet on the chest pocket but decided against it at the last minute. On his feet he wore his favourite blue suede brothel creepers. In his inside jacket pocket, he kept his insurance, the brass knuckle duster Deano had given him on their first dust up. As always, Deano looked what he was, King of the Teds, with Deano the Dog stitched in gold thread onto his top pocket.

"Hello mate," Ricky said to the barman. "Two pints of Carling and whatever the lads in the corner are having."

The barman nodded, smiled and began to pour the drinks.

"Alright Deano," one Ted leader said.

"Good to see you," another said.

"Pleased to meet you mate," said a third.

Deano took his seat at the head of the table. Ricky pulled out a chair from another table and put it by Deano's side so that the other Teds had to move around slightly.

"What a great venue," Deano said. "It seemed right that we meet with the Teddy Boy leaders of East London in this historical place. Besides that, I heard that they pour a good pint."

A few of the Teds laughed.

"I think that most of you will either know me or know of me. I'm Deano the Dog. Up until a few weeks ago we had just over seven hundred Teds from across London in our alliance, the Ted Army. My number two, Ricky and I, visited the leaders of the Teds in Islington, Tottenham, Clerkenwell, Finsbury Park, Haringey, Barnet and Enfield. Without exception they have all agreed to become an active part of the alliance. Each of those leaders, whether they have ten or forty in their gang will take a seat on the governing board and have the opportunity to run the alliance and build on it further. No one, and I do mean no one, interferes with day to day business, but if any one of those gangs in the alliance needs help, then we march on their enemies as one. Today we have just over twelve hundred Teds in the alliance and I'm hoping that we can increase that number to over sixteen hundred with the support of the Teds of East London.

One by one the leaders of the East London Teds nodded and agreed to join the alliance.

"I don't know about the rest of you, but I ain't following no thumb sucker from South of the river," Carly Thompson, the leader of the Mile End Teds said in an aggressive tone.

All eyes turned on Carly. He had the largest of all the gangs in East London with over fifty handy lads at his disposal. Carly had a vicious and violent reputation and had served time in Borstal twice for violent assaults.

"Carly, I don't give a toss about all this South and East London divide," Deano said firmly. "What I do care about is the love of Rock 'n' Roll music, the drape suit and all those that wear it."

The barman and a pretty young bar maid brought two large trays of drinks to the table.

"Thank you," Ricky said, putting two ten-pound notes on the table. Get yourselves a drink with us."

"We heard about the stunt your Ted Army pulled with that lot over in Fulham, but," Carly paused and pulled a switchblade out of his pocket. He pressed the button and a six-inch blade shot out and locked into place. "We don't scare so easily. I'll have it with you,

Ricky Turrell, or anybody else that fancies their chances." Carly turned and faced Deano head on. "We are the Mile End Teds, unlike some here, we're East London born and bred and proud of it. We stand alone."

Ricky sensed Deano was being pushed into a corner and that any Ted-on-Ted violence could destabilise and ruin the alliance. He took a sip of his lager and faced Carly.

"It's a shame that you can't see the bigger picture, Carly. Both Deano and I have the utmost respect for you and the Mile End Teds. As Deano's second in command, do you mind if I speak directly to, Mack, your number two?"

"You can say what you like," Carly said before leaning back in his chair.

"Good to meet you, Mack. It's always good to talk with an opposite number. I don't know about you, but I've always thought the role of a good, responsible, number two is to play the devil's advocate at times. Maybe challenge the leaders thinking on any given subject. Even if it's what we believe ourselves to be right, but just to put it out there for further consideration because sometimes these off the cuff decisions can have an impact on every member of the gang. I mean none of us would want to end up in the nick just because the leader thought it would be a good idea to storm a police station or kick the shit out of some copper on his night beat, right?"

Mack nodded.

"Allow me to lay this out for you. What kind of numbers do you have? Fifty teds?" Ricky said.

Mack Nodded, "Yeah, just over."

"Okay, so now imagine twelve hundred battle ready Teds. With fifty to a coach load that's twenty-four coach loads of drape wearing Teds and two thousand four hundred clenched fists ready to slaughter any perceived enemy at a moment's notice. What Deano and the alliance would like is for the Mile End Teds to leave here as friends and talk through this proposal. You lads would add great value to the Ted Army, so I'm truly hoping that we can find a way for this to work. Does that sound reasonable to you, Mack?" Ricky said as he reached for his pint.

"Carly is number one and under normal circumstances what he says goes, but on something as big as this I'm sure he wouldn't mind if we took some time to talk through your proposal with the greater good of the gang and Ted movement in mind," Mack said.

"You are a very fair and reasonable man," Ricky said. "So, if you lads don't mind, Deano has business with the newest additions to the alliance.

Carly stood up and pushed his chair over, shot both Deano and Ricky a menacing look as he strode off across the pub to the exit. Ricky held out his hand and Mack shook it.

"I look forward to hearing something positive from you soon. Here's my work number," Ricky said, handing Mack his business card. It read:

London Tyre Co.
Ricky Turrell
Managing Director
01 647 7684

"Yeah, we'll speak soon, Ricky. Deano mate," Mack said before turning and shaking his hand. "King of the Teds, it's been an honour."

Ricky waved the barman over to take another order.

"So what do you think?" Ricky muttered.

"It's lucky you spoke out when you did because I was all set to give that mouthy fucker twenty-four hours to disband, drop wearing the drape or face the consequences. Who does he think he is placing a blade on the table like that? I'd bury that piece of shit along with his blade," Deano hissed.

Ricky had a vision of Deano plunging Eddy Boyce's own blade deep into his chest before having him buried alive in Addington Woods.

"Yeah, I figured Carly was on thin ice which was why I spoke out mate. I just thought that Ted-on-Ted violence could really hurt the alliance," Ricky said.

"You did the right thing. So, not only have you built a reputation for being able to have a decent row but now you're a bloody diplomat too," Deano chuckled. "Maybe you'll be looking for my place one day."

"Nah, not for me thanks. I'm happy where I am," Ricky said.

"You might be right, Deano," Ricky thought. *"Maybe I will take your spot one day when the time is right."*

Deano took his seat at the head of the table and began to lay out how the alliance had been formed and what would be expected from all the gang leaders.

Chapter 25

Ricky arrived at the Arms early in the evening. It had been a good day at work and he wanted a couple of pints before going home.

"I can't believe the amount of nicking's happening around the estate," Ronnie said. "Some dirty low life is grassing, because there's no way the gavvers have done all this on their own."

"It's all old-school villains too," Ricky said.

"Those dirty slags will fit up anyone and everyone to clear the books," Ronnie said. "They would have the general public believe that the Met are greatest police force in the world and that they all act like Sherlock Holmes and Watson running around London solving crimes. When in reality they're mostly lying two faced bastards with a history of planting evidence or beating lesser men to confess to crimes they never did. All that fair play and innocent stuff is complete and utter bollocks, believe me Ricky. I've been banged up with blokes that were hundreds of miles away, with reliable witnesses, who still ended up getting weighed off based on the evidence of some corrupt copper. Your average man in the street would be horrified if they really knew how the boys in blue behaved out of sight in the cells where they beat the confessions out of people. Not quite the Dixon of Dock Green they would have us all believe,"

Ronnie handed Ricky a pint of Carlsberg lager.

"Cheers mate," Ricky said. "The grass needs to be found, that's for sure."

Ricky took his pint and sat over by the jukebox. It wasn't playing and the pub had only a few customers. Ricky took a sip and sat back in his chair.

"I thought that was you."

Ricky looked up to see Trudy, the local brass.

"How are you Trudy, do you want a drink?" Ricky said motioning the barman to bring over Trudy's usual drink.

"Yeah, sure, thank you," Trudy said, pulling out a chair and sitting down.

"I know something Ricky and I'm not sure what to do about it," Trudy whispered.

"Is it something you think I could help you with?" Ricky said.

"It's definitely something that I think you should know," Trudy said.

As the barman approached carrying her drink, she went quiet.

"Okay, this sounds pretty serious. What is it?" Ricky said, leaning forward and lowering his voice.

"It's Double Bubble," Trudy whispered.

"What about him?"

"I think he's a grass," Trudy whispered.

"A grass? What makes you think that?" Ricky said.

"Look, business hasn't been as good as it should be and I'm into Double Bubble for a few quid. I needed money for the rent, bills, food and that just until business picked up again," Trudy continued.

"And?"

"Well, I didn't think too much about it at first, but Double Bubble suggested that I work some of my debt off by, well, you know…?"

"What?"

"Going around to his place and… what, do I have to spell it out for you?"

"No, no of course not," Ricky said.

"Well he likes me to stay over so I have to do my business at night and then again in the morning. It's just his thing. Anyway a few months back, that copper, what's his name Detective Sergeant Ray White and the other copper came steaming through the door saying that they had business with Double Bubble and I was fucked off sharpish."

Trudy stopped to take a sip of her drink.

"I didn't think much of it at first. I mean he's a money lender with a dubious background so it's odds on that he's going to get a tug from the old bill sooner or later. Anyway, a couple of days later I was due to go back to Double Bubble's place when I heard the voices of those coppers coming out of his flat, so I quickly shot off and hid behind the wall by the lift. I heard the dopey one with him asking if he trusted Double Bubble and that DS White said that he hadn't steered them wrong so far. It didn't take a mastermind to put two and two together and I figured he must be the grass. Anyway, I went to his flat just as I'd promised and Double Bubble was really full of himself, you know? He didn't act like a guy that had just been turned over by the filth."

"Did he say anything to you?" Ricky whispered.

"What, are you joking or what? I just did what I was there to do. If he got the slightest inkling that I knew anything, my little girl would be growing up without her mum," Trudy said.

"Who else have you told?" Ricky asked harshly.

"No one! I've been walking around thinking what I should do for the last few days and then I thought I saw you come in here," Trudy said taking another sip of her drink. "What are you going to do?"

"Well first things first. Is this about you owing money and looking for a way not to pay it back?" Ricky said.

"Ricky, what do you take me for?" Trudy said.

"A clever woman that owes a money lender because her usual income has temporarily dried up," Ricky said.

"Well, all that is true, but I know what I heard, and I know what I saw and he's the grass that has been having all our friends and neighbours carted off by the old bill," Trudy said, raising her voice slightly.

"Alright, I believe you, but you've got to keep this to yourself, Trudy, because information like that could lead to serious stuff. You do know that, don't you?" Ricky said.

Trudy nodded her head.

"Right, what do you owe him?" Ricky said, reaching into his pocket.

"Sixty-five quid," Trudy said.

Ricky lowered his hands below the table, peeled off one hundred pounds and passed it over to her out of sight.

"This is for you to clear your debt and there's a little extra to keep your head above water. I will, in my own time, take care of the grass but you are not to say a dickie bird, alright?" Ricky said before sinking back into his chair.

"I won't say anything, cross my heart," Trudy said before swallowing the last of her drink.

"I hope you make the bastard pay," Trudy whispered as she got up to leave.

"Well, well Double Bubble, you slag, it looks like your days of informing are soon to be over," thought Ricky as he gulped down the remainder of his pint.

Ricky decided to give the second pint a miss and left the pub.

"Ricky!"

Ricky turned and saw his mum, Caroline, standing by the wall outside the community centre. He trotted over towards her.

"Hello Mum, what are you doing here?"

Caroline closed her eyes and shook her head slowly.

"What's up Mum, is it Dad?" Ricky said as he stroked her arm.

"It's nothing like that," Caroline said.

"Good," Ricky said, "but what's up? I can tell something isn't right…"

"I don't like to bother you with it," Caroline said.

"Mum," Ricky said firmly, "Just tell me what's up."

"Your dad lost his job. He was made redundant, and things have been tight. We used all our savings in the hope that your dad would get another job quickly. He's been pretty down about it and…"

"And what Mum?"

"When the savings ran out and the bills kept coming in, we didn't have any choice but to borrow money from Double Bubble," Caroline said.

"Why didn't you come to me?" Ricky said with a sigh.

"We haven't seen you in months and you know what your dad is like," Caroline said.

"Yeah, I do know what he's like, but he's still my dad and I would have helped," Ricky said.

"Double Bubble stopped your dad in the street yesterday and, well, he threatened him with violence. Your dad was quite shook up when he got home last night, which is why I'm here now. I was hoping to reason with him and ask for another few weeks to try and get ourselves sorted out," Caroline said.

"That fucking Double Bubble," Ricky said. "Sorry Mum, I didn't mean to swear."

"I've heard worse from your father," Caroline said with a chuckle.

"Here," Ricky said, pulling a large wad of money from his pocket and forcing it into Caroline's hand.

"Ricky that's far too much," Caroline said.

"Business has been good Mum, so take that and pay off what you owe to Double Bubble, any bills you've got and then fill your cupboard with food," Ricky said. "You can tell Dad it's an interest free loan if it makes him feel better but it's not Mum, alright? Look, here's my business card. If you need some money to tide you over until Dad is working again then call me, alright and I'll be there, okay?"

Caroline nodded.

"I need you to promise me that you'll call me, Mum or you'll have me worrying and I know you wouldn't want that," Ricky said.

Caroline nodded and tightened her hand around the wad of notes.

"I promise Ricky, and thank you," Caroline said.

Ricky held open his arms and gave his mum a tight squeeze.

"I love you Ricky," Caroline whispered.

"I love you too Mum," Ricky said. "I've got to go, but we'll catch up soon."

Ricky kissed his mum on the cheek and then raced over to his Rover and drove back to his flat in Carshalton Beeches.

"You are going to pay for this Double Bubble. I promise you that, sunshine, you're done!" Ricky thought.

Ricky had planned to have a night in to catch up on some book work and write out another batch of cash sales invoices so he could launder some more cash through the business. Instead, he showered, shaved and put on a grey drape suit with mustard coloured velvet collars, pocket tops and cuffs and ordered a taxi to take him to the Cadillac Club.

***

The taxi dropped him off right by the club's entrance. Ricky didn't stop to look up at the flashing lights as he normally did, but paid his entry fee and wandered through the club and upstairs to the VIP lounge where Cookie, Frank Allen's personal minder, welcomed him in.

"Hi Frank," Ricky said placing a large glass of malt whiskey on his table.

"Hello Ricky, I didn't know we had a meeting scheduled for tonight," Frank said before pouring the last drops of his drink into the new one.

"No, we haven't. I was wondering if you had the name of a good trustworthy Madame. I'm going to need a girl next door type brass that operates off the manor. Being able to act would be an advantage," Ricky said.

Frank chuckled and then reached for his pen and note pad and tore off a slip of paper. He wrote 'Fiona' and a telephone number.

"I'm not even going to ask you why," Frank said, handing him the piece of paper.

"It's just business," Ricky said.

"It always is," chuckled Frank.

"Cheers Frank. I need to see Sean and Denis, so I'll catch you later if that's okay," Ricky said.

"Of course it is," said Frank. "No problem with our bit of business is there?"

"Absolutely not," Ricky said.

"Good, I'll see you later then," Frank said.

Ricky found an empty table and motioned Sean and Denis, who were standing by the bar, over to join him.

"You alright lads?" Ricky said.

"Yeah, not bad," Sean said, "But business could always be better. Why, what have you got for us?"

Ricky told them about the opportunity to take a full truck load of tyres while the driver, who would be in on it, was eating breakfast at a café on the outskirts of London. Sean threw in a number which Ricky halved and they shook hands. Ricky went on to say that he was always in the market for new car tyres, inner tubes or good quality plant from fitting bays. He would take delivery at London Tyre Co and handed Sean a business card. Ricky stressed that whilst he would take everything they could get, the tyres couldn't be stolen locally. Sean shrugged his shoulders and said that they would take a wander down into the Kent Medway towns to check things out and get back to him within a few weeks.

Ricky used the phone behind the bar and called Fiona on the telephone number Frank had given him. When she answered Ricky explained that he was a friend of Frank's and that he had an unusual, but well-paid job that he'd like to discuss with her. Fiona was a little reluctant at first until Ricky said that he was at Cadillac Club in the VIP lounge right now and would ask Frank to come to the phone to vouch for him. Fiona gave him an address in Islington and agreed to meet him there at 11.00pm.

Chapter 26

"We deserve this," DS Ray White said. "I could do with a right good drink."

"Yeah, I can only stay until about nine Guv," DC Bernard Jacobs said.

"What, are you on a promise or something?" DS White said.

"No, nothing like that. I just said that I'd help her with things she needs to get sorted for the weekend Guv."

"You need to get your priorities right my son. We're making good, solid, progress with bringing down the more notorious elements of the Milton Road Estate and I reckon we're onto something bigger with Deano Derenzie and his number two Ricky Turrell. My money is they know a lot more than either of them are letting on about the missing skinhead, Eddy Boyce. He's out there somewhere pushing up daisies, and it's just good police work and time before we bring them down, Bernie. I don't know how, yet anyway, but there is a link here to Frank Allen. All my cop instincts tell me there's more and I will find out. Once this sniffer," DS White said, pointing to his nose, "Goes to work, there's no stopping me."

"Do you think Frank Allen is involved with the missing skinhead Guv?"

"Wake up Bernie and get with the program. Frank Allen is a major villain and hasn't had a single charge stick on him since the early 1950s. The man is made of Teflon because nothing sticks. He has eyes and ears everywhere and that includes our own factory," DS White said with a sneer.

"Do you think he has cops on his payroll?" DC Jacobs asked.

"It wouldn't surprise me, Bernie. When we pulled Deano Derenzie and Ricky Turrell in, no one, anywhere, was any the wiser and then just a few hours later we had that brief all over us again. The same one that turned up over that suicide when we pulled in that Teddy Boy. That can only mean one thing… we have dirty cops on the payroll. There's a connection here because I did some digging, and that brief is one of three that work for Frank Allen. Trust me, Bernie, there is a connection. I don't know what it is yet, but the clouds are parting, slowly but surely," DS White said, tapping the side of his head with his index finger.

"I still don't get what a missing Skinhead has to do with Frank Allen.," DC Jacobs said.

"Just trust me, it will all come together and, in the meantime, you can get your Guvnor a very large whiskey over ice," DS White said.

DC Jacobs pushed open the doors to The Swan pub.

The Swan pub was a regular haunt for police officers. DS White had been using it as his local ever since he joined the force. It was a place where police officers could chat about work and relax before going home. Thursday and Friday nights had been notorious for late night binge drinking as both junior and senior officers shook off the stress connected to the job. There was an unwritten rule abided to by all the police officers that used The Swan… 'What happened in the Swan… stayed in The Swan.'

"Harry, can we have two extremely large whiskeys and put them on Bernie's slate," DS White said.

"Coming right up lads," Harry, the landlord said.

"Do you ever regret leaving the force Harry?" DC Jacobs asked.

"No, not me. I had my boots filled back in the early sixties. Those were good days, chasing around after real criminals and not so much of the paper work you boys get these days," Harry said.

"And it's only going to get worse," DS White said. "You've got to get as high as you can in the shortest time possible to avoid the mess that's coming. That's my plan Harry. I want to be Chief Inspector in five to six years and then ride the job out behind a desk until I collect my pension."

"Sounds like a plan to me," Harry said as he placed two large whiskeys on the bar.

"It looks like another busy Thursday is on the cards," DS White said. "Are we alright for a late one? I've got a right thirst on."

Harry winked and moved down the bar to serve another customer.

***

"Hello Roger, what are you doing here? I thought you'd been transferred up town," DS White said.

"I was, but was called back to tie up some loose ends on an old case," Roger said.

"You want a drink?" DS White said.

"Cheers Ray, I'll have a large scotch," Roger said.

"Harry, when you're ready mate. Same again and one for Roger," DS White said.

"I bumped into one of our old lot the other day," Roger said.

"Yeah, who was that then?"

"He was uniform, good lad with potential. A bit head strong but then the most effective coppers are," Roger said. "Kevin, you must remember him. He came in here a lot until he got on the firm with some bird. Michelle, I think her name was. Yeah, he would rattle on about her in here all the time. Saying how they were made for each other and were getting married and all that. Got on your wick after a bit, but he was alright. Well, it did come as a bit of a surprise when some queer bashers turned his place over and gave him a right good hiding. That poor bugger was in hospital for weeks. They broke his jaw and ribs, and knocked out a couple of teeth. Vicious little bastards, we never did catch them. We pulled in the usual Skinhead suspects from the Bedford Estate but couldn't come up with anything that we could make stick. I have to say I never had him down for batting for the other side what with this bird of his."

"I remember hearing about that," DS White said. "Nasty business."

"Didn't he leave the force?" DC Jacobs said.

"I don't think he had much of a choice," Roger said. "They spray painted his wall with 'Queer' so everyone saw it and you know what it's like. The word went around like wildfire. One of the last things he told me was he was having some trouble with a Teddy Boy; you know those lads on the Milton Road Estate. Apparently, this lad had made a hit on his girl. He wasn't best pleased."

"Really?" DS White said. "Did he give a name?"

"I can't remember to be honest," Roger said.

"Was it Deano Derenzie or Ricky Turrell?"

"The name Ricky rings a bell, but I wouldn't swear to it. He just said some Teddy Boy from the Estate," Roger said.

"Where did you see him? Did you get an address?" DS White asked.

"I bumped into him on Waterloo Station. He was travelling to see family in Portsmouth or something. I tried to make conversation, but he wanted to be off. You can tell these things, can't you? Probably a bit embarrassed by it all I suspect. What's your interest then, Ray?"

"I've got an on-going investigation and the names Deano Derenzie and Ricky Turrell just keep coming up," DS White said.

"Well, if I see or hear from him Ray, I'll get some contact details," Roger said.

"Yeah, you do that please Roger, cheers," DS White said.

"Here Bernie what are you like for pub games?" Roger asked.

"I've never played any," DC Jacobs said.

Roger turned and winked slyly at DS White.

"First things first, we need a few more of these," Roger said, holding up his empty glass.

"You'll like this, Bernie. Roger was the wooden spoon champion. It'd be good to see someone take his crown," DS White said.

"What, you have championships?" DC Jacobs said.

"We certainly have, and Roger was unbeaten. He came close to losing to me a few years back, before you were transferred here Bernie, but he managed to hold on to that prestigious title."

Harry put-six double whiskeys on the bar along with two large wooden spoons.

The three men took a glass each, clinked glasses and cheered each other. Both DS White and Roger sank theirs in one gulp. DC Jacobs watched as their glasses emptied and then, reluctantly, did the same. DS White let out a cheer as the last of Bernie's drink disappeared down his throat. Roger patted him on the back.

"I have a feeling you're going to be some adversary," Roger said.

"He has the all the makings of a champion," DS White said.

"Right, so how do we do this?" DC Jacobs asked.

"Watch and learn my son," DS White said.

Roger handed Bernie a wooden spoon.

"What you do is just place the end of the spoon in your mouth, like so," Roger said.

DC Jacobs copied him.

"Then we take turns to hit each other over the head with just our head and neck movement," Roger said.

"Okay," DC Jacobs said.

"You go first Bernie," Roger said.

Bernie leant forward so that he was in good striking distance. With the wooden spoon fixed firmly between his teeth he tipped his head back and then lunged forward so it tapped Roger on the head.

"Not bad," Roger said.

Drinkers from around the pub began to circle around the pair. Harry smiled and handed DS White a third wooden spoon which he held behind his back.

"Right, my go," Roger said through clenched teeth.

DC Jacobs removed the spoon from his mouth and leaned forward. Roger tipped his head and lunged forward, stopping short of striking DC Jacob's head. DS White, sitting behind DC Jacobs and out of sight, raised the wooden spoon above his head and struck Bernie.

"Argh!" DC Jacobs yelled out.

The growing crowd let out a laugh.

"Right, your go," Roger said. "Remember it's all in the head and neck movement."

Roger removed his spoon and leaned forward. DC Jacobs put the wooden spoon back into his mouth, tipped his head back and lunged forward again, gently tapping Roger on the head. The lads in the pub let out a unanimous cheer.

"You're getting the hang of it," Roger said as he put the wooden spoon back between his teeth.

DC Jacobs took a quick swig of his whiskey and then reluctantly leaned forward. Once again Roger tipped his head back and lunged forward, stopping just short of Bernie's head. DS White held the spoon above his head and then sent it crashing down. DC Jacobs let out a yell and rubbed his head frantically.

"That bloody hurt!" DC Jacobs said.

The crowd let out a boozy, laddish, cheer as DS White delivered the mighty blow.

"It's your go Bernie. Now try to really give it some. I can take it," Roger said as he leant forward on his bar stool.

DC Jacobs stopped rubbing his head and put the wooden spoon back between his teeth. With a determined grip between his teeth, he rocked his head and neck back and then lunged forward. The spoon gently tapped Roger on the head. The crowd in the pub let out a cheer.

"You're definitely getting there," Roger said. "My go."

DC Jacobs removed the spoon from his mouth and took another quick swig of his drink before leaning forward, ready for Roger to strike. Roger leaned as far back as he could and bolted forward, stopping just short of DC Jacob's head again. DS White had raised the spoon well above his head and slammed it down with all the force he could muster.

CRACK!

"Fuck, fuck, fuck!" DC Jacobs yelled out, holding his head with both hands. "That bloody hurt!"

Everyone in the pub was laughing out loud and cheering the two men on.

"I think you might need some practice," Roger said as he put his wooden spoon on the bar.

Harry quickly took DS White's spoon before collecting the other two.

"You did well for a first time," Roger said. "You've definitely got the right kind of moves. I could really feel that last blow."

"Yeah, like a fly landing on your head," DS White said as he wiped the tears of laughter from his eyes. "As the loser, Bernie, you have to get the next round of drinks."

"Same again Harry," DC Jacobs said, still rubbing his sore head.

DS White spotted a beautiful woman in the far corner of the bar. She was in her late twenties with moon-gleam golden hair that toppled over her shoulders. Even from that distance he could clearly make out her pert little nose and blossom-pink lips. The woman looked over at DS White, smiled briefly, and then looked back at her drink.

"Here, Harry who is the bird?" DS White asked.

Harry looked over at the girl and shook his head. "I don't know, Ray. She's had the same gin and tonic now for well over an hour.

"Give us a large G & T would you Harry, and another of these," DS White said.

"What do you think of the bird in the corner?" DS White said.

"Very nice," Roger said. "I wouldn't mind some of that."

"She looks nice Guv," DC Jacobs said.

"I'm going to pull that," DS White said.

"Yeah, course you are," Roger said.

"Just watch the master go to work," DS White said as he took both drinks from the bar, winked, and walked over to the table where the pretty blonde sat.

"Hello darling. I hope you don't mind but I saw you sitting alone and thought I'd get you a drink," DS White said.

The woman looked up, fluttered her eyelashes and smiled.

"That was very thoughtful," the woman said. "That was very funny, what you were doing to your friend."

"It's good to let yourself go occasionally and have a good time. Sorry, my name is Ray, Ray White and you are?"

"Charlotte It's nice to meet you Ray," Charlotte said with a warm smile. "Please, take a seat."

"Don't mind if I do," DS White said as he pulled out the chair and sat down. "So, what brings a pretty girl like you to this den of inequity?"

"Well I was supposed to be meeting a friend, but it looks like he's stood me up," Charlotte said.

"Well that's his loss," DS White said.

Charlotte beamed.

"Do all you men work together?" Charlotte asked, looking over at the crowd of men laughing and joking around the bar.

"Yes, well sort of. We're all police officers," DS White said.

"Oh, wow, what an interesting job," Charlotte said.

DS White looked down at her tapered waist and perfectly formed breasts and then turned back to DC Jacobs and Roger. He pouted his lips and winked. They both raised their glasses.

"I think your friends are calling you back," Charlotte said, looking over his shoulder.

"Well I'd much rather be in the company of a beautiful woman than two hairy arsed coppers," DS White said.

"Do you drive a police car with the lights and sirens?" Charlotte asked.

"No, no," DS White said. "I'm a Detective Sergeant sweetheart, a plain clothes officer. I'm only interested in taking down major villains."

"That must be so exciting! You mean big villains like the Kray Twins?" Charlotte said leaning towards him.

"Well, the Krays were in a different part of London to me back in sixties," DS White said.

Charlotte leaned back in her chair and took a sip of her drink.

"But I did get to meet them," DS Ray White said, fearing he was losing Charlotte's attention.

"Yeah, me and a few of the lads had to go and interview Ron about an unsolved crime," DS White said.

"Really," Charlotte said, leaning back towards him.

"Yeah, I had him in the interview room and really laid into him about clearing up this crime that was still sitting on the books," DS White said softly.

"What did he say?" Charlotte asked.

"Nothing at first but then, like all criminals, he buckled and just spilled the beans like they all do," DS White said. "He just said, 'Ray, I wish it had been you that nicked me'.

"So he really respected you then, Ray?" Charlotte said.

"Well, you know…" DS White said, shrugging his shoulders.

"You must be a very good police officer Ray," Charlotte said.

"I've been at this game a long time, Charlotte. You have to keep the streets clean of low lives and villains for normal people like you sweetheart," DS White said.

"Well on behalf of the general public Ray, thank you," Charlotte said with a broad smile.

"You, darling, are very welcome," DS White said.

"It must be very frustrating sometimes though," Charlotte said softly. "I mean if you know someone has committed a crime, but you just can't prove it."

"I always get my man," DS Ray White said.

"But what if they have just covered their tracks too well," Charlotte said.

"If we know they did it but can't get them bang to rights, I'll make the crime fit. I mean if you can't get them on one crime, then you get them on another. It's all part of the cops and robbers thing. They, that's the villains, understand that just as we do," DS White.

"That's not right though, is it?" Charlotte said, uncrossing and crossing her legs.

DS White caught a glimpse of her stocking tops. He cleared his throat before answering.

"It's better that these menaces to society are banged up, darling, so that normal people can go about their daily business without the fear of being robbed, beaten up or," DS White said, casting his eyes over Charlotte's shapely figure, "worse."

"Tell me Ray, are you married?"

"Me? No, are you?"

"No, not me. I've had a few boyfriends but nothing serious," Charlotte said.

"So, tell me Charlotte, what does a beautiful girl like you look for in a man?"

"I went out with a fireman once, he was fun. Then there was this sailor, but he wasn't around that much, you know, what with travelling overseas for long periods," Charlotte said.

"You like a man in a uniform then," DS Ray White said.

"Doesn't everyone?" beamed Charlotte. "I was seeing this policeman, but we kind of split up and it was me that asked to meet him here tonight."

"So it was a copper that stood you up. That's just plain rude," DS White said. "What was it, the long hours at work that caused the problem?"

"No, nothing like that," Charlotte said. "Our problem was more personal."

DS White's ears pricked up.

"Can I ask what it was? You can trust me, I am a policeman after all," DS Ray White said.

Charlotte became a little flushed and lowered her voice.

"You promise not to tell anyone?" Charlotte said, lowering her voice.

"Cross my heart," DS White said running his finger across his chest in the shape of a cross.

"I like uniforms, Ray," Charlotte said. "You know,"

"What, you like to dress up?" DS White said.

"No, silly," Charlotte chuckled. "I like to see men in their uniforms. Well, part of their uniform."

"Right, okay," DS White said.

"Oh, have I said something wrong, Ray?"

"No, no, I just think that it's very liberating of you to know what you like and what you want," DS White said.

"I do know what I like Ray, and in these modern times I think it's okay for a girl to like sex and not only that, but to have the kind of sex she wants and enjoys. It is 1975 after all!" Charlotte said.

"Good for you," DS White said dropping his hand below the table to adjust his trousers. "It's refreshing to come across an open-minded young woman."

"Here Guv, it's well after ten and I'm already late so I'm going to get off, alright?" DC Jacobs said.

"Yeah, right Bernie. I'll see you back at the factory in the morning," DS White said. "Here, wait a minute."

DS White stood up and stepped around the table.

"Just a minute sweetheart," DS White said as he led Bernie a few feet away and out of earshot.

"What's up Guv?" DC Jacobs said.

"I need you to do me a favour," DS White whispered as he placed his arm around DC Jacobs' shoulders.

"I think I'm right in here Bernie. She's a right little sort. I need you to phone the enemy and tell her I'm on an all-night stake out. We're following some major villains, alright?" DS White said.

DC Jacobs turned his head to look at Charlotte. She smiled.

"I'm not happy about lying to your wife Guv," DC Jacobs said.

"Come on Bernie. Listen, right, opportunities to shag a right good-looking sort like that don't come along every day, so give me a break and just make the call Bernie," DS White pleaded.

"Alright Guv, I'll make the call but I ain't happy about it."

"That's the spirit Bernie," DS White said. "Ask Harry to send over a couple more drinks on your way out"

DC Jacobs tutted loudly and stomped off towards the bar.

"Is everything alright?" Charlotte asked.

"Yeah, there was some business that needed to be taken care of and as his superior officer I handed him the task," DS White said.

"He didn't look too happy," Charlotte said.

"I told him that I can't always be around to hold his hand and if he wants to wear the big boy's pants like me, he has to step up and just get the job done," DS White said.

Harry put a tray of drinks on the table. "Shall I stick this on your tab, Ray?"

"Cheers Harry," DS White said, handing a drink to Charlotte.

"Do you fancy going on to a club or something after this?" DS White said.

"Not really," Charlotte said.

"Oh, oh okay," DS White said.

"I don't live far from here; we could have a night cap back at my place or a coffee. That's if you want to," Charlotte said.

"Yeah, yeah, that would be great. I'd love a night cap back at yours," DS White said.

"I have whiskey," Charlotte said.

"You never cease to amaze me," DS White said.

"Come on then," Charlotte said.

DS White followed Charlotte across the bar towards the exit.

"Harry, I'll be in tomorrow night to sort out my tab," DS White said as he passed the bar.

Once DS White stepped out of the pub and into the fresh night air, he stopped momentarily and took a deep breath.

"There's nothing like London air," DS White said. "It's the greatest city on the planet."

Charlotte waved a black taxi cab down and they both got in.

"Where too, treacle?" the driver asked.

Charlotte gave him an address while DS White sat back in the seat and closed his eyes.

"Are you okay, Ray? You look a bit peaky," Charlotte said.

"I'm tip top darling. Never better," DS White slurred.

"Maybe just the one too many," Charlotte chuckled.

The taxi driver drove across town and within a few minutes stopped outside a block of private apartments.

"This is nice sweetheart. You must be doing alright for yourself," DS White said as he staggered out of the cab and handed the driver two one-pound notes. "Keep the change mate."

"I like it," Charlotte said.

DS White followed her up the pathway and into the building. The lights automatically came on as they climbed the stairs to the second floor. Charlotte took a set of keys from her bag and opened the front door.

"Home sweet home," she said closing the front door behind them. "Go through to the lounge and I'll fix us both a drink.

DS White staggered down the hallway and stepped into the lounge. It was decorated with beige wallpaper and had floor to ceiling brown curtains at the window. The suite was a brown leather chesterfield with matching armchairs.

"This is a lovely place you've got here," DS White said.

"Thank you, Ray," Charlotte called out from another room.

"How does she afford all this?" DS White muttered to himself.

"Ray, why don't you come and join me in here," Charlotte called out.

"Yes!" DS White whispered and punched the air.

DS White walked gingerly up the hallway and stopped by the bedroom. He paused at the door and looked in. The lights were dimmed and at each corner of the large double bed were rope restraints.

"This looks very kinky," DS White said.

Charlotte was in the en-suite with the door closed.

"Just how I like it, Ray. There's a drink on the bedside cabinet for you," Charlotte called. "Make yourself... comfortable."

DS White slipped his jacket and shirt off. He undid his trousers and ran them down his legs. Dressed in just white underwear, black socks and shoes he stood in front of the mirror faced wardrobe and admired his physique.

"You've still got it my son," he muttered to himself and then took a long swig of the whiskey on the bedside cabinet.

He slipped off his shoes, socks and underwear and slid on to the large bed. The en-suite bathroom door opened, and Charlotte stepped out wearing a sexy skin-tight black leather mini dress that amplified her curves. Her thigh high black leather stiletto boots left just a hint of flesh. Charlotte had styled her blonde hair into a bun on top of her head. She wore a tight leather eye mask. In her left hand she carried a black leather horse whip

DS White's jaw dropped as he muttered 'Fucking hell' to himself.

"I am Mistress Jezebel, Mr Policeman."

"You look amazing," DS White said.

"You," Charlotte said, raising her voice and slapping the whip across the top of the dressing table, "Call me mistress. Do you understand?"

"Yes Mistress," DS White said.

"Good, because policeman or not, in this place I am Mistress, do you understand me?"

"Yes Mistress," DS White said.

"Place your feet and hands inside the rope restraints," Charlotte commanded.

"Err…"

"Do it now!" Charlotte yelled.

"Yes Mistress," DS White said as he quickly slipped his feet and hands through the thick rope.

Charlotte strutted around the bed and pulled on the rope, so his feet were secured and held firmly. She then ran the whip along DS White's naked body and stopped so she could secure booth his hands.

"Now Mr Policeman, you want me, don't you?"

"Yes Mistress," DS White answered meekly.

Charlotte reached up and opened the door at the top of the wardrobe and took out a police constable's helmet. She held it up for him to see and then ran her tongue around the silver badge before strolling back and placing it on DS White's head.

"You're a naughty policeman, aren't you?" Charlotte said.

"Yes Mistress," DS White said.

"You like to catch criminals in any way you can, don't you Mr Policeman even if you have to bend the rules?"

"Yes Mistress."

"Well, you better start working harder, Mr Policeman, because I have no time for slackers."

"I will Mistress."

Charlotte leant forward and kissed him gently on the head, slid slowly onto the bed and over DS White. Her tight black mini dress rode up as she straddled his manhood.

"You are going to work hard, aren't you Mr Policeman?"

"Yes Mistress."

DS White spent the night with Charlotte and was kept busy until the early hours, then, utterly exhausted, he fell into a deep sleep. While he slept, Charlotte gathered up the recording equipment she had been wearing at the pub and left the flat with a professional photographer who had taken pictures throughout their liaison from the wardrobe opposite the bed. The final picture was of DS White, still tightly bound and fast asleep wearing the police constable's helmet. At just after 10.00am Charlotte met with Ricky at a café and handed him the tapes, the developed photographs and the police constable's helmet that Lee had taken during the street battle on Bedford Estate.

"Nice job Fiona, or is it Charlotte? Well done," Ricky said as he handed her an envelope full of money.

"I don't normally do this kind of stuff," Fiona said.

"I know, which is why I've put a little more in there than was agreed. You'll be able to return to North London a few quid richer," Ricky said.

"I don't want any come backs," Fiona said.

"There will be no come backs Fiona. He's well and truly done. No one will be hearing any more from Detective Sergeant Ray White. His days in the force are over," Ricky said.

Chapter 27

At London Tyre Co business was booming, with customers in every bay and several cars waiting outside for new tyres, puncture repairs and wheel balancing.

"Perfect," Ricky thought. *"Just as I planned. Step one complete."*

The phone rang on Ricky's desk. After two rings he picked it up.

Ricky: London Tyre Company, Ricky speaking, how can I help you?

Male Voice: Ricky Turrell?

Ricky: That's me, who wants to know?

Male Voice: Hello mate, its Mack from the Mile End Teds.

Ricky: Hello Mack, how are you mate?"

Mack: I'm fine mate, but things are not that good my end.

Ricky: Why, what's up?

Mack: I've tried talking with Carly and he's got a right hard on for you and Deano.

Ricky: Really.

Mack: Every time I bring up joining the alliance and the Ted Army, he just goes right off on one talking about how he's going to bring you lot down to size.

Ricky: What about the rest of the gang?

Mack: Most of us admire and respect Deano; he's the number one. We've all heard about his exploits and knowing how big the alliance has got. I'd say that 90% of my Teds, given a choice, would sign up tomorrow.

Ricky: Look that's good to know.

Mack: I'm not sure how we're going to make this work.

Ricky: You'll have to leave with this with me awhile, alright?

Mack: Sure, I just don't want to get into something that none of us really want. No one here is going to stand up to Carly. He'll just cut them. It wouldn't be the first time.

Ricky: Are the lads loyal to you, Mack?

There was a moment's silence.

Mack: I believe so.

Ricky: Then our problem isn't with the Mile End Teds, it's with a maverick who has a history of turning on his own lads, right?

Mack: Yeah, I suppose so. Are you going to sort this with Deano?

Ricky: I need a few days to get my thoughts together. Deano doesn't take bad news too well and I need to make sure he understands that this has nothing to do with you or the vast majority of the Mile End Teds. Leave it with me, Mack, and don't worry, we will get this sorted.

Mack: Alright Ricky, good to speak with you mate. Here's my home number so you can get hold of me: 01 377 6790.

Ricky scribbled it down in his daybook.

Ricky: Cheers Mack, take care and we'll speak soon.

Ricky hung up the phone.

"That Carly must be off his rocker thinking he's going to take on me, Deano and the rest of the alliance," Ricky thought. *"He will pay with pain, broken bones and blood and you, Mack, will take his place and run the Mile End Teds."*

***

It had been a record-breaking day for the London Tyre Company. Barry, the new manager, had brought in additional trade business and the marketing campaign, aided by knocked off tyres from Justin, had brought in profitable retail work. Barry left just after 6.30pm and Ricky stayed on as he was expecting company. He cast his eye over his daybook and slowly ticked off all the things that he set himself to do that day and then added more actions.

It was just after 7.15pm when there was a knock at the office door. Ricky sauntered over and opened it.

"Alright, Terry, Steve," Ricky said.

The two lads both nodded and entered the shop.

"Do you want a drink or something?" Ricky said.

Terry and Steve both shook their heads.

"What's up Ricky?" said Terry. "This is all a bit cloak and dagger, isn't it?"

"I've called you here for a reason. It's not safe for us to talk openly at the Arms," Ricky said.

"What do you mean not safe?"

"We have a grass on the Estate," Ricky said.

"We know that Ricky. We've all sat back and watched people we know get carted off by the gavvers and there is no way on this green earth that the old bill did it without any help from someone close. Someone in the know," Terry said.

"Precisely Terry, and I know who it is," Ricky said.

"Who?" Steve said.

"Double Bubble," Ricky said.

"Bollocks is it," Terry said with a look of complete surprise.

"I'm afraid so Terry," Ricky said.

"I don't like the fella but a grass? He's an old-school villain! I just don't see it," Terry said, shaking his head.

"You have to stand on me, it is him," Ricky said.

"I'm not doubting you Ricky, but what makes you so sure?" Terry persisted.

"You know Trudy, the brass?" Ricky said.

"Yeah," Terry replied, but my brother knows her better.

"Shut it," Steve said.

Terry laughed. "What about her?"

"Well, she's been working off some loans to Double Bubble and after an overnight session Detective Ray White and his side kick turn up at his flat giving it the big one about having business with Double Bubble and according to her it was shortly after that when people started getting collared from around the estate. Look, I don't have a bloody confession, but I do have solid information and we've seen enough people getting carted off. I can't sit back and do nothing knowing what I know," Ricky said firmly.

"So what do you want to do?" Terry asked.

"This isn't Ted business, so I've not involved Deano or any of the others. This is about looking out for people on the Estate and taking care of business if we have a known grass."

"Okay," Terry said with a manic grin.

"Yeah, okay," Steve said as he slowly nodded his head.

"Okay?" Ricky said.

"You want us to pay a visit to Double Bubble, right?"

"I want the three of us to pay the grass a visit. He needs to be served up good and proper," Ricky said.

"When?" Terry asked.

"Tonight," Ricky said.

Terry glanced over at Steve and they both nodded.

"Ricky, tell us straight. Do you work with Frank Allen?"

Ricky paused for a few moments and then took a breath.

"Under normal circumstances this is not a thing that I would openly talk about. I'm sure that you both understand that," Ricky said.

Both Terry and Steve nodded.

"I don't work directly for Frank Allen, but we do work together. You might say that we share similar business interests," Ricky confirmed "Why would you ask?"

"We want to move up, Ricky. Neither of us have done a proper day's work since leaving the Army. We look around us and it's people like you that are making moves and getting ahead. I don't want a nine to five dead end job with some old sort indoors giving me grief for having one pint too many before coming home. We have skills, Ricky, you've seen how Eddy Boyce was dealt with. He was not the first, and I'm pretty damn sure that he won't be our last. All we're asking is that when opportunities present themselves to make a few quid then remember us. Will you do that Ricky?" Terry said.

"Have either of you ever nicked a motor before?" Ricky asked.

"I did as a kid," Steve said.

"Right, I can give you a start, if you want it. I need stolen motors weekly. Nothing too fancy, just new Cortinas, Granadas and Escorts, you know the kind of stuff. It has to be between a year and two years old. I pay a standard unit rate regardless of the car's make and model. I'll give you the spec, you know colour, XL, GXL or Ghia and you take that motor and bring it here after dark. I will pay you out straight away, there's no hanging about.

"That sounds interesting. Are you up for that Steve?" Terry said as he turned to his brother.

Steve nodded. "No problem, we can learn on the job."

"What kind of numbers are we talking?" Terry said.

"I can start you on Monday with at least five motors, all Fords. That's five hundred quid," Ricky said.

Terry's eyes lit up.

"We're in!" Terry said.

"Good, now once you've got some experience under your belt, I can move you on to more upmarket motors, like Jags, Daimlers and the odd Porsche. It pays the same money but its more volume and good, regular, business, week in and week out," Ricky said. "If you're in then you're in, because, as you know, Frank Allen is not the kind of bloke to mess around," Ricky said seriously.

"Yeah, we're in," Terry said.

"Now if something comes up that involves violence, then we talk about money depending on the scale of the job. Right now there's nothing, and this thing with Double Bubble is about doing the right thing for those on the Estate by taking out a grass who is responsible for having our own people put away."

Terry and Steve both nodded in agreement.

Ricky walked over to the filing cabinet and took out three new sets of plain overalls and three black balaclavas. He put them on the desk.

Terry picked up one of the black balaclavas and pulled it over his head. It left only his eyes on show.

"Nice, very nice," Steve said.

"We don't want any backlash. This is a quick in and out job. We hurt him and leave," Ricky said. "Do you have any tools with you?"

Terry pulled out a short rubber covered steel bar and grinned.

"This is my favourite cosh," Terry said.

"So you have a favourite," Ricky chuckled.

"I've got mine too," Steve said with a broad smile. "It's like my American Express card... I never leave home without it."

All three of the lads laughed. Ricky checked the time on his watch.

"Shall we make a move?" Ricky said, rising from his chair.

"Sure, we'll follow you back to the Estate," Terry said, taking two sets of overalls and a balaclava from the desk.

Ricky closed and locked the door to the office.

"That's another tick off the 'to do' list," Ricky thought. *"I'm gutted that it's come to this Neil, but it's all about words and actions and what I witnessed at the salvage yard was a bloke that's pussy whipped, and I'm not putting my business at risk over some bird that did the dirty on my weak mate. I'll keep using Neil, but Terry and Steve will become my primary suppliers of hot motors."*

Ricky had brought his Rover P5B in to work and parked up the Zodiac MK2 in one of his lock- up garages. The car attracted attention and when he was working, the last thing he wanted was people remembering that they saw his motor in a particular vicinity. The Rover, Ricky had concluded, fitted in easily and nobody, not even the old bill, looked at it.

Ricky parked the Rover outside the Milton Arms pub. Terry and Steve parked behind him in a blue mini. He slipped the overalls over his clothes, took his brass knuckle duster out of the glove box and slid it into his side pocket. Ricky rolled the balaclava up tight and held it in his hand. He got out of the car and walked slowly over to Terry and Steve.

"Right let's do this," Ricky hissed.

The three lads walked around the back of the precinct and on to Double Bubble's block of flats. They bounded up the stairs and stood together outside Double Bubble's front door. The kitchen light was on. Ricky took a quick peek and saw a figure leave and turn out the light.

Ricky took a couple of steps back until he was up against the concrete barrier. He took a deep breath, turned sideways and charged forward. His shoulder connected with the front door and sent it flying open. Terry and Steve raced down the dimly lit hallway towards the front room holding out their coshes, ready to strike.

Terry was the first to reach the lounge. Double Bubble was up and off the sofa with both fists clenched. Terry swung the cosh and missed. It flew just inches past Double Bubble's face. A single punch sent Terry flying backwards. He crashed into the television set and fell to the floor. Steve ducked as a giant fist flew towards him. He spun back around and smashed the cosh over Double Bubble's left arm. The crack of broken bone resonated around the room followed by screams of pain.

"I'll fucking do you the lot of you!" Double Bubble yelled as he cradled his arm momentarily, and then turned quickly towards his dinner plate still on the sofa. He grabbed the large steak knife.

"I'll fucking cut you to ribbons," Double Bubble screamed, thrusting the steak knife back and forth.

Terry got up off the floor. The three men stood around Double Bubble as he waved the knife frantically from left to right. Steve broke the stand-off by lunging forward and swinging his cosh. Double Bubble side stepped him, turned and ran the steak knife down his upper arm. The blade sliced through the cotton overalls and deep into his arm. Ricky saw the opening and fired his right fist.

CRACK!

Double Bubble yelled again as the knuckle duster broke and splintered bone in his face. Terry swung his cosh and caught Double Bubble off guard. He dropped the steak knife.

CRACK!

Steve, now on one knee, threw himself forward and smashed Double Bubble across his left knee.

CRACK!

His leg collapsed from under him. The giant of a man fell clumsily to the floor.

"I will have you!" Double Bubble muttered. "Mark my words I will have each and every one of you!"

Ricky bent down and let him have a powerful right hander. There was a sickening crack as his nose shattered. Blood shot from his nostrils and onto Ricky's hand. Ricky hit him again and then again, until Double Bubble lay motionless on the floor.

"Pass me the blade," Ricky called as he sat astride Double Bubble's motionless body.

Terry didn't hesitate to hand Ricky the blade. Ricky threw his head back and took a deep breath, then grabbed Double Bubble around the throat with his left hand. Taking the knife firmly in his right hand, Ricky carved the word 'GRASS' into Double Bubble's forehead.

"That's him done now," Ricky said. "His days of money lending are over. How's your arm?"

Steve cradled his left arm and then nodded.

"It's fine," Steve said.

"Do you think you'll need stitches?"

"Nah, I'd rather have the scar," Steve said.

"Here," Terry said as he reached for an object on the coffee table, "This is Double Bubble's black book on who owes what."

Terry handed Ricky the book. He looked through it briefly and then put it into his pocket.

"We need to a make a move," Terry said when he spotted a couple of dark figures standing on the landing by the front door.

The three lads checked around the room quickly and then bolted up the corridor and out onto the landing into the cold night air, down the dimly lit concrete stairway and into the night.

Ricky took the lads' overalls and balaclavas, put them into a metal dustbin at the back of the garages and poured petrol over them. He threw a match in and watched as the flames spread and leapt up over the top of the dustbin. Ricky wiped the blood from his hand with a tissue and threw it onto the fire, then brushed himself down and strolled back around to the Milton Arms. He stopped outside the pub entrance as an ambulance, with sirens and lights blazing, raced past.

"You're a grass and you threatened my mum," Ricky thought, *"and now you've paid the price."*

Ricky patted Double Bubble's black book through his trouser pocket, smiled and then stepped into the pub. It was packed with regulars. The sound of *"I Can't Give You Anything (But My Love)'* by The Stylistics was playing. He saw Kaz and Donna down by the jukebox, raised his head and strolled over to the bar, acknowledging people with 'alright' and nods.

"Alright Ronnie," Ricky said. "Can I have a pint of Carling please mate?"

Ronnie nodded and placed a straight pint glass under the draught tap.

"I've been here all night tonight, is that alright with you?" Ricky asked as he reached for the pint.

"That must be your fourth pint then," Ronnie replied with a mischievous grin. "You don't want to be driving."

Ricky winked and looked down the bar to where Deano, Lee, Terry and Steve were sitting.

Chapter 28

Ricky invited Terry and Steve parker to join him for a drink in the VIP Lounge at the Cadillac Club. Ricky explained to Cookie, who was managing the door, that Terry and Steve Parker were good friends and business associates and would be regular visitors. Cookie smiled and beckoned them in. Ricky led the brothers to the bar where Doreen was standing.

"I'll get Doreen's drink and I'll have a couple of malt whiskies please," Ricky said to the barman.

"That's very good of you," Doreen said. "If I wasn't old enough to be your mum, I might think you were trying to chat me up,"

Doreen giggled.

"What can I say Doreen, I've always had a thing for the mature lady," Ricky said. "Do you know Terry and Steve Parker, Doreen?" Ricky asked.

Doreen turned to face the two lads.

"Oh my," Doreen said looking the lads up and down and then placing her finger on her lip. "What is it about Teddy Boys that just wants to bring out the worst in me?"

Doreen shook both their hands.

"I've seen you at the Milton Arms with Deano and of course, Ricky. In fact, and this will be showing my age, but I think I know your mum," Doreen said.

"Do you mind if I just go and have a word with Frank? He's expecting me," Ricky said.

"Not at all, you bugger off and leave me to find out all these lads' darkest and deepest secrets," Doreen chuckled.

"Doreen, sweetheart, you'd turn grey if you knew just half of them," Ricky thought as he approached Frank Allen's table.

***

Take a seat Ricky," Frank said as he motioned him to sit down, "and have a drink with me."

"Cheers Frank," Ricky said.

Frank motioned the barman to bring over two large malt whiskeys.

"You have been very busy tidying things up. I'm impressed," Frank said with an admiring nod of his head, "Very impressed!"

"How do you mean?" Ricky said.

"You don't need to be coy around me. You had a problem with an active grass on your estate, but you sniffed him out and took care of business. It was the right thing to do, well done."

"You know about that?" Ricky said.

"If there was anybody on Milton Road estate to suss out who was informing, my money would have been on you, Ricky, and I have to say I thought it was a nice touch to mark him up like you did. There is no hiding for him anywhere now. Inside or out here those in the know will see Double Bubble for what he is…. a low life grass," Frank said.

Ricky nodded.

The barman placed two crystal cut tumblers with a healthy measure of malt whiskey on Frank's table.

"Cheers," Ricky said.

The two men clinked glasses.

"My understanding is that the plod who was making a nuisance of himself and running around using all that information given to him by Double Bubble, has also been taken care of. My sources tell me that he's off the force and his wife has left him too. I heard he was a broken man, Ricky. How do you feel about that?" Frank said.

"He was a hindrance and an obstacle Frank, so I removed him," Ricky said bluntly.

"It takes a lot of bottle to go up against the old bill, Ricky, and believe me, those bastards have long memories, especially if you come out on top. All that said, another job well done," Frank said.

"In a relatively short period of time you've proved and handled yourself well Ricky, I knew that you would. I have a nose for good operators," Frank said before taking a sip of his drink. "This world that you're getting deeper into, is cloak and dagger. Take my advice and always remain vigilant, guarded and cautious. If you let your guard down and let the wrong person in, you could end up paying with time spent in a prison cell and believe me you do not want that. In our world, Ricky, there is always the potential for infiltrators, informers and grasses at every turn. People can and will betray your trust in them. Now that could be to avoid criminal charges against them, family or a loved one. There are scum out there that will just dob you in for a few measly quid, drink or drugs and then use that as an excuse to turn on their own."

Ricky nodded his head and listened intently.

"Most of us proper people like the Kray Twins and the Richardsons have lived by a code but those days, my friend, are well and truly over. The gavvers are the biggest gang in the land and have unlimited resources to catch and put people like us away. Have you ever heard of The Wembley Mob?"

"Can't say I have, Frank," Ricky answered with a shrug of his shoulders.

"Well they were a handy mob led by a bloke called Bertie Smalls and a good friend of mine Mickey Green. They did a raid on a Barclays Bank in Ilford. It was a nice little touch. They got away with over two hundred and thirty grand. Most of the lads had it on their toes to sunny Spain. In the meantime, some scummy little bastard has given up the name of the firm to the old bill. Now with all the names in the frame they just waited patiently for each member of the gang to return to blighty one by one. Bertie Smalls was the first to get pulled in. The gavvers had him bang to rights and his brief told him that he was looking at a twenty-five stretch for his part in the robbery. Bertie was a proper old-school villain who you would have expected to keep his mouth shut and just do his bird, but he didn't. A deal was done so he had immunity from prosecution and in return he sang like a lark. In May this year those lads all got weighed off for a total of one hundred and six years, with my friend Mickey Green getting an eighteen stretch.

"That is well out of order," Ricky said.

"That isn't all. That slag Smalls is still dobbing faces in from all over the manor. This is a new era Ricky, and the 'once upon a time' faces that you would have sworn were staunch could turn you in for a free ride," Frank said.

"What about you Frank, are you safe?" Ricky asked.

"Me, I'm fine. Well as fine as one could be, Ricky. There isn't a place on the planet a grass could hide where I wouldn't have him or her found. As you have probably gathered, I have contacts in the force, politicians and access to the real power. I'll know if they're coming before the ink on the warrant is dry."

"What's all this I hear about you and Deano Derenzie?" Frank said. "There's talk about a Teddy Boy Army with over a thousand heads. Is that right?"

"Yeah, it's probably closer to fifteen hundred," Ricky said.

"Now that is impressive, and they're all over London?" Frank said.

"Almost every Estate in London has a Teddy Boy presence. Some areas have more than others, so we've been recruiting. I'm saying we, but this has been Deano's baby," Ricky said.

"But you're right up there, right?" Frank said.

"Yeah, I'm number two to Deano," Ricky said.

"Now I've heard lots about Deano the Dog, King of the Teds. He's extremely handy, fearless and now heads arguably the largest gang in London. Is he game for a bit of business?" Frank asked.

"I'd like to say yes, Frank, but unless it's Ted related, he doesn't have a lot of interest in leveraging his skills and contacts," Ricky said.

"Leveraging is a bloody good word Ricky, I like that. You see, I'm working on something, and this could be huge - and I mean hundreds of thousands - if not millions. It's still very early days but I'm going to take a trip to Spain in the next month or so to explore it further. Tell you what, have you got a passport?"

"No, but I could get one," Ricky said.

"Well you go ahead and get yourself a passport and we'll take a trip out there together," Frank said. "That is if you want to."

"Yes, of course Frank. I'm more than interested.

"Remember, we keep this quiet, alright?" Frank said.

"Mums the word," Ricky said.

"I have some more business to attend to," Frank said.

Ricky swallowed the last of his drink and stood up. The two men shook hands.

"Keep up the good work and get that passport sorted sooner rather than later.

"Will do," Ricky said.

Ricky walked over to the bar and ordered a drink. He turned back to see two burly men in black suits sit down at Frank's table.

"Everything alright?" Terry said.

"Yeah, all is good," Ricky said.

"It's all business as usual so you guys can keep those motors coming in," Ricky said.

"Sorted," Steve said.

Ricky waved to two girls that he knew to be escorts in the club. One was a blonde with long wavy hair and blue eyes and the other was a brunette with a short, bobbed hair style and elf like features. They wore midi length sparkling dresses with high heels. It was the standard uniform for the club's escorts.

"Terry, Steve, this is Nicky," Ricky said, pointing towards the blonde, "and this is Sandra."

"Hello," the girls replied together.

"Terry and Steve are both very good friends of mine, girls, and this is their first time in the Cadillac Club's VIP lounge. I would like, very much, for you to show my friends around and help them to enjoy themselves," Ricky said, pulling out a large wad of notes from his pocket. He placed them on the bar and called the barman over. "My friends and the ladies here are not to pay for a drink tonight, okay? They are my guests. Now if there's any more owed, then I'm back in here on Saturday to meet with Frank and I'll sort whatever I owe."

"Yes, Ricky," the barman said.

"I'm going to get myself off. I have some pressing business to get sorted but, in the meantime, have a bloody good night," Ricky said with a broad grin.

"Wow, are you twins," Nicky said as she felt Terry's shirt collar, "like the Kray twins?"

Ricky shook his head and winked. He put his empty glass on the bar and left the VIP lounge. He walked down the stairs while the DJ played *'Money Honey'* by the Bay City Rollers.

"Ricky, is that you?" a voice called out.

Ricky turned and looked back up the stairs. There at the top in a short cream coloured skirt and brown blouse stood Michelle. Ricky's throat went dry, and his heart began to pound. She looked stunning.

"Michelle?"

"Well hello stranger," Michelle said with an animated smile.

Ricky walked back up the stairs. He was trying to look cool and calm, but his heart was racing and his mind throwing up a hundred and one reasons why she should be at the club.

"You look great, Michelle, how are you?" Ricky said.

"Look, I'm sitting over there," Michelle said pointing to a small group of girls. "It's a friend's birthday and I said I'd come along."

Michelle took him by the hand and led him over to the bar.

"Now I'd like to buy you a drink," Michelle said.

"The usual, Ricky?" the barman said.

Ricky nodded. He knew the barman from the VIP lounge and had made a habit, ever since his first meeting with Frank Allen, to drink a single malt whiskey.

"The usual, eh?" Michelle said with a curious expression. "I'll have a Vodka and Lime please."

"So, how have you been?" Ricky said. "Did you go back and finish your course at university?"

"I did and I have," Michelle said. "I didn't think so before, but it was the right thing for me."

"Good, I'm pleased for you." Ricky said.

"I see you're still a Teddy Boy," Michelle said. "You look good."

The barman put the drinks on the bar. Michelle reached into her bag for her purse, but Ricky was too quick and put a five-pound note on the bar and told the barman to get one for himself.

"What can I say, Michelle, I like the clothes," Ricky said as he fingered the lapel on his drape jacket.

"What are the chances of you being here?" Ricky thought. "I have bloody missed you, Michelle. You look incredible!"

"You shouldn't have done that Ricky. I wanted it to be my treat," Michelle said.

"You can get the next one. So tell me, are you all done now and back for good?" Ricky said.

"Well, I did have my own place in Southampton but after Daddy's accident I came back home to be with Mum.

"Accident?" Ricky said.

"Yes, somebody stole his car and Daddy, being Daddy, tried to stop him. The thief just drove off with Daddy still clinging to the car. He lost his grip and rolled off down the road fracturing his legs, feet, arms, hands and ribs. He also had some head injuries but fortunately nothing too serious. He's on the mend but it has really shaken him," Michelle said.

"I'm sorry to hear that," Ricky said. "Was that his Jaguar?"

"It was a new one. Daddy part exchanged his older one and bought a new one. It wasn't the car that he was so upset about, it was losing all his freemasonry bits and pieces," Michelle said.

"Shit!" Ricky thought. "That must have been the bloke that Neil was telling me about. Well, that motor has well and truly gone now. It's in Africa and frankly it couldn't have happened to a nicer bloke. Not good enough for your daughter, am I?"

"As long as he's making a recovery, that's the main thing. I mean he can always buy new masonic stuff, can't he?" Ricky said.

"Yes, but it just meant a lot to him. He got a really good look at the thief who stole his car and has given the description to the authorities. He has a lot of friends in the police force, and they said that would find the thief. It was just a matter of time." Michelle said.

"That doesn't sound good," Ricky thought.

"How is your mum coping?" Ricky said.

"She's finding the whole thing quite difficult to be honest, Ricky. Mummy isn't good with Daddy being at home this much. She's used to having her independence. Mummy likes to shop with friends or meet them for coffee or lunch but Daddy's just being so demanding. The doctor says it's depression from the head injuries and that he will get better with time," Michelle said.

"How have you been?" Michelle said.

"Life has been good. I did start my own business, just like I told you I would, and it seems to be going well. I have my own place now and, well, you know, it's all good," Ricky said.

"Your own business. Look at you," Michelle said with a slight nod of her head.

In the background the DJ slowed the pace down and put on *'I'm Not In Love'* by 10cc.

"I love this record," Michelle said.

"Don't tell anyone, but yeah, me too. Would you like to dance?"

Michelle smiled and reached for his hand.

"I'd love to," she said as she led him onto the smaller upstairs dance floor.

Ricky took her into his arms and pulled her body in close to his. Michelle rested her head on his chest. The aroma of her perfume was almost intoxicating. Memories came flooding back of their short but exciting time together.

"I think I'm still in love with you Michelle," Ricky thought.

"I am sorry that my daddy told you not to call again," Michelle whispered. "I tried to tell him that all that trouble and fighting wouldn't have had anything to do with you, but he just wouldn't listen. All he saw was Teddy Boys in the newspapers and that was it. You were guilty,"

"I've missed you," Ricky said.

"I bet you've not given me a second thought. There's probably been scores of girls since me," Michelle whispered.

Ricky pulled her body closer and kissed the top of her head.

"You were very special to me Michelle," Ricky said.

"Were," Michelle whispered.

"Are… special Michelle. You are still very special to me," Ricky whispered into her ear.

Michelle raised her head slightly, so their eyes met. Ricky leaned forward and their lips touched. As they kissed passionately all the feelings that Ricky had felt before came rushing back with such a force that he felt his knees weaken.

"I never stopped loving you, Ricky Turrell, and thought about you every day," Michelle said.

The record stopped but Ricky and Michelle stayed on the dance floor still swaying to their own special melody. *"I Only Have Eyes for You'* by Art Garfunkel played, and the dance floor very quickly filled again with couples slow dancing.

"I hoped, no, I willed for you to be here tonight," Michelle said.

"I'm thrilled we've bumped into each other," Ricky said.

"Me too," Michelle said.

"Michelle, there's a big show on Friday with a special guest DJ, Steve Maxted, The Wild One," Ricky said.

"Ricky I've seen him perform before, and he's absolutely brilliant. None of that sitting by the turn table and just playing random records like most of the DJ's we have in clubs like this. Steve Maxted is up and dancing about to the latest tracks while performing all sorts of tricks and crazy stunts. I've seen him at The Witchdoctor in Catford and a group of us even travelled down to the Star Ballroom in Maidstone because he was so good. He's a legend but none of us could get tickets. It was all sold out."

"Don't worry about that, you're with me," Ricky said. "I can't get tickets for all your friends, but I can certainly get one for you. That's if you want to come with me?"

"I can't think of a better way to spend to spend a Friday night," Michelle said before leaning forward and kissing Ricky gently on the lips.

"Are you hungry?"

"I don't think they do food here," Michelle said.

"No, not in here," Ricky chuckled. "There's a Chinese restaurant called the Wong Kei in Soho that I've been meaning to try for some time. I just thought if you were hungry, we could catch up over spareribs."

"Okay, yeah, I'd like that," Michelle said. "Let me just have a quick word with my friends."

***

Ricky and Michelle took a taxi to Soho where they ate and chatted at the Wong Kei Chinese restaurant until after 1.00a.m. In the taxi on the way back to South London, Michelle confessed that she had called her mother earlier to tell her she would be staying over at her friend's house and not to wait up.

Chapter 29

The Cadillac Club: The Steve Maxted 'The Wild One' Show

Ricky handed Deano a pint of Carlsberg lager.

"Deano, mate, I've had a phone call from Mack from the Mile End Teds," Ricky said.

"Hold that a just a minute will you Ricky. There's something I've got to do," Deano said as he put his beer on the table and walked over to Kenny.

"Kenny, I need a word," Deano said gruffly.

"Yes, mate, of course," Kenny said as he followed Deano to an empty table.

"Sit down," Deano ordered.

Kenny did as he was told and pulled out a seat.

"I've got to tell you Kenny, I've really struggled with how to deal with you in recent months. For as long as I've known you you've been chasing skirt, and truth be told, you would rather try to get your end away than hang out with us lot," Deano said.

Kenny held his hands and hung his head.

"That's true, ain't it?" Deano said.

Kenny nodded.

"Birds mean naff all to you, do they? They're just a notch on the headboard for Kenny! I've watched you flirt like some kind of peacock until you've had your end away and then they're nothing. Birds are just play things to you, which is why it's taken all my strength to not just tear you apart for what you did to Specs. He never had the kind of charm you have. Specs could never chat birds up like you did. He even swallowed all his pride and took up with Denise after you dumped her for what, another bird? However, with all that said we have been friends for a long time, and we've stood side by side against whatever came up against the Milton Road Teds. In all our time as friends you never once let me down and proved yourself many times over, and it's because of that that I can finally forgive you, Kenny, and let it go," Deano said.

Kenny raised his head slowly. His eyes were red and teary.

"Thank you, Deano," Kenny muttered.

Deano held out his hand and Kenny shook it.

"I don't want no sentimental stuff now, but what has been said needed to be said, and now we can just park it up and move on," Deano said before turning to Ricky and waving him over.

"Right, I understand," Kenny said, wiping a stray tear from his eye.

"Alright Deano," Ricky said as he put his pint down next to Deano's.

"Yeah, now what's all this about Mack and the Mile End Teds?" Deano said.

"Mack said that Carly Thompson didn't want anything to do with a Ted Army and that he wanted the Mile End Teds to stand alone," Ricky said.

"What, is he off his rocker?" Deano said.

"It's a bit more than that. According to Mack most of the lads want in and it's just Carly who is calling the shots. He's got a right bee in his bonnet about both you and me Deano. He's been talking about coming down and making an example of us," Ricky said.

"He's definitely out of his tree. Well it looks like these boys are going to get totally bashed up," Deano said with a manic grin. "What do you think Kenny?"

"Sure, Deano. I'm there!" Kenny said.

"It's like I said Deano. Most of the lads respect you and want to be part of the Ted Army. I think we can be a bit clever here; sort out Carly Thompson and forge an alliance with Mack as the new leader," Ricky said, waving the cigarette smoke away that had wafted over from a small group of girls behind them.

"Alright, Ricky, for now you have a word with Mack and make your plans together and then fill me in on the details, but I will not wait around. All eyes will be on us and how we deal with those that decline our offer. I cannot and will not be seen to be weak," Deano said.

"Alright, what's going on here then?" Lee said as he joined the lads at the table.

"We were just looking down at our empty glasses, Lee, and wondered why you hadn't been over and offered to get the beers in," Deano said, handing Lee a five-pound note. "Get yourself one too."

Lee looked hurt and disheartened, but reluctantly took the money and returned to the bar.

"Here Kaz," Lee said interrupting her conversation with Melanie.

"What?" replied Kaz.

"I might have put this girl in the family way, and I don't know what to do," Lee muttered.

"You're joking," Kaz said.

Kaz, Donna and Melanie stopped their conversation and turned to face Lee.

"Who is it?" Melanie asked.

"I'd rather not say just yet?" Lee whispered.

"Do we know her?" Kaz said.

"Probably, she lives on the estate," Lee said.

"I know this probably sounds silly, Lee, but did you definitely have sex with her?" Melanie said.

"If you mean did we get naked and do the business, then yes," Lee said.

"Did you wear something?" Kaz asked.

"What do mean?" Lee said.

"You know," Kaz said softly. "Did you wear a rubber Johnny?"

"Well kind of, but it might have been too late," Lee said.

"Oh, right so you couldn't hold it back," Melanie said.

"Please, give it a rest," Lee said, looking around for stray ears.

"Don't worry we'll not say anything," Donna said. "What makes you think she's pregnant?"

"I saw her yesterday and she said that she'd missed her period," Lee said.

"Did she say how late she was?" Kaz said.

"She said she was a week late and that she was never late. She looked frightened and I've not slept a bloody wink," Lee said.

"Okay, you can calm down Lee. Being just a week late doesn't automatically mean that you're pregnant," Melanie said. "I've been late countless times since I've been with Deano so I can talk from experience."

"Me too," Kaz said.

"Well don't look at me," Donna said.

"Your girlfriend missing her period might mean that there are other things happening that's holding up her menstrual cycle. Has she said anything about feeling tired?"

"No," Lee said.

"My sister," Melanie said, "Became really tired during the early weeks of her pregnancy. She would constantly complain about feeling exhausted and would actually fall asleep on the sofa some days while the six 'o' clock news was on."

"Has she mentioned anything about her breasts becoming swollen, enlarged or sore?" Kaz said.

"No, she didn't mention her tits at all, only that she was a week late for her period and that was it?" Lee said.

"I think the best thing is we have a word with her Lee. Don't worry, we'll say nothing to that lot," Kaz said, pointing to Deano, Ricky and Kenny. "Your secret is safe with us."

"I don't want to become a dad yet," Lee said.

"What about your girlfriend, has she spoken about becoming a mum?" Melanie said.

"She doesn't want a baby either. We just kind of got off together one night and that was it," Lee said.

"We'll have a chat Sunday lunchtime in the Arms and then we'll go and have a word with your… friend," Kaz said.

"Here, what happened to those beers," Kenny called. "We're all getting right parched over here."

"I'm not your bloody servant Kenny," Lee said harshly.

"Do you know what Lee? You're about as useful as an ashtray on a motorbike," Kenny said before turning to face the barman. "Here mate when you're ready, we're dying of thirst over there."

"Deano might have forgiven you, Kenny, but I fucking haven't," Lee growled through gritted teeth.

"Lee," Kenny said as he slowly looked Lee up and down and smiled "You have an inferiority complex, you do know that, don't you? Well, my old son I'm here to tell you that it's completely justified."

"Fuck off," Lee hissed.

Melanie, Kaz and Donna turned away and continued their conversation.

Kenny leaned forward and whispered "Speak to me out of turn again Lee, and I will take you outside and open you up. Now look me in the fucking eyes and tell me I'm joking."

The barman put a pint of Carlsberg on the bar. "Nice one, mate," Kenny said before looking back over at Deano and noticing that both Terry and Steve Parker had joined them "I'll have four more of those for the lads and one for Lee here."

Kenny returned to Deano and the lads and put the tray of lagers on the table.

"I was just telling Terry and Steve about Carly Thompson thinking he's going to sort me out," Deano said. "Do you know he had the front to put a blade on the table while we were talking about bringing the Mile End Teds into the Ted Army?"

Terry shook his head.

"That is well out of order," Steve said.

"I'm thinking that he should be taught a lesson," Deano said. "What do you think Kenny?"

"Mate, whatever you want to do, I'm there," Kenny said.

"I thought we'd sorted this," Ricky thought. *"Mack and I will work it out."*

"I'm thinking we should pay them a visit and after I've served him up, we'll take scissors and cut off his hair, strip him of his drape suit and then you two can take a hammer to his kneecaps," Deano said before turning slightly and winking at Kenny. "Of course, that's only if Ricky doesn't get something sorted."

"You, Deano, are a bloody wind up," Ricky said.

"Yeah well, you bite easily," Deano said with a grin.

"Ricky?"

Ricky turned and saw Michelle standing just a few feet away. He looked her up and down and beamed.

"Hello Michelle, you look great," Ricky said as he leaned forward and kissed her gently on the lips.

"Thank you," Michelle said before doing a little twirl.

"New outfit?" Ricky said, stepping back to admire her royal blue midi-skirt, brown leather high heel boots, two-tone tonic coloured blouse with butterfly collar and paisley cardigan.

"I thought I'd try something different," Michelle said. "Do you like it?"

"Like it? No… I love it," Ricky said.

Michelle beamed,

"Let me introduce you to some of my friends."

Ricky took Michelle by the hand and introduced her to Deano, all the lads and Melanie and the girls. The girls took quite an interest and engaged Michelle in a conversation about fashion.

"Michelle, fancy a drink upstairs before the Steve Maxted show?"

"Sure," Michelle said. "It's been really nice meeting you all. Hopefully we'll see each other again."

Melanie, Kaz and Donna all kissed her on the cheek.

"You've done well there," Melanie whispered. "I'm pleased for you both."

"Thanks Melanie," Ricky said. "We'll be back in time for Steve Maxted."

Ricky and Michelle walked towards the door of the VIP Lounge arm in arm.

"Are you sure we'll be allowed in here?" Michelle said, squeezing Ricky's arm. "It'll be embarrassing if we get turned away."

"We'll be fine," Ricky said.

"Good evening Ricky," Cookie said as he stepped to one side to allow Ricky and Michelle to enter the VIP Lounge.

"Thanks Cookie," Ricky said before squeezing Michelle's arm back.

"You!" Michelle said with a giggle. "Why didn't you say you were a member?"

Ricky shrugged his shoulders and smiled.

The VIP Lounge was busy with most of the tables taken. Ricky spotted Neil sitting with Jackie. He looked away quickly not wanting to join them at their table.

"Alright Ricky," Sean said. "Can we have a quick word later about that bit of business?"

"Yeah sure, Sean," Ricky said, shaking his hand. "Sean, this is Michelle and Michelle this is a friend of mine, Sean.

"Nice to meet you Michelle, I'm not surprised he's been hiding a little cracker like you away," Sean said before throwing his head back and laughing out loud.

"Err, thank you," Michelle said.

"I'll come and find you in a while," Ricky said.

"Yeah, see you later," Sean.

"How do you know him?" Michelle said as they approached the bar.

"Oh, Sean and his partner Denis find bankrupt stock and sometimes they come up with stuff that's of interest," Ricky said.

"I hate lying to you Michelle, but this place is a den of iniquity, full of thieves, robbers and serious villains and I don't want you thinking badly of me," Ricky thought.

"The usual for you, Ricky?" the barman asked, putting a tumbler on the bar and reaching for a bottle of single malt whiskey.

Ricky nodded.

"And for the lady?" the barman said as he finished pouring.

"Gin and tonic, please," Michelle said.

"Make it a double," Ricky said with a wink, handing the barman a couple of notes. "Have one for yourself."

"The usual?" Michelle said.

"Yeah, well I do like to pop in every so often," Ricky said awkwardly.

"Are people expecting to see you with someone else?" Michelle said, turning to face him. "Not that it's anything to do with me."

Ricky smiled.

"No, it's a place I come to meet some friends, talk a little business and relax. I've never brought a girl here," Ricky said.

The barman put Michelle's drink on the bar and tried to hand Ricky back his change. Ricky held up his hand indicating that the barman should keep the change.

Ricky turned and saw that Frank Allen was shaking hands with two men in dark suits. They stood up to leave and Frank caught Ricky's eye. He waved him over. Ricky tilted his head to one side. Frank smiled and waved them both over to join him.

"Michelle, come and meet Mr Frank Allen," Ricky said.

"Frank Allen? You mean *the* Frank Allen?" Michelle said.

"Come on, he's a nice guy," Ricky said, leading her towards Frank's table.

"Hello Frank," Ricky said.

Frank stood up and shook Ricky warmly by the hand and then faced Michelle.

"Good evening, Miss. I'm Frank Allen. It's lovely to meet you. Please, take a seat."

Ricky pulled out a chair for Michelle.

As Frank sat down, he looked up at the bar and held up three fingers.

"Hello Mr Allen, I'm Michelle."

"Please, Michelle, call me Frank. All my friends call me Frank. I hope you don't mind but I've taken the liberty of ordering us drinks," Frank said.

"No not at all, that's very kind of you," Michelle said.

"So tell me Michelle, have you known Ricky long?"

Michelle put her hand over her mouth and giggled.

"Frank, it's a long story but we've only just met again. I've been away at university," Michelle said.

"Education; the corner stone of every successful career," Frank said. "What industry do you think you'll work in?"

"Architecture," Michelle said.

"Fascinating. You know I have a portfolio of land in London that will need to be developed at some point. Maybe that is something you could help me with in the future?" Frank said as he leaned back in his chair and patted Ricky on the shoulder.

"Initially I'll be working in the family business, but plan to go on my own once I've become established," Michelle said.

"Good for you," Frank said. "Then, Michelle, when you're ready, I will be your first client. You just let my friend Ricky here know when that day arrives."

"Thank you, Frank," Michelle said.

"You're very welcome," Frank said.

The barman put a tray on Frank's table with three large cut crystal tumblers of malt whiskey. Frank reached forward and placed one in front of both his guests.

"Cheers Frank," Ricky said, raising his glass.

"Did you have some business with Sean and Denis?" Frank asked, looking over at the two men standing by the bar.

"Yes, but that can wait Frank," Ricky said.

"Tell you what, why don't you go and sort your business out and Michelle and I can talk about what could be done with some of my land," Frank said.

"Okay, are you alright with that Michelle?" Ricky said as he stood up.

"Yes, of course," Michelle said with a reassuring smile.

"See you shortly," Ricky said as he left the table.

Ricky joined Sean and Denis at the bar. He looked back and saw that Frank and Michelle were fully engaged in conversation.

"Alright lads," Ricky said.

"Yeah, sweet," Denis said. "We've met with the driver, Justin, and we're ready to do that bit of business next week. That's if you're ready to take delivery."

"No problem," Ricky said. "It's like I said, I'll take everything you can get."

"Good, because we took a trip down to Kent last week on the look out for work, and we came across this tyre bay in Gillingham. Denis had a good look around the place and it's minted with stock from floor to ceiling. We went back that night and all they have protecting the place is a padlock, but, and this will crack you up, it's one of those hasp and staple brackets with the screws on show. So a couple of one inch screws is all that stands between us and a nice pay day," Sean said.

"Sounds good," Ricky said. "I'll take everything; tyres, inner tubes, wheel balance weights, the lot.

"Sweet," Denis said, "but we'll need to off load it quickly."

"Just give me a ring," Ricky said, handing Sean a business card, "And we'll make the arrangements.

"Hello mate."

Ricky turned to see Neil standing beside him.

"Neil, hello mate I didn't see you in here," Ricky lied.

"Yeah, I've got a table at the back with Jackie, and I thought, I know that drape suit, so I came down to say hello and ask if you wanted to join us?"

"One minute mate," Ricky said, turning back to Sean and Denis, "Give me a bell when you're ready."

"Will do," Sean said.

"Catch you later," Denis said.

"Sorry mate I just needed to finish up a bit of business," Ricky said.

"Come and say hello to Jackie," Neil said.

"I can't mate, I'm with Michelle and right now she's chatting with Frank Allen so I better get back," Ricky said.

"Oh, okay then. Another time maybe?" Neil said.

"Yeah, of course mate," Ricky said.

There were a few moments of awkward silence.

"I better get back to Michelle," Ricky said.

Neil nodded and walked slowly back to his table.

"Sorry Frank, business is all sorted," Ricky said.

"Well Ricky, I have to say that you have the most amazing young lady, beautiful and intelligent. I'm pleased for you both," Frank said.

Michelle looked at her watch and stood up. "It's almost time for the Steve Maxted show, if you don't mind."

"Not at all," Frank said. "It was a pleasure meeting you, go ahead and enjoy the rest of your evening."

"Cheers Frank," Ricky said, shaking Frank by the hand.

"You have a keeper there," Frank whispered.

Ricky swallowed the last of his drink and put the empty glass on the bar before leaving the VIP Lounge.

"I can't believe that was the actual Frank Allen," Michelle said. "If you believe what's in the newspapers, you'd think he was some kind of super villain when actually he's a real gentleman."

"You can't believe everything you read in the newspapers for sure," Ricky said. "Frank is a businessman and an easy target for the press because of the company he kept back in the sixties."

"He was telling me about land that he has along the Thames. It's all just dilapidated industrial warehouses now, but in the future it'll be perfect for development for office space or residential," Michelle said. "Do you think he meant it when he said he'd give me some projects?"

"Without any doubt," Ricky said. "If Frank Allen says something you can take it as gospel. He's a man of his word."

"That could be exciting to know that there's work available for when I go on my own," Michelle said, "And he likes you."

"Really?" Ricky said.

"Destined for great things is what he said," Michelle said.

The couple walked back downstairs and joined Deano and the others.

"I think it's about to start," Michelle said, looking around as people began to fill the dance floor.

The lights dimmed and three spotlights shone down on the stage. The crowd stood still as a husky male voice boomed out from the speakers.

"There is a place where you can be truly free and only music will fill you with energy. Be prepared for a musical show unlike any other on earth. Get ready to be transported to this place

***

Ladies and Gentlemen! Please welcome England's Number One Live DJ ... I give you ... Steve Maxted ... The Wild One!"

The audience erupted with applause, cheers and whistles.

The spotlight shone down onto the right-hand corner as Steve Maxted stepped out onto the stage dressed like Clint Eastwood in a Spaghetti Western movie. He strutted forward, stopped to adjust his hat and then stood legs apart with his right hand over his holstered Colt 45 handgun. The lights whisked around the top of the stage and then Steve Maxted drew his weapon and fired three rapid shots. There was a flash of brightly coloured lights and an explosion with vibrantly coloured confetti falling from the ceiling and littering the stage.

The crowd cheered excitedly as Steve Maxted put the weapon back into his holster and strutted slowly over to the record decks.

"*Let's Dance*' by Chris Montez boomed out of the speakers with multi coloured lights racing around the floors, walls, and ceiling. Steve Maxted took his cowboy hat off, held it high above his head and then tossed it across the stage like a frisbee.

The dance floor was heaving with sweating bodies rubbing up against each other as they danced joyfully to the rhythm of the music. No one cared if you were a Teddy Boy, Skinhead, Boot Boy or just one of the lads, because everyone was just having fun and enjoying the release of a stressful week.

Ricky looked around him and everyone from the Milton Road Estate was dancing and jigging around. He spotted the two sharp eyed jovial bouncers that regularly patrolled the club on the look out for trouble or just looking at the pretty girls dancing.

Ricky and Michelle immersed themselves in the happy, carefree atmosphere 'The Wild One' had created. With his eyes closed, Ricky could feel all thoughts about Teds, violence and villainy just being swept away. It was pure and utter escapism.

The dance floor remained full throughout the Steve Maxted 'The Wild One' show. The DJ had walked across the stage on his hands, taken a chair and balanced it on his chin while he changed records to '*Let's Twist Again*' by Chubby Checker. The show had gone down a storm with everyone still talking about his act long after he had left the stage.

"That was brilliant!" Michelle said. "Can we go and see him again Ricky?"

"Yeah, of course," Ricky said.

"Promise?" Michelle said before kissing him on the cheek.

Ricky smiled and nodded.

"Well Deano and I have some news," Melanie said.

The group stopped talking.

"We've set a date to get married and… you're all invited," Melanie said, holding up her engagement ring, "And that includes you, Michelle."

"That's great news!" Kenny said.

"We've not quite settled on the honeymoon yet. I want to go to Playa de las Americas in Tenerife and Deano wants to stay at the Grand Hotel in Brighton," Melanie said.

"Oh, come on Deano," Kaz said, her hands on her hips. "You've got to go to Tenerife."

"We'll see," Deano said.

"Yes we will," Melanie said before kissing him on the lips. "Tenerife?"

"Oh, go on then," Deano said.

The group cheered and raised their glasses,

"Tell you what, this calls for a celebratory round of drinks," Ricky said, motioning the barman over, "And I'm in the chair."

The group cheered again.

"Same again all round," Ricky said as he put a couple of ten pound notes on the bar.

"Ricky," Deano said.

"Yes mate."

"I've been thinking about who I should have as my best man," Deano said. "It's not easy, so what I've decided is that I want you, Kenny and Lee to all be my best men. Are you alright with that?"

"Deano, it would be an honour mate," Ricky said as he put a pint of Carlsberg lager in front of his friend.

"It would have been Specs, if he was still here," Deano said.

"I know mate," Ricky said, "But he's up there looking down mate, and wishing all the best for you."

"Specs mate, rest in peace," Deano muttered and then took a long swig from his pint.

"I'm going to get to some air, this cigarette smoke is killing me," Deano said, fanning away cigarette smoke from Melanie, Kaz and Donna.

"I'll join you mate," Ricky said. "Michelle, I'm just going to grab some air with Deano. Are you alright with Melanie?"

Michelle smiled, nodded and continued her conversation with the girls.

Deano and Ricky strolled through the club, acknowledging Teds from all over South London on their way to the exit. The two lads stood at the entrance door, and both took deep breaths of clean, cigarette smoke free air.

"DEANO!" a voice yelled.

Ricky looked up to see Fat Pat walking towards them with a sawn-off shotgun. Deano darted away to the left.

BANG!

Deano yelled out in pain and fell to the ground, grasping his side.

Ricky looked on. It was all happening so fast.

Fat Pat stood above Deano and pointed the sawn-off shotgun at his chest.

"This is for my nephew Eddy Boyce!" Fat Pat hissed as he pulled the trigger at point blank range.

BANG!

Deano's body lifted and fell back to the ground. Blood covered the pavement.

"No!" Ricky yelled as Fat Pat ran back to the main road and a waiting Jaguar MK2 with the engine running. Ricky spotted Clifford Tate at the steering wheel.

Books by Dave Bartram

With Dean Rinaldi

King of the Teds: Inception

King of the Teds II: Unification

King of the Teds III: Infiltration

Coming Soon!

King of the Teds IV: Subversion

King of the Teds V: Misdirection

King of the Teds VI: Retribution

Facebook: Dean Rinaldi Ghostwriter Publisher & Mentor

www.deanrinaldi-ghostwriter.com

Printed in Great Britain
by Amazon